"LOOK AT THE SIZE OF IT!"

The crawling giant pulled itself slowly toward Ranger MacNeil and the Dancer, and they backed cautiously away as they realized it wasn't alone. Behind it came another giant, and another. From farther down the tunnel came the sound of still more giants.

The great white form filled the tunnel. MacNeil tried to reach the giant's throat, but couldn't get past the hammering fists. The Dancer moved forward to stand beside MacNeil, but even he, Blademaster though he was, couldn't do more than slow the giant's advance. Slowly, step by step, the two Rangers were forced back down the tunnel. They'd almost reached the steps leading up and out when the giant suddenly lunged forward. The left hand caught hold of MacNeil's shoulder, and the right fastened onto the Dancer's sword arm. Despite their frantic struggles, the giant pulled them slowly forward, its mouth stretching wide to reveal huge, jagged teeth. . . .

Down Among
the Dead Men

by

Simon R. Green

A ROC BOOK

ROC
Published by the Penguin Group
Penguin Books USA Inc., 375 Hudson Street,
New York, New York 10014, U.S.A.
Penguin Books Ltd, 27 Wrights Lane,
London W8 5TZ, England
Penguin Books Australia Ltd, Ringwood,
Victoria, Australia
Penguin Books Canada Ltd, 10 Alcorn Avenue,
Toronto, Ontario, Canada M4V 3B2
Penguin Books (N.Z.) Ltd, 182-190 Wairau Road,
Auckland 10, New Zealand

Penguin Books Ltd, Registered Offices:
Harmondsworth, Middlesex, England
First published by Roc, an imprint of Dutton Signet,
a division of Penguin Books USA Inc.

First Printing, December, 1993
10 9 8 7 6 5 4 3 2 1

"It's the Beast. It knows what scares us."

There is a part of the Forest where it is always night. The tall trees bow together to shut out the light, and whatever lives there has never known the sun. Mapmakers call this area the Darkwood, and add the warning: *Here Be Demons*.

Ten years ago the Darkwood's boundaries slowly began to expand, and for the first time in uncounted centuries the long night spread its dominion over more and more of the Forest Kingdom. Demons swarmed ahead of the enveloping darkness, an endless tide of twisted and misshapen creatures that slaughtered every living thing in their path. They were finally stopped and driven back, but only at great cost to the Forest Land and those who lived there. The long night retreated with the demons, and the Darkwood resumed its original boundaries. A quiet, weary pace fell across the broken Land, and the slow rebuilding began.

Ten years have passed since the Demon War. The Forest's scars are slowly healing, the Darkwood is still and silent, and few demons ever venture out of the endless night. But in a clearing not far from the Darkwood boundary, in a darkness where a sun has never risen and a moon has never shone, an ancient evil stirs in its sleep and dreams foul dreams.

1

Silence Carved in Stone

Duncan MacNeil reined in his horse and looked around him. Narrow shafts of golden sunlight pierced the Forest gloom, shining down through the occasional gaps in the overhead canopy. Tall trees stood close together on either side of the beaten trail, their branches heavy with the summer's greenery. The hot, muggy air was thick with the scent of earth and leaf and bark. A handful of birds sang in the higher branches, warning the creatures of the wild that man was moving through the Forest.

MacNeil stirred impatiently in his saddle. After two weeks' hard traveling, the Forest's charms had begun to pall. In fact, MacNeil was beginning to think he could live quite happily if he never saw another tree again. He glanced back down the trail, but there was still no sign of the rest of his party. MacNeil scowled. He hated being kept waiting. He looked at the trail ahead, but the tightly packed trees cut short his view. MacNeil signaled his horse to move on again at a slow pace. The border fort couldn't be far ahead, and he was itching to take his first look at it.

The Forest moved slowly by him, his horse's steady muffled hoofbeats sounding loud and clear in the quiet. The birds slowly stopped singing, and no game moved in the surrounding shadows. MacNeil dropped one hand to the sword at his side and eased the blade in its scabbard. Everything seemed peaceful, but he didn't believe in taking unnecessary chances. His gaze fell on a clump of dead trees to his left. They were twisted and hollow, eaten away from within by decay. The gnarled branches were bare, the bark mottled with lichen. Even after ten years there were still parts of the Forest that had never recovered from the long night.

The trees fell suddenly away to either side of him, and MacNeil jerked his horse to a halt at the edge of a clearing. He leaned forward in his saddle, shading his watering eyes against the bright sunlight, and smiled slowly. Square in the middle of the huge clearing stood the border fort, a vast stone edifice with two massive iron-bound doors and only a series of arrow slits for windows. MacNeil looked the fort over carefully. The two doors were firmly shut, and there was no trace of movement anywhere in or around the fort. The great stone walls brooded silently and enigmatically in the late afternoon sunshine.

MacNeil sat back in his saddle and frowned thoughtfully. There were no guards at the doors, and no one walked the high battlements. There were no flags flying, no pennants at the watchtowers, and no smoke curled up from the dozen or more chimney pots. If there was anyone in the fort, they were going to great pains to hide the fact. MacNeil looked back over his shoulder. There was still no sign of the rest of his party. He looked back at the fort, scowling unhappily. Normally he'd have more sense than to get so far ahead of his own people, but this business with the border fort worried him, and the sooner he got to grips with it, the better he'd feel.

There was a storm coming. He could feel it. Dark clouds were gathering in the sky, and the air had been close and muggy all day. MacNeil looked up at the lowering sky and cursed mildly. He had planned to look the fort over thoroughly from the outside and then spend the night in the Forest, but all the signs suggested it was going to be a filthy night. And MacNeil had no intention of sleeping on muddy ground in a thunderstorm when there were comfortable beds to be had close at hand. He and his team had spent too many nights in the field of late, and this summer had to be the wettest he'd ever known.

He stretched slowly and eased himself in the saddle. Somehow he'd thought the border fort would look more impressive, given the commotion it had caused at court. The panic had begun when it was discovered the fort hadn't communicated with the outside world in almost a month. No messengers, no carrier pigeons, nothing. The king sent messengers to the fort. None of them ever returned. Magicians and sorcerers tried to make mental contact with the fort, but some kind of barrier kept them out. The king listened to all the reports and grew steadily more worried. This particular fort lay on the border between the Forest Kingdom and its neighbor, the Duchy of Hillsdown. It had always been a disputed boundary, even to the point of war, and in the chaos that had followed the long night, Hillsdown had made several attempts to settle the question permanently in its favor. The new border fort had been built at the Forest King's command expressly to discourage such actions, and shortly after it was completed, that particular stretch of the frontier became suddenly very peaceful again. The Duke of Hillsdown sent several threatening letters and backed unobtrusively down, and that was that. Until last month.

MacNeil's hand settled comfortably on the pommel of his sword as he studied the silent fort. There were no outward signs that anything was wrong—the great stone walls were unmarked by fire or violence, and the clearing looked still and peaceful—and yet there were no signs of life either. MacNeil stirred restlessly, and his horse shook its head uneasily, responding to his mood. He patted the horse's neck comfortingly, but his eyes never left the fort.

Duncan MacNeil was a tall, muscular man in his late twenties. Long blond hair fell raggedly to his shoulders, kept out of his face by a simple leather headband. Cool gray eyes studied the world from a broad, smiling face. His shoulders were wide, his chest was broad, and there wasn't an ounce of spare fat on him. He worked hard to keep it that way. His clothes were simple and functional, and he sat his horse with the unthinking ease of a man who'd spent most of his working life in the saddle. His sword hung at his side in a well-worn scabbard, and his hand rarely moved far from it.

He'd lied about his age and joined the guards at fifteen, keen as mustard for a life of action and adventure. The Demon War had knocked most of that nonsense out of him, but deep down he was never content just to do his job and pull his pay. He needed a little excitement in his life to give it spice. His constant search for a little excitement had got him into trouble more than once, and lost him as many promotions as he gained. After one particularly unfortunate incident, involving the wrecking of a fashionable tavern after the innkeeper objected to MacNeil's complaint about watered ale, he was presented with a simple choice by his superiors: join the Rangers or spend the rest of his life turning large rocks into smaller ones in a military prison.

Rangers worked in small mobile teams, sent out ahead of a main force to investigate dangerous or suspicious situations. Such teams tended to be brave, competent, and ultimately expendable. The money was good, but truth be told, MacNeil would have done the job for nothing. Though of course he never told them that. They might have taken him up on it. Being a Ranger had given him all the excitement he could handle and then some. It was his life. He studied the fort before him and smiled happily. This one was going to be a challenge, he could tell. MacNeil loved challenges.

His smile faded slowly away. The trouble with challenges was that they were often time-consuming, and he was working under a strict deadline. He and his team had just three more days to find out what had happened at the fort. After that a full brigade of armed guards would arrive to man the fort again. And if there wasn't an answer ready and waiting for the commander of that brigade, Ranger Sergeant Duncan MacNeil and his team were going to be in big trouble. Heads would roll. Possibly quite literally.

Hoofbeats sounded on the path behind him as the witch called Constance rode out of the Forest gloom to join him. She steered her horse in beside MacNeil's, flashed him a quick smile, and looked out into the clearing with darting, eager eyes. The witch was a tall, striking brunette who sat her horse with more determination than style. She was only just out of her teens, and wore a smart blouse and trousers of black cotton topped with a billowing cloak of bright scarlet trimmed with gold. MacNeil thought she looked like a mobile target. He got nervous just riding beside her. Her face was raw-boned and sensual, with sparkling dark eyes that missed nothing and a great mane of night black hair held back out of her face by strategically placed ivory combs. She was a bit skinny for MacNeil's taste, but she moved with an unself-conscious grace, and her smile was bright and challenging.

MacNeil still wasn't quite sure what to make of Constance. She'd only joined his team a few weeks back, and this was her first mission, her first chance to show what she could really do. If she was half as good as she claimed to be, she'd be worth watching. MacNeil frowned slightly. Constance was replacing a witch called Salamander, who had died three months before. Three months almost to the day. Salamander had been a pretty good witch, in her way, but she had always thought herself a swordswoman as well as a magic-user, and in the end that killed her. She had drawn her sword when she should have cast a spell, and the bandit had been just that little bit faster with his ax. She took a bad wound in the gut, the wound became infected, and Salamander died in a filthy village tavern, out of her mind with fever and calling for a husband who'd been dead five years.

MacNeil had killed the bandit, but it didn't help. He'd led his team into that village. He'd told them it was safe.

He'd had a lot of trouble finding someone to replace Salamander. Every Ranger team had to have a magic-user; there were far too many magical creatures and occurrences lying in wait in the Forest these days, left over from the Demon War. Unfortunately, most of the kingdom's magic-users had been killed in the war, so instead of a sorcerer or sorceress he'd had to settle for a witch—first Salamander, then Constance.

Although he hadn't exactly chosen Constance. Truth was, he'd spent so long hedging over his choice that his superiors got impatient and appointed a witch for him. Constance had been a lot younger than he'd expected, but since she'd been raised and trained in the all-woman Academy of the Sisters of the Moon, he had no doubt as to the power of her magic. The sisterhood didn't turn out underachievers. You either graduated with honor or they buried you in an unmarked grave and scratched your name off the academy rolls.

He bowed politely to the witch beside him. "Well, Constance, this is it. That fort is what all the fuss is about."

"Poxy-looking place," said Constance airily. "Any sign of life?"

"Not so far. As soon as the others catch up, we'll go and take a closer look. See if it's still habitable."

Constance looked at him quickly. "You're not thinking of spending the night in there?"

MacNeil shrugged. "There's a storm coming, and a bad one by the feel of it. You can sleep out here in the rain if you want to, but personally speaking, I'm not at all averse to the idea of having a solid roof over my head for a change. You're new to field work, Constance; the first thing you learn in this business is to take your comforts when you can, and be grateful for them. They're few and far between in our line of work. There's plenty of time to give the fort a thorough inspection before nightfall."

Constance shook her head. "I don't know, Sergeant, I—"

"Constance," said MacNeil easily, "there's only one leader in this team, and that's me. I've taken the time to explain some of my reasoning to you because you're new to this group and this is your first mission, but I'm not going to make a habit of it. When I give an order I expect it to be obeyed, without question. Is that clear?"

"Perfectly clear," said Constance coldly. She turned away from him and studied the fort with great concentration. "I take it you have noticed that there are no guards on the battlements."

"Yes."

"Could they all have deserted, do you think?"

MacNeil shrugged. "It's possible. But if that's the case, what happened to all the messengers the king sent?"

Constance pursed her lips thoughtfully and tried to look like she was thinking hard. She wanted very much to impress MacNeil, but at this distance she couldn't See anything useful about the apparently deserted fort. She was still learning how to use her Sight, that mystical mixture of foresight and insight, and there were limits to what she could do with it. Unfortunately, the only cure for that was experience, which was why she'd applied to become a Ranger. It was one of the quickest ways to graduate from witch to sorceress. If you survived.

She heard a noise behind her and looked back sharply into the Forest as the rest of the party appeared out of the shadows. Flint and the Dancer guided their horses along the difficult trail with casual ease. They both looked extremely competent and completely relaxed.

Jessica Flint was a good-looking brunette in her late twenties. She was a little over average height, wore her hair cropped like a man, and had a figure that would have been voluptuous if she hadn't been so muscular. Flint was a trained swordswoman and looked it. She wore a long chain mail vest that had seen better days but left her sinewy arms bare. Her cotton blouse and leggings were old but well maintained. Her face was open and cheerful, even in the heat of battle, of which she'd seen more than her fair share. She was one of the few survivors of those who'd fought in the last great battle of the Demon War, outside the Forest Castle itself. She still bore some of the scars, and there were only three fingers on her left hand. She carried her sword in a long, curved scabbard covered with delicate silver scrollwork. The scabbard was worth more than her sword and her horse put together, and Flint was very proud of it.

Giles Dancer rode at her side, as he always did. He wore quiet, nondescript clothes and no armor. He was just a little shorter than average and slight of build, and his flat, bland face showed little trace of personality. Put him in a crowd and you'd never notice him, until it was too late. The Dancer was a Bladesmaster, a man trained to such a peak of perfection that he was almost literally unbeatable with a sword in his hand. Bladesmasters had been rare even before the Demon

War; now there were said to be only two left alive in all the Forest Kingdom, and the Dancer was one of them. He was always quiet and polite, and his eyes had a vague, fey, and faraway look. No one knew exactly how many men he'd killed in his time; rumor had it even he was no longer sure. He and Flint had been partners from well before they joined MacNeil's team, and they had a reputation for getting the job done, no matter what the cost. They weren't always popular, but they were always respected. They'd been with MacNeil almost seven years, at least partly because he was the only one able to keep them under control. They respected MacNeil. Mostly.

The Dancer looked absently at Flint as they rode forward to join the others. "We're almost there now, aren't we, Jessica?"

"Almost," said Flint patiently. "I don't know why you're so eager to get there. So far everyone else who's approached this fort has disappeared off the face of the earth."

"They were amateurs," said the Dancer. "We're professionals."

"You're getting complacent," said Flint. "One of these days you're going to run into someone who's as good with a sword as you think you are, and I won't be there to back-stab him for you."

"Never happen," said the Dancer.

Flint snorted loudly.

"I'm quite looking forward to poking around inside the fort," said the Dancer. "Investigating a baffling mystery will make a pleasant change from chasing footpads through the Forest. A deserted fort, alone and abandoned to the elements ... doesn't it just make your flesh creep?"

"You've been listening to those damned minstrels again," said Flint disgustedly.

"Can I help it if I'm a romantic at heart?"

"You're morbid, that's what you are. Don't blame me if you get nightmares. You know those Gothic tales upset you."

The Dancer ignored her. Flint looked at Constance, waiting patiently beside MacNeil at the end of the trail.

"Giles," she said thoughtfully, "what do you make of our new witch?"

"She seems competent enough."

"Green, though. Never been on a real mission before. Never been tested under pressure."

"She'll settle in. Give her time."

"She's certainly no replacement for Salamander; she knew her job."

The Dancer looked at Flint affectionately. "You couldn't stand Salamander and you know it."

"I didn't like her much, but she always pulled her weight. A vital mission like this is no way to break in a new witch. If she fouls up, we could all end up dead."

"If there's a storm tonight we could get hit by lightning," said the Dancer. "But there's no point in worrying about it, is there? You worry too much, Jessica."

"And you don't worry enough."

"Then you can worry for me."

"I do," said Flint. "I do."

They fell silent as they drew up their horses beside MacNeil's. He nodded to them briefly. "Anything to report?"

"Nothing so far," said Flint. "We backtracked a way, just in case we were being followed, but we didn't see anyone. In fact, we haven't seen anyone for days. This part of the Forest is practically deserted. I haven't seen a village or a hamlet or a farm in almost a week."

"Hardly surprising, with the Darkwood boundary so close," said MacNeil.

"The Darkwood's quiet now," said the Dancer. "It won't rise again in our lifetime."

"We can't be sure of that," said Flint.

"No," said Constance oddly. "We can't."

MacNeil looked quickly at the witch. She was staring out into the clearing, her eyes dark and hooded.

"What is it?" said MacNeil quietly. "Do you See something?"

"I'm not sure," said Constance. "It's the fort. . . ."

"What about it?"

"There were giants in the earth in those days," she whispered, and then shuddered suddenly, looked away, and pulled her cloak about her. "I don't like this place. It's got a bad feel to it."

MacNeil frowned. "Do you See . . . anything specific?"

"No. My Sight is clouded here. But I've dreamed about this fort for the last three nights, terrible dreams, and now that I'm here . . . The clearing is cold, Duncan. Cold as a tomb. And the fort is dark. It feels . . . old, very old."

MacNeil shook his head slowly. "I think you're letting your feelings interfere with your magic, Constance. There's nothing old about this fort. It was only built four or five years ago. Before that, there was nothing here."

"Something was here," said Constance. "And it's been here for a very long time. . . ."

Her voice trailed away. Flint and the Dancer looked at each other but said nothing. They didn't have to. MacNeil knew what they were thinking. If Salamander had said such things, they would have taken it seriously. She'd had the Sight, and if she said a place was dangerous, it was. No argument. But this new witch . . . as yet her magic hadn't been tested under pressure, and until it had, no one was going to take her warnings seriously. Constance looked at MacNeil for his reaction, and he was careful to keep his voice calm and even.

"We're not going to learn anything about the fort just sitting here looking at it. The sooner we get in there and check the place out, the sooner we'll know where we'll be spending the night."

He urged his horse forward into the clearing. Flint and the Dancer followed him, and Constance brought up the rear. Her mouth was grim and set, and her eyes were very cold.

MacNeil tensed automatically as he left the cover of the trees for the open clearing. So far there'd been nothing to suggest there was an enemy presence anywhere nearby, but after so long in the Forest he felt naked and vulnerable in the wide-open space. The clearing had to be a good half-mile wide, shaped into a perfect circle by ax and saw. MacNeil peered unobtrusively about him, but there was no sign of anything moving in the surrounding trees. He frowned slightly as he suddenly realized just how quiet the clearing was. There were no birdsongs, no buzzing insects, nothing. Now that he thought about it, the Forest had been unusually quiet all day. No birds flew in the summer sky, and no game moved among the trees. Maybe the approaching storm had driven them all to cover. . . . The party's hoofbeats sounded loud and carrying in the quiet, and MacNeil felt a growing conviction that he and his team were being watched.

They drew steadily nearer the fort. Its high stone walls were a pale yellow in color, the pure white of the local stone already discolored by wind and rain and sun. The embrasures were empty, the battlements were deserted, and the great double doors were firmly closed. It was like looking at a fort under siege. MacNeil looked closely at the grassy floor of the clearing. There were no tracks to show that anyone else had crossed the clearing recently. MacNeil scowled unhappily. Maybe none of the messengers had actually got this far. This part of the Forest was notorious for its footpads and liers-in-wait.

The guards did their best to keep the roads open, but once off the beaten trail, a lone traveler took his life in his hands. Thieves and cutthroats and outlaws of all kinds had made the Forest wilds their own in the chaos following the Demon War. The most notorious gangs, like those led by Jimmy Squarefoot and Hob in Chains, had since been ruthlessly hunted down and hanged, but their successors were still active in the more remote parts of the Forest. Not that the Forest attracted only evil men; there were also those like Tom o' the Heath, who watched over lost travelers on the moors, and Scarecrow Jack, self-styled protector of the trees, a wild spirit of the greenwood who sometimes aided those in need with bounty he stole from the rich and prosperous who passed through his territory. But still and all, the Forest was a dangerous place for a man traveling on his own, and king's messengers were just as vulnerable as any other man.

MacNeil shook his head and glared at the border fort. He'd had enough of ifs and maybes; he wanted some answers. And one way or another, the fort was going to provide them. He looked across at the sun, hanging low on the sky just above the treetops. Two hours of light remaining at most. That meant he only had tonight and three more days before the main party arrived. Three days and four nights to find the answers. MacNeil sighed heavily. He hated working to deadlines. That was the trouble with being the best, he thought sourly. After a while they not only expect the impossible, they want it to a timetable as well.

He finally drew up his horse before the closed main doors, and the others reined in beside him. The fort stood still and silent before them, the last of the sunlight gleaming brightly from the yellow stone. MacNeil stared uneasily at the closed doors. The air was very still, and the continuous quiet preyed on his nerves. It was as though the fort was watching and waiting to see what he would do, defying him to solve its mystery. He pushed the thought from his mind, sat up straight in the saddle, and raised his voice in a carrying shout.

"Hello, the fort! This is Ranger Sergeant Duncan MacNeil. Open, in the name of the King!"

There was no response. The only sound to be heard was the low whickering of the horses.

"You don't really expect an answer, do you?" said Constance.

"Not really, no," said MacNeil patiently, "but we have

to go through the motions. It's standard procedure, and sometimes it gets results."

"But not this time."

"No. Not this time. Flint . . ."

"Yes, sir?"

"Try those doors. See how secure they are."

"Yes, sir." Flint swung down out of the saddle and handed her reins to the Dancer, who looped them loosely over his left arm. Flint drew her sword and walked unhurriedly forward to examine the closed doors. Her sword was a scimitar, and light gleamed brightly on the long curved blade as she hefted it. The doors loomed over her, huge and forboding. Flint studied the dark iron-bound wood carefully, and then reached out and tried each door with her left hand. They didn't give an inch, no matter how much pressure she applied. Flint beat on the left-hand door with her fist. The sound carried loudly for a moment, and then fell away in a series of dying echoes. Flint looked back at MacNeil.

"Locked and bolted by the feel of it."

"Surprise, surprise," said Constance impatiently. "Allow me."

A gust of wind swirled suddenly around the party, and the temperature dropped sharply. The horses rolled their eyes and tossed their heads nervously. MacNeil muttered soothing phrases to his horse and tightly clutched the reins. Magic beat on the air like the wings of a captured bird, and the great wooden doors creaked and groaned. They shuddered visibly, as though some invisible presence was pressing strongly against them. And then, quite clearly, there came the sound of metal rasping on metal as the heavy bolts slid back into their sockets, followed by the sharp clicking of tumblers turning in a lock. Constance let out a juddering sigh, and the two huge doors swung smoothly open, revealing an open, empty courtyard. The doors ground to a halt, and Constance smiled triumphantly. The gusting wind died away quickly, but it was still unseasonably cold, despite the bright sunshine. Constance looked challengingly at MacNeil, and he bowed politely to her.

"Not bad, Constance. But Salamander would have done it in half the time."

"To hear the three of you talk," said Constance, "you'd think this Salamander was one of the greatest witches who ever lived."

"She was good at her job," said MacNeil.

"If she was so good at it, why is she dead?"

"Bad luck," said Flint sharply. "It can happen to anyone." She walked back to her horse and took the reins from the Dancer.

Thank you, Jessica, thought MacNeil. *You always were the diplomatic one.*

Flint looked at him calmly. "Ready to take a look, sir?"

"Sure," said MacNeil. "Lead the way, Flint."

She nodded and led her horse into the open courtyard. MacNeil and the Dancer moved forward to flank her with their horses, and Constance brought up the rear. The wide cobbled yard stretched away beneath the lowering summer sky, but no horses stood at the hitching rails, and the surrounding doors and windows were dark and empty, like so many blank, unseeing eyes. The Dancer drew his sword, and MacNeil followed suit. There is a sound the sword makes as it clears the scabbard, a grim rasping whisper that promises blood and horror and sudden death. The sound seemed to echo on and on in the empty courtyard, as though reluctant to die away. MacNeil looked at the Dancer's sword, and not for the first time his hackles stirred uneasily. The Dancer's sword was long and broad and double-edged. There was no grace or beauty about the weapon; it was simply a brutal killing tool, and that was how the Dancer used it. MacNeil carried a long, slender sword that allowed him to work with the point as well as the edge. There was more to swordsmanship than butchery—at least, as far as he was concerned.

He looked around him, taking in the fort's courtyard. The wide-open space was deserted, but the feeling of being watched was stronger than ever. MacNeil scowled. There was something about the place that put his teeth on edge. Where the hell was everybody? The doors had been locked and bolted from the inside; there had to be someone here . . . somewhere. . . . MacNeil shivered suddenly. *A ghost just walked over my grave,* he thought wryly, and yet somehow he knew it was more than that. On a level so deep within him he was hardly aware of its presence, an old and secret fear cast a shadow across his thoughts. He looked around him at the darkened windows and felt a tremor in his soul, a stark and basic horror he hadn't felt for many years. Not since he faced the demon horde in the depths of the long night, and knew he couldn't stand against them. . . .

MacNeil shook his head quickly. He'd think about that later. He had work to do. He steered his horse over to the nearest hitching rail, and the memory faded from his mind, as it had so many times before. He dismounted and wrapped the reins around the low wooden rail. The others moved in beside him to see to their horses, and MacNeil looked quickly around at the various doorways, getting his bearings. One fort is much like any other, and it didn't take him long to work out which was the main entrance. The door was opposite the courtyard doors and stood slightly ajar. Beyond it was nothing but an impenetrable gloom. MacNeil started toward the door, and then stopped and looked back suddenly. For a moment he'd thought he heard something. . . . He stood listening, but the only sound was the soft murmur of the rising wind outside the fort. MacNeil frowned as he realized that many of the windows looking out onto the courtyard were hidden behind closed shutters, despite the heat of the day. *That's crazy,* he thought confusedly, *it must be like an oven in there.* His mind seized on the word *crazy,* and it repeated over and over in his thoughts like an echo. To get away from it, he concentrated on what he was looking at. The stables were to his right, the barracks to his left. In both cases, the doors stood slightly ajar. He became aware that Constance was standing beside him, her eyes darting nervously around the courtyard, as though searching for something safe to settle on.

"You said this was a new fort," she said suddenly, not looking at MacNeil. "Do you know why it was built here? Is there anything about this location I ought to know?"

"You already know most of it," said MacNeil. "The border between the Forest Kingdom and Hillsdown runs right through the middle of this clearing. The fort is here to stabilize this stretch of the frontier, nothing more. It worked quite well . . . until just recently."

Constance frowned. "Hillsdown doesn't have much in the way of sorcerers or magicians, not that I've ever heard of. Taking out a fort this size would require sorcery far beyond Hillsdown's means."

MacNeil looked at her thoughtfully. "Can you sense anything here? Anything magical, or immediately dangerous?"

Constance closed her eyes and gave herself to the Sight. Her mind's eye opened, and scenes and feelings came to her. The fort was cold and empty, like an abandoned coffin, but still there was something . . . something awful, not far away. She concentrated, trying for more detail, but her Sight remained obstinately vague. There was definitely something dangerous close at hand; there was a feeling of power about it, and a stronger feeling of *wrongness*. A slow beat of pain began in her forehead, and the images became blurred and muddy. Constance sighed and opened her eyes again. As always, the Sight left her feeling drained and tired, but she kept her voice calm and steady as she spoke to MacNeil. She didn't want him thinking of her as the weak link in his team. It was obvious he already considered her no replacement for his precious Salamander.

"There's something here, Sergeant, but I can't get a clear picture of it. It's some kind of magical presence, very powerful and very old, but that's all I can See."

Something old, thought MacNeil. *That's twice she's used the word* old *in connection with this fort, despite knowing how recent it is.*

"All right," he said finally. "First things first. If we're going to spend the night here, we need a place we can defend, and this courtyard definitely isn't it. Flint, Dancer, you check out the stables and then see to the horses. Constance, you come with me. I want to take a look at those barracks."

Flint and the Dancer nodded, and moved off toward the stables. MacNeil headed for the barracks on the opposite side of the courtyard and the witch hurried after him, not wanting to be left on her own, even for a moment. The silence was beginning to get to her, and the vague image she'd Seen disturbed her deeply. In some strange way she felt as though she ought to recognize it.

MacNeil noticed her haste in joining him, and was careful not to smile. He was grateful for the company himself. He came to a halt before the barracks door and studied it closely. Like all the other doors he'd seen in the courtyard, it stood slightly ajar. MacNeil pursed his lips thoughtfully. If there was a pattern or reason to it, he couldn't see it yet. He pushed the door gently with the toe of his boot, and it swung smoothly open. MacNeil hefted his sword and stepped forward into the gloom of the barracks.

Light filtered past the closed shutters and spilled in from the open door. MacNeil stepped quickly in and to one side. A silhouette against an open door made too good a target. He pulled Constance over beside him and they stood together in silence a moment, letting their eyes adjust to the gloom. There was a thick layer of dust everywhere, and dust motes spun slowly in the narrow shafts of sunlight. The air had a damp, musty smell that was subtly disturbing. *It smells more like a mausoleum than a barracks,* thought MacNeil, and then wondered why that particular comparison had occurred to him. A single chair lay on its side in the middle of the floor, between two rows of beds. There were dark stains spattered across the chair, as though it had been flecked with paint. MacNeil heard Constance draw in a sharp breath, and then a sudden brilliance flooded the barracks as the witch held up her right hand. MacNeil cursed irritably and shielded his dazzled eyes with his free hand.

"Next time, warn me first."

"I'm sorry," said Constance breathlessly, "but look at the chair, Duncan. Look at the chair. . . ."

The dark stains on the chair were blood—old, dried blood. MacNeil lowered his hand and looked quickly about him. There were fifty beds in all, set back against the walls in two neat rows. On every bed the rumpled blankets were soaked with long-dried blood.

"My God," said Constance quietly. "What the hell happened here?"

MacNeil shook his head, unable to speak. In the silvery light that glowed from the witch's upraised hand, he could clearly see the great crimson splashes on the walls and floor and ceiling. It was like walking into an abandoned abattoir. Most of the bedclothes had been hacked and cut apart by swords or axes, while two beds had been literally torn to pieces. Splinters lay scattered across the floor, and a half-dozen thick wooden spikes had been driven into one wall like so many jagged nails.

MacNeil moved forward slowly. Constance stayed where she was by the door, the silver light still blazing from her hand. MacNeil vaguely prodded the nearest bed with his sword. He felt strangely numb, unable to take in what had happened. He was no stranger to blood and violence and sudden death, but there was something horribly pathetic about the empty blood-stained beds. What kind of creature could have killed

fifty guards in their barracks and then disposed of their
bodies, all without leaving any trace of its own presence? He hadn't seen an atrocity like this since the Demon War. And there were no demons in the Forest
anymore. MacNeil crouched beside the bed and looked
underneath it. There was nothing there but more dust
and dried blood.

So much blood . . .

He straightened up and looked back at the witch by
the door. "Constance."

"Yes, sir?"

"What can you See here?"

The witch closed her eyes and opened her mind.
The light from her hand snapped off, and darkness fell
upon the barracks once again. MacNeil gripped his
sword tightly, blinded by the sudden loss of light. He
peered about him into the gloom, listening warily for
any sound of something sneaking up on him under
cover of the sudden darkness, but all was still and silent. His eyes slowly adjusted again, and he could just
make out Constance standing very still beside the open
door. As he watched, she sighed and turned her head
to look at him.

"I'm sorry," she said tightly, "I can't See anything. I
should be able to, but I can't. Something here in the
fort, or very close by, is blocking my Sight."

MacNeil frowned. "Could it be a natural blind spot?"

"I don't know. But haven't you noticed? It's cold in
here. Very cold."

"It's bound to be, now we're out of the sun. It's the
thick stone walls."

"No," said the witch. "It's more than that."

MacNeil noticed for the first time that his breath

was steaming on the still air. He tightened his grip on his sword hilt, and found he could barely feel it. His fingers were numb from the cold. It had crept up on him so slowly he hadn't even noticed.

"I think we'd better get out of here," he said softly. "For the time being." He backed away toward the door, his sword held out before him. There was no sign of any immediate danger, but for some reason he didn't want to turn his back on the bloodstained beds. He reached the open door and found Constance had already stepped out into the courtyard. MacNeil paused a moment in the doorway. Fifty beds. So much blood ... He stepped out into the courtyard and pulled the door firmly shut. He scowled at the closed door and then looked at Constance. Her face was pale but composed.

"Where next?" she said evenly.

MacNeil nodded at the main entrance. "That door should lead into the reception hall. Perhaps we'll find some answers there."

He strode quickly across the courtyard, and Constance followed close behind him. The open yard seemed almost uncomfortably warm after the chill of the barracks. He pushed the door open and entered the reception hall with his sword at the ready. It looked like any other hall in any other fort, a simple, unadorned chamber with one desk and a half-dozen uncomfortable-looking chairs. Everything seemed normal, apart from the four nooses that hung from the overhead beam, the thick ropes dangling limply in the still air. The hangman's knots looked amateurish but effective. Beneath the nooses, four chairs lay on their sides on the floor. MacNeil stood just inside the door and swallowed dryly. It was only too easy to visualize four men being forced to stand on the chairs while the nooses were tightened around their necks. And then the chairs would have been kicked away, one by one. . . .

"Maybe some of them went mad," said Constance slowly.

"It can happen," said MacNeil. "Like cabin fever. Take a group of armed men and confine them in a limited space for a long period with nothing to do, and they'll crack sooner or later. But any commander worth his salt knows the danger signs and takes steps to deal with it. No one said anything about this fort having a bad record; as far as I know there were no indications that anything was wrong . . . No, it doesn't make sense. If four men were hanged here, where are their bodies? Why take them down and leave the nooses? Nothing about this place makes any sense. Yet. But more and more I get the feeling something terrible must have happened here."

"Yes," said Constance oddly. "Something terrible. And I think it's still happening."

MacNeil looked at her sharply. The witch's eyes were vague and faraway, and there was something in her face that might have been fear.

Flint and the Dancer stood just inside the stable doors and stared silently about them. Light poured in from the open doors, pushing back the shadows. The heavy wooden stalls had been smashed into kindling. The walls were scarred and gouged, as though they'd been scored repeatedly by claws. There was no sign of any of the horses, but blood had splashed and dried on the floor and walls.

"Nasty," said Flint.

The Dancer nodded. "Very."

"Demons?"

"Unlikely."

"It's their style."

"The Demon War ended ten years ago. No one's seen a demon outside the Darkwood since."

Flint scowled unhappily. "They came out of the long night once before; maybe they're on the move again."

The Dancer knelt down and studied the blood-stained straw covering the earth floor. "Interesting."

"What is?" Flint knelt down beside him.

"Look at the floor, Jessica. There's blood everywhere but no footprints, only hoof marks. And if the horses were killed and dragged out, where are the tracks? There should be some traces to show what happened to the bodies."

"You're right," said Flint. "It is interesting."

They straightened up quickly and automatically fell into their usual fighting position, back to back with swords held out before them. The shadows all around were suddenly dark and menacing. The air was dry and still and unnaturally cold. It smelled faintly of death and corruption. Flint stirred uneasily and flexed the three fingers of her left hand. The scar tissue where the missing two fingers had been throbbed dully. It didn't like the cold. Flint shuddered suddenly. There was something dangerous here in the fort with them; she could feel it. She had no idea what or where it might be, but she had no doubt it was there. Flint trusted her instincts implicitly.

"Yes," said the Dancer quietly. "I feel it too. Whatever happened to the people in this fort, I don't think they died a clean death."

"We can't leave our horses here," said Flint. "They'd spook before we could get them through the door. Let's take a look at the main building, see if we can find a suitable place there."

"Good idea," said the Dancer.

"Then let's get out of here. I'm getting spooked myself."

"You're not alone," the Dancer assured her.

"I told you not to listen to those minstrels. You'll be having bad dreams tonight."

"Wouldn't surprise me. I don't think this is a good place to sleep, Jessica."

Flint smiled slightly. "You might just be right, Giles. But can you think of a better way to get to the bottom of what happened here?"

"There is that," said the Dancer. "Let's go."

He led the way back out into the sunshine, and Flint pulled the doors shut after her. She and the Dancer crossed the courtyard side by side, swords at the ready, their eyes wary and watchful. Their footsteps echoed hollowly back from the high stone walls. The sky was darkening toward evening, and the shadows were growing longer.

Flint and the Dancer eventually settled the horses in the main reception hall. It wasn't ideal, it wasn't even a lot better than anywhere else, but the horses seemed prepared to tolerate it. They rolled their eyes as they were led through the door, and regarded the bare wooden floor with grave suspicion, but finally settled down. Flint lit a lantern, and then she and the Dancer made their way deeper into the main building. Finding MacNeil and Constance was easy enough; they just followed the tracks in the thick dust on the floor. Flint eventually rounded a corner and found MacNeil waiting for her, sword in hand.

"I thought I heard somebody following us," said MacNeil dryly, lowering his sword.

"Have you found anything?" asked the Dancer.

"Nothing helpful. Just empty rooms, dust, and blood."

The bloodstains were everywhere. They splashed across the ceiling, ran down the walls, and pooled on the floor. So much blood . . .

"What are the chances on finding anyone alive?" said Constance.

"Not good," said MacNeil. "But we'll keep looking anyway. Just in case."

The four of them slowly made their way through the fort, corridor by corridor, room by room. The corridors were for the most part bare and unadorned, with little in the way of matting or tapestries to break up the monotony of bare stone. All the rooms were empty and covered with a thick layer of undisturbed dust. But wherever they went they found bloodstains and broken furniture and enigmatic claw marks gouged deep into the stone walls.

And finally they came to the cellar, and there was nowhere left to go. The cellar was a featureless stone chamber some fifty feet square, littered with accumulated rubbish. Two open doorways led into smaller storage areas. MacNeil picked his way carefully through the mess, and the others followed him as best they could. There were piles of firewood, bags of rags, and stacks of old paper waiting to be pulped, along with broken furniture, wine casks, and general filth and garbage, all strewn across the bare floor without rhyme or reason. MacNeil made his way to the center of the cellar, being very careful about where he trod and what he trod in, and then stopped and looked disgustedly about him.

"I've seen cess pits that were cleaner than this."

"It is rather untidy," said the Dancer. "But have you noticed the walls?"

"Yeah." said MacNeil. "There aren't any bloodstains down here."

"Is that a good sign or a bad sign?" said Flint.

"Beats me," said MacNeil.

"We've got to get out of here," said Constance suddenly. "Something's wrong here."

The others turned to look at her. The witch was shivering violently.

"How do you mean, something's wrong?" said MacNeil. "Have you Seen something?"

"It's *wrong* here," said Constance, staring blindly ahead of her as though she hadn't heard him.

MacNeil looked at the others, and then looked quickly around the cellar one more time. He shook his head slightly, as though disappointed, and then moved back to take the witch's arm. "There's nothing down here that matters. Let's go, Constance."

She nodded gratefully and let him help her back to the cellar door. Flint and the Dancer followed them out.

Eventually they ended up in the main dining hall, at the rear of the fort. It was a good-sized hall, some forty feet long and twenty wide, with trestle tables set out in neat rows. As in the cellar, the walls were unscarred and there were no bloodstains anywhere. The tables were set for a meal long abandoned. Food still lay on some of the plates, dry and dusty and covered with mold. Bottles of wine stood open and unopened on the tables. It was as though people had come in for a meal as usual, and then halfway through had just got up and walked away. . . .

"We'll sleep here tonight," said MacNeil. "It's comparatively untouched by the madness, and since there's only the one entrance, it should be easy enough to defend."

"You're really prepared to spend the night here?" said Constance. "After everything we've seen?"

MacNeil looked at her coldly. "We've seen nothing that's immediately threatening. Whatever killed all these people, it's obviously been gone some time. We'll be a lot safer here, and a great deal more comfortable, than we would be out in the Forest during a thunderstorm. We'll set a guard tonight, and first thing tomorrow morning we'll start tearing this place apart. There's got to be an answer here somewhere."

"I don't think we should disturb anything," said Constance. "I mean, it could be evidence."

"She's right," said the Dancer.

MacNeil shrugged. "Anything that looks significant we can leave alone. Either way, it can all wait till the morning. They don't pay me enough to go wandering around this place in the dark."

"Right," said Flint. "There isn't that much money in the world."

"All right, then, let's get our bedrolls in here and get ourselves settled," said MacNeil. "It'll be dark soon."

"Dark," said Constance quietly. "Yes. It gets very dark here at night."

They all looked at her, but the witch didn't notice, lost in her own thoughts.

Out in the Forest, a lone figure watched the fort curiously, and then faded back into the shadows between the trees and was gone.

2

In the Darkness
of the Night

Night fell suddenly. Less than an hour after the Rangers entered the dining hall, darkness swept over the border fort. Flint and Constance busied themselves lighting the torches on the walls as the daylight faded, while MacNeil and the Dancer arranged burning candles and oil lamps in a circle around the sleeping area they'd chosen. Though none of them admitted it aloud, they were all wary of what the darkness might bring, and none of them wanted to face the unknown without plenty of light to see it by.

Flint and the Dancer collected the saddle rolls from the horses and brought them back to the hall. They stayed close together in the narrow passageways and held their lanterns high. The lengthening shadows were very dark. Flint and Constance laid out the bedrolls in the middle of the dining hall, while MacNeil and the Dancer arranged the trestle tables around them in a simple barricade. The lightweight tables weren't very sturdy, but they gave a feeling of protection and security, and that was what mattered. Even with all the candles and torches and lamps, the dining hall was still disturbingly gloomy and full of restless shadows. The size of the hall gave every sound a faint echo that was subtly unnerving, and outside the fort a strong wind was blowing, moaning in the night. And yet when all was said and done, none of the Rangers really gave much of a damn. After the day's hard journey they were all bone weary and half asleep on their feet.

Flint volunteered to take the first watch, and nobody argued with her. They unwrapped their sleeping rolls and laid the blankets side by side. There was something comforting and reassuring in the simple proximity, and there was also no denying that the dining hall had grown uncomfortably cold.

MacNeil considered starting a fire in the open hearth, and then decided against it. A fire would be more trouble than it was worth, and anyway, it was a summer's night, dammit. It couldn't be that cold. . . . He climbed into his blankets and pulled them up around his ears. The floor was cold and hard and uneven, but he'd slept on worse. Already he was so tired he could hardly keep his eyes open. He yawned, scratched his ribs, and sighed contentedly. It felt good to be off his feet at last.

Flint fussed over the Dancer's blankets, sorting them out for him while he watched patiently. The Dancer was hopeless at the little practicalities of life. He couldn't saddle his own horse either, and if he had to live on his own cooking, he'd starve. No one ever said anything. The Dancer's talents lay in other directions. Flint finally got him settled and sat down beside him.

"We should have looked for a room with an adjoining bath," she said quietly. "We could both use one."

"Speak for yourself," said the Dancer.

"I am," said Flint. "I once fought a walking corpse that had been buried in soft peat for six months, and it smelled better than I do right now. But that can wait till tomorrow. Get some sleep, Giles. I'll wake you when it's time for the next watch."

The Dancer nodded sleepily, laid back, and closed his eyes. Flint smiled at him affectionately for a moment, and then drew her sword and rested it across her knees, ready to hand. Flint believed in being prepared.

Constance came back from the closed-off corner they'd designated as the latrine, and clambered stiffly between her blankets, next to MacNeil's. "First thing tomorrow morning we find a room with its own jakes and move there," she said determinedly. "That soup tureen is no substitute for a chamber pot."

MacNeil chuckled drowsily without opening his eyes. "Good night, Constance. Pleasant dreams."

The dining hall grew quiet as the four Rangers settled down for the night. The only sounds were the rising moan of the wind outside and faint snores from the Dancer, who was already well away. The Dancer could sleep through a thunderstorm, and often had. Constance tossed and turned for a while, unhappy with the hard stone floor, but eventually grew still. Her breathing became slow and regular, and some of the harshness went out of her face as her features slowly relaxed. MacNeil lay on his back, comfortably drowsing, occasionally staring up at the shadowed ceiling past drooping eyelids. Sleeping in the fort was a calculated risk, but he didn't think there was any real danger in it. Not yet. Whatever it was that had gone on a killing spree, there was no sign of it in the fort now.

Whatever it was . . . The Demon War had awakened a great many creatures that might otherwise have slumbered on, undisturbed by the world of man. The Forest's past lay buried deep in the earth, but after the time of the long night, the past no longer slept as soundly as it used to. Some of the deeper mine shafts were still sealed off because of what the miners had found there.

There were giants in the earth in those days. . . .

MacNeil stirred restlessly. If by some chance he was wrong, and whatever it was hadn't left the fort yet, well, at least this way there was some bait to draw it out of cover. Bait. MacNeil smiled sadly. That's what Rangers were when you got right down to it. Rangers were expendable troops, used to draw out an enemy and expose its strengths and weaknesses. The only difference was that this bait had teeth. MacNeil glanced across at Flint, who was staring straight ahead of her with one hand resting comfortably on her sword hilt. He was glad Flint had volunteered to take the first watch. He trusted her. The Dancer meant well, but if he got too comfortable he had a tendency to doze off. Which meant he spent most of his watches pacing up and down to keep himself alert. Things like that didn't help at all when you were trying to get to sleep. And Constance . . . was untried. MacNeil closed his eyes and let himself drift away. He could trust Flint. She was dependable. He yawned widely. It had been a long, hard day. . . .

Time passed. Flint watched over the sleepers, and the lights burned steadily lower.

The demons came swarming out of the long night, vile and malevolent, and the guards at the town barricades met them with cold steel and boiling oil and what little courage they had left. Duncan MacNeil stood his ground and swung his sword in short, vicious arcs, cutting down creature after creature as they threw themselves at the barricades in a never-ending stream. Shapes out of nightmares and fever dreams reached for him with clawed hands and bared fangs, and their eyes glowed hungrily in the endless night. Blood flew on the air in a ghastly rain as the guards swung their swords and axes, and the demons died, but there were always more to take the place of those who fell. There were always more.

A tall, spindly creature with a spiked back and taloned hands reared up before MacNeil. He ducked beneath a flailing blow and gutted the demon with one swift cut. Long ropes of writhing intestines fell down to tangle the demon's legs, but still it pressed forward until MacNeil sheared off its bony head with a two-handed blow. Its mouth snarled soundlessly on the blood-soaked ground, and the body swung this way and that for long moments before realizing it was dead. None of the demons made a sound, even when they died. Forever silent, in life or death, like evil thoughts given shape and substance.

Something the size of a man's head, with thick black fur and a dozen legs, came flapping out of the darkness on bat's wings. MacNeil cut it out of the air and it exploded wetly, showering him with foul-smelling blood that burned where it touched his bare skin. And while he was distracted, shaking and cursing, a patchwork demon with a vast corpse-pale body and huge scything jaws slammed into him from nowhere and threw him to the ground.

For a moment all MacNeil could see was a confusion of human and demon feet all around him, slipping and stamping in the crimson mud. He lashed out at the pale demon as it bent over him, and screamed shrilly as its claws tore through his ragged chain mail. He wriggled away through the mud, then drove his boot up into the creature's gut, desperation lending him strength. The demon lurched backward, caught off balance, and MacNeil surged to his feet. By the time he had his feet under him again, the pale demon was gone, carried away by the shifting press of bodies, but there were still more demons to be faced. MacNeil wiped blood and tears from his face with his sleeve and hacked about him with his sword to try to clear himself some space. He put all his remaining strength into his blows, and the power from his muscular arms and broad chest drove his sword deep into demon flesh and out again in steady butchery.

The demons came from all sides now, vicious and unrelenting, and the night wasn't dark enough to hide the horror of what they did. MacNeil fought on. He had no idea of how many demons he'd killed. He'd lost count long ago. It didn't make any difference. There were always more. He swung his sword double-handed now, and the hilt jarred in his hands as he hacked through a demon's spine. There were screams all through the night, and somewhere close at hand a man was cursing endlessly, his voice thick and empty. A woman sobbed, loud and anguished, until the sound broke off suddenly. And then the demons were retreating as suddenly as they'd come, melting silently back into the endless night.

MacNeil lowered his dripping sword and leaned on it, fighting for breath. The air was full of the stench of blood and death. The great muscles in his arms and back ached horribly, and he was deathly tired. There was no end to the demons, and the intervals between their attacks were getting shorter. They came to the slaughter like pigs at a trough, and there was no end to their appetite for carnage. And strong as he was, MacNeil knew there were limits to his strength, and he was fast approaching them.

He slowly straightened up and looked about him. There were bodies everywhere, and the barricades had been all but torn apart. The dead and the wounded lay where they had fallen on the blood-soaked ground. No one had the time or the strength to drag them away. Many of the bodies showed signs of feasting. The demons were always hungry. The long night was bitterly cold, and MacNeil pulled his tattered cloak about him. His hands shook, not entirely from the cold. High above, the Blue Moon shone down from a starless night, and the Darkwood held dominion over all the Forest. Demons swarmed everywhere in the darkness surrounding the small besieged town of King's Deep. The town had been cut off from the outside world for so long its defenders were no longer sure how long it had been. The nightmare seemed to go on forever, as though it had always been happening and always would. No sun rose or set in the Darkwood; there was only the endless night and the creatures that moved in it.

MacNeil clutched his sword tightly, but it had lost all power to comfort him. He'd always thought of himself as brave, but that was before the Darkwood. In the past he'd fought footpads and smugglers and Hillsdown spies, and never given a damn for the danger. He was strong and fast and good with a sword, and he'd never once backed down from a fight. Unlike many of his fellow guards, he'd always looked forward to going into action; he loved the thrill in his blood and the chance for glory. But that was before he came to defend King's Deep and found himself facing a ravenous horde of inhuman creatures that came swarming out of the dark in never ending numbers. He'd taken his place at the barricade and fought and killed and slaughtered until his sword arm ached and his armor was soaked with demon blood, and none of it mattered a damn. One by one the defenders fell, and a growing desperation gnawed at MacNeil as the siege continued with no end in sight.

He leaned against the barricade and closed his eyes for a moment. His whole body trembled with fatigue, and sweat and blood trickled down his face. He couldn't face another attack. He just couldn't. He opened his eyes and glanced back at the town behind him. Here and there in King's Deep a few lights flickered defiantly against the darkness, but the light didn't carry far. There weren't many people left to look at them anyway. MacNeil looked down at his sword. Demon blood dripped steadily from the long blade, but he couldn't find the energy to clean it.

He'd always thought he was brave. For almost two years he'd used his sword to enforce the king's law, hunting down criminals and keeping the roads safe. He was proud of his strength and his courage, and neither of them had ever let him down. Until he came to King's Deep, and the demons taught him fear. He killed them over and over again, and still they came swarming out of the darkness, driven by hatred and a never-ending hunger. MacNeil had given everything he had to stop them, and it hadn't been enough. He looked out into the endless night and waited for the demons to come again. He thought he would die soon, and he doubted his death would be easy.

The demons had taught him fear. It felt like panic and despair.

He looked at the broken barricade before him and wondered why he still stayed at his post. King's Deep was nothing to him, just another small country town in the back of beyond, of no importance to anyone but its inhabitants. The town was bound to fall sooner or later, and if he stayed he'd fall with it. If he stayed. He turned the thought over in his mind, studying it warily. He didn't have to stay. The guard captain who'd given him his orders was dead and gone, along with most of the other guards. He could just slip quietly away from his post and run, trusting to the dark to hide him. No one would ever know. Except him.

MacNeil shook his head to clear it. In all the minstrels' songs the heroes never once considered turning and running. They just stood their ground and died nobly. It was different here in the darkness, facing an enemy without end. . . . He looked up sharply as he sensed rather than heard a stirring in the night. There was a clatter of running feet around him as others sensed the disturbance and moved forward to block some of the larger gaps in the barricades. MacNeil gripped his sword tightly and wondered vaguely why he was crying. The tears ran jerkily down his face, cutting furrows in the drying blood. He tried to stop crying and couldn't. He was cold and tired and hurt so badly he could hardly stand up straight, and still he had to fight. It wasn't fair. They had no right to expect so much of him. He'd done his best for as long as he could, but he just couldn't do it anymore. Not anymore.

Demons came boiling out of the darkness, throwing themselves at the barricades in a silent, murderous frenzy. MacNeil stood his ground and swung his sword double-handed, the long blade biting deep into demon flesh. Foul-smelling blood flew thickly through the air, and his footing grew slippery. His arm and back muscles screamed in agony, but still he fought, his sword rising and falling again and again. He started to whimper, and bit his lips until the blood came to keep from crying out. The demons burst through the barricades, and he was forced to retreat. He fell back, fighting every step of the way, and all around him the town's defenders were pulled down and slaughtered. Their screams lasted a long time. MacNeil swung his sword with failing arms, and the demons came at him from all sides.

No. No, this isn't how it was. The long night broke, the dawn came, and the demons and the darkness retreated. King's Deep was saved, and I survived. I remember! I was there! This isn't how it was!

The demons swarmed over him and pulled him down, and there was only the blood and the darkness.

A low wind murmured across the deserted moor, and moonlight shone silver on the early morning mists. The sun would be up in less than an hour, and still Jessica Flint stood alone in the old graveyard. She pulled her cloak tightly about her, and vowed that once she got back to her nice warm barracks nothing short of a declaration of war would get her out on night duty again.

She also vowed to do something extremely unpleasant to the sergeant who'd volunteered her for this duty.

Flint looked about her, but apart from the graveyard the open moor stretched away in every direction, all silver and shadows in the half moon's light. Half a mile away, over the down-curving horizon, lay the small village of Castle Mills, to whom the graveyard belonged. It was on the villagers' behalf that Flint was freezing her butt off on the moor at this unearthly hour of the morning. Six months before, they'd caught a rapist and murderer attacking his latest victim. The villagers dragged him out onto the street and hanged him on the spot, amid general celebration. Rather than pollute their graveyard, they threw the body into a peat bog out on the moor. One month later the dead man dug his way out of the mire and made his way back to the village. He killed four women with his bare hands before the villagers banded together and drove him off with flaring torches. He returned to the peat bog and disappeared beneath the mud. But the next month he rose again, and every month after that. The villagers learned to patrol their streets as soon as the sun went down, and the lich turned his attentions to the local graveyard, which comfort he'd been denied. He dug up graves, smashed coffins, and violated the bodies. The villagers sent to the guards for help, and Flint was the unlucky one.

She glanced at the oil-soaked torch standing unlit beside a tombstone. She didn't dare light it before the lich appeared, for fear of frightening him off. In order for it to be effective, she'd have to use the torch at very close range.

Flint frowned and rested her hand on the pommel of

the sword at her side. She'd never fought a lich before. Fire was the usual defense, but by all accounts the lich had proved too elusive for that, so far. Maybe if she hacked him into small pieces first. . . . She shrugged and looked around her.

It wasn't much of a graveyard. Just a wide patch of uneven earth, with a dozen weatherbeaten headstones and a scattering of sagging wooden crosses. It smelled pretty bad too. Flint doubted if the people of Castle Mills had even heard of embalming.

A faint noise caught her attention, and she spun around, sword in hand. The peat bog where the murderer's body had been dumped lay less than a hundred yards away, its dark, wet surface gleaming coldly in the moonlight. Flint licked her dry lips, and then froze where she stood as a claw-like hand thrust up through the mire. Mud dripped from the bony fingers as they flexed jerkily. The hand rose slowly out of the mire, followed by a long, crooked arm and a bony head. Flint snapped out of her daze, and drawing flint and steel from her pocket, she lit the torch she'd brought with her. For a moment she thought it had got too damp to catch, but the oil-soaked head finally burst into flames, and she turned back to face the peat bog with the flaring torch in one hand and her sword in the other. The mire's surface parted reluctantly with a long sucking sound, and the dead man pulled himself out into the night air. He stood wavering on the edge of the bog, and slowly turned his head to look at Flint. His skin was stained and shrunken, but had been mostly preserved by his time in the bog. The eyes were gone, eaten away by decay, but Flint somehow knew that he could still see her. The lich wore a series of filthy tat-

ters that might once have been clothes, held together
by muck and foulness. Mud dripped steadily from him
as he started forward, heading for Flint.

All right, thought Flint. *This is where I earn my pay.*

She stepped forward to meet the lich, holding the
torch up high. Moonlight shimmered brightly on the
curved blade of her scimitar as she held it out before
her. The lich walked unsteadily toward her, his bony
fingers clenching and unclenching spasmodically. Flint
waited until the last possible moment, and then cut at
the lich with her sword. The dead man swayed aside
horribly quickly, and the blade whistled through empty
air. Flint quickly recovered her balance and jumped
backward, but the lich's hand shot out and fastened
onto her left wrist. The bony fingers sank deep into her
flesh, and blood ran down her hand, but she wouldn't
drop the torch. Flint swung her sword down in a short,
brutal arc and cut through the lich's wrist. She fell
backward, the dead hand still clutching her wrist, and
landed awkwardly. Somehow she still managed to hang
onto the torch and her sword.

The lich stopped and looked at the stump of his
wrist. No blood spurted from the severed arm, though
bone fragments showed clearly in the moonlight. Flint
stealthily drew her feet under her and shook the dead
hand free from her wrist. Cut off the head and then
the legs, and the thing would be helpless. Burn the
remnants to ashes with the torch, and the lich would
never trouble the villagers again. All it took was a
steady nerve and a steady hand.

She scrambled quickly to her feet, and then tripped
on the uneven ground. She fell heavily, jarring the
breath from her lungs, and dropped both her sword and

the torch. The flame flickered and went out. Flint
struggled to her knees, gasping for breath, and reached
for her sword. The lich got there first.

No. That's not right.

The lich picked up the sword with its remaining
hand and hefted it thoughtfully. The eyeless face
turned slowly to grin at Flint. She scrambled frantically
backward.

No! That isn't the way it happened! I beat the lich!

The walking dead man loomed over her, huge and
dark and awful. Moonlight gleamed on the sword as he
lifted it above his head, and then the blade came flashing down and blood ran darkly on the moonlit ground.
The sword rose and fell, rose and fell. . . .

Giles Dancer walked down a long stone passage that
had no beginning and no end. Torches burned on the
walls to either side of him, but made little impression
on the darkness that filled the passage like a living
thing. The Dancer walked through the corridors of
Castle Lancing with his sword in his hand, searching
for the werewolf.

The shapeshifter was as cunning as it was deadly,
and it had taken the Dancer some time to work out
which of the baron's guests was the werewolf, but now
he knew. The creature couldn't be far ahead of him. He
padded softly down the narrow corridor, his calm, cold
eyes searching the gloom for any trace of his prey. It
seemed to him that he'd been searching for the werewolf for a long time, but the Dancer was patient. He
knew he'd find it eventually, and then he would kill it.

He walked on down the passage, and a slight frown
creased his forehead. He hadn't known Castle Lancing

was this big. Surely he should have got somewhere by now. And there was something about this case he ought to remember; he was sure of it, but he couldn't quite place what it was. A sudden sound caught his attention, and he stopped where he was and listened carefully. The sound came again: a low, coughing growl, not far away. The Dancer smiled. This should be interesting. He'd never killed a werewolf before. He hoped the creature would put up a good fight; it had been a long time since anyone had been able to challenge his skill. Man or beast, sorcerer or shapeshifter, it made no difference to him. He was a Blademaster, and he was unbeatable. He moved slowly forward, listening carefully all the way, but there was only the silence and the shadows. And then he rounded a corner in the passage, and the werewolf came out of the darkness to meet him.

It was tall, well over seven feet in height, its shaggy head brushing the roof of the corridor. Its thick fur was matted with sweat and blood, and it smelled rank, like a filthy butcher's shop. The close-set eyes were yellow as urine, and its wide, grinning mouth was full of heavy pointed teeth. The werewolf snarled at the Dancer, and ropy saliva fell from its mouth. The two of them stood looking at each other for a long moment, and then the Dancer smiled and hefted his sword lightly. The werewolf howled and threw itself at the Dancer's throat. He sidestepped easily, and his sword cut into and out of the werewolf's stomach in a single fluid movement. The creature howled again and spun around to claw the Dancer, the horrid wound in its gut healing even as it moved. The Dancer slipped the silver dagger out of the top of his boot and drove it between the werewolf's ribs with a practiced twist of the wrist. The creature screamed in a human voice and fell limply to the stone floor. Its blood was as red as any human's. The Dancer stepped carefully back out of range, and watched calmly as the werewolf's panting breath slowed and stopped.

And as he watched, the creature's shape blurred and changed, the fur and fangs and claws slowly melting away, until there before him on the floor lay Jessica Flint, with his knife in her heart.

The witch called Constance stood in the reception hall. A cold wind was blowing from nowhere, and the shadows were too dark. Four men were tying nooses and throwing the ropes over the supporting beam above them. They paid the witch no attention as they worked, and though their mouths were smiling, their eyes were puzzled and confused.

The first man to finish took a chair from beside the wall and positioned it carefully under the noose he'd arranged. He stood on the chair, slipped the noose around his neck, and then waited patiently while the others did the same. Finally all four men were standing on chairs with nooses around their necks. They pulled the nooses tight, and without looking at each other, one by one they stepped off the chairs. They hung unmoving from the roof beam, slowly strangling. Their hands hung freely at their sides as they choked.

Constance stepped around them, giving their twitching feet a wide berth, and ran into the main corridor that led off from the reception hall. A guard was hacking a trader to pieces as he tried to crawl away. A lengthy trail of blood on the corridor floor showed how

long the trader had been crawling. Neither the guard
nor the trader noticed Constance at all. She walked on
through the fort, and everywhere she went it was the
same: scenes of madness and murder and grotesque su-
icide. One man sat in a corner and stabbed himself repeatedly in the gut until his arm became too weak to
wield the knife. A woman drowned her two children in
a hip bath, and then sat them both in her lap and sang
them lullabies. Two men duelled fiercely with axes,
hacking at each other again and again with no thought
of defending themselves. They gave and took terrible
wounds, but would not fall. Blood flew in the freezing
air and steamed in wide puddles on the floor. All
through the fort it was the same; men, women, and
children died horribly for no reason that Constance
could see or understand. Their eyes were not sane. It
was very cold in the fort, and darkness gathered around
the shrinking pools of light.

Above and beyond all the madness and death Constance could hear a continual dull thudding, like a
great bass drumbeat that went on and on. It seemed to
come from everywhere and nowhere, and it was a long
time before Constance realized she was listening to the
beating of a giant heart, immeasurably far away.

She came at last to the dining hall, where hundreds
of men and women and children sat at dinner. She entered the hall warily, but still no one knew that she was
there. She moved over to the nearest table, and her
face twisted with disgust as she saw what they were
eating. The meat on the platters was raw and bloody,
and maggots writhed in it, twisting and wriggling as
they squirmed out onto the table. Lengths of purple intestines hung over the edges of the table, twitching and

dripping, and bowls were full of bird's heads, the dark little eyes alive and knowing. The witch looked away and realized for the first time that the man sitting before her at the table was dead. His throat had been cut, twice. Blood had run down his neck and soaked into his shirtfront. He smiled politely at Constance and offered her a wineglass. It was full to the brim with blood.

Constance backed quickly away as she realized he could see her, and one by one all the guests turned to look at her. They were all dead. Some had been stabbed, some had been burned. Some had died easily, while others had been all but hacked apart. Four carried their necks at a stiff angle to show the livid rope marks on their throats. Constance shook her head dazedly, pressed her lips together, and tried not to scream. And then, one by one, the gathering of the dead raised their arms and pointed behind her. Constance turned slowly, unwillingly. Whatever it was they wanted her to see, she knew she didn't want to see it. But still she turned, and a scream rose in her throat as she saw MacNeil, Flint, and the Dancer hanging on the wall behind her. They'd been pinned to the stonework by dozens of long-bladed knives. Their dangling feet were a good six inches off the ground, and from the amount of blood that had pooled on the floor beneath them, they'd been a long time dying.

Constance whimpered faintly. There was a series of scuffing noises behind her, and she turned back to find the dead rising unhurriedly to their feet. They advanced slowly on her, each carrying a long-bladed knife. Constance started to back away and slammed up against the closed door. She frantically pulled the handle, but the door wouldn't open. She spun around, and the knives were very close. Constance screamed.

MacNeil snapped awake as the scream broke through his dream. He tore at his tangled bedding and sat bolt upright, his mind still howling *demons demons demons*. He thrashed wildly about him for his sword, and then stopped as he realized where he was. He let out his breath in a long, slow sigh, and the dream fell away from him. His face was covered with a cold sweat, and he rubbed it dry with the edge of his blanket. His hands were still shaking slightly. He took a deep breath and held it a moment. It didn't help as much as he'd hoped. He looked quickly about him. Constance was sitting up beside him. Her face was buried in her hands, and her shoulders were shaking. The echo of her scream was only just fading away. The Dancer was standing by his blankets, sword in hand, looking around the empty hall for a target. Flint stood at his side, also clutching her sword. Her eyes were vague and only just beginning to focus.

MacNeil slowly relaxed. *It's all right now. It was just a dream. You're safe now.* The last of the panic died away, and he was himself again. He reached out and put a comforting hand on Constance's shoulder. She cried out at his touch and flinched away from him. And then she looked up and saw who it was, and some of the tension went out of her. The calm poise of her face was gone, shattered by her nightmare, and MacNeil was strangely touched as he saw how open and vulnerable she looked. He wanted to take her in his arms and comfort her, promise to keep her safe from the world. Even as he thought it, the familiar calm features reappeared as Constance regained control of herself. She sniffed once and rubbed her face with her sleeve.

"I'm sorry," she said muffledly, "I had a bad dream . . . a nightmare."

"I guessed that," said MacNeil dryly. "Are you all right now?"

"Yes, I'm fine. I'm sorry I woke you."

"I'm not," said MacNeil. "I was having a pretty bad dream of my own, and I can't say I'm sorry it was interrupted. If you hadn't woken me up, I'd have probably felt a bit like screaming myself."

"You had a nightmare?" said the Dancer, frowning.

"Yes," said MacNeil. "So what? Everyone has nightmares."

"Including me," said the Dancer quietly. "What are the odds on three of us having nightmares at the same time?"

"Four," said Flint.

MacNeil looked at her sternly. "You fell asleep on watch?"

Flint nodded unhappily. "I must have dozed off for a moment."

"That's not like you," said the Dancer.

"No," said MacNeil thoughtfully. "It isn't."

Constance looked at Flint, started to say something, and then changed her mind. "Your dream," she said finally. "What was it?"

Flint frowned. "I dreamed about the time I fought a walking dead man. Only in my dream, I lost."

"I dreamed about a werewolf I killed a few years back," said the Dancer. "Only . . . things were different in the dream."

Constance looked at MacNeil. "What about you, Duncan? What was your dream?"

"What does it matter?" said MacNeil. "It was just a nightmare."

"It might be significant. Tell me."

No, Constance. I can't tell you. I can't tell anyone. I can't tell anyone about the time I almost turned and ran.

"I dreamed I was back in the long night," he said finally. "Fighting the demons again."

Constance frowned. "Demons . . ."

"I hardly think that's significant," said MacNeil. "I mean, we were talking about them earlier on, weren't we?"

"Yes," said Constance, "we were." She thought for a moment, and then looked seriously at MacNeil. "My dream was different. You all dreamed of things that happened to you in the past. I dreamed of what happened here in the fort, not long ago."

"A kind of Seeing?" said Flint.

"I don't know. Maybe." Constance shuddered suddenly. "I saw the people here go insane and kill each other and themselves."

For a while, no one said anything.

"That's certainly one explanation," said MacNeil. "But if that is what happened, where are all the bodies?"

"They haven't left the fort," said Flint. "We'd have seen the tracks."

"I don't know," said Constance. "But what I dreamed is what happened here."

"Are you sure?" said MacNeil.

"Of course I'm sure! I'm a witch! There's something in this fort with us. Something powerful. It sent us those nightmares. It's testing how strong we are, looking for weak points. Only I was stronger than it thought, and I Saw something of the truth."

MacNeil chose his words carefully. "I think you're reading too much into this, Constance. I'll agree it seems likely these dreams were sent to us, but that's all they were—dreams. Anything else is just guesswork. We've been through every room and corridor in this fort; there's no one here but us."

"Don't look now," said the Dancer very quietly, "but that's no longer true. Someone's watching us from the door."

In the quiet of the night, a lone figure stepped out of the trees at the edge of the Forest, and scurried quickly across the clearing toward the fort. Moonlight filled the clearing as bright as day, and there wasn't a shadow anywhere for Scarecrow Jack to hide in. He ran on, head down and arms pumping. If the guards had left a lookout on the battlements he was a dead man; they couldn't avoid seeing him in this much light. But he'd waited almost an hour, hoping in vain for a cloud to cover the moon, and in the end all he could do was make a run for it and trust to his luck. Given the small number of guards he'd seen, the odds were they hadn't bothered to post a lookout, but Jack hadn't survived this long in the Forest by trusting his luck. Except when he had to. His nerves crawled in anticipation of the arrow he'd never see before it killed him. The fort finally loomed up before him, and he threw himself forward into its concealing shadows. He sank down on his haunches and leaned against the cold stone wall until he got his breath back. The night lay dark and silent all around him.

Scarecrow Jack was a tall, slight man in his mid-twenties. Long dark hair fell to his shoulders in a great shaggy mane that hadn't known a brush or comb in years. A thin length of cloth knotted around his brow kept the hair out of his eyes, which were dark and narrowed and always alert. He wore a collection of roughly stitched green and brown rags that barely qualified as clothes and seemed to be largely held together by accumulated dirt. They smelled rather pungent, but in the Forest the green and brown rags enabled him to blend perfectly into the background, hiding him from even the most experienced of trackers. No one found Scarecrow Jack unless he wanted to be found.

Jack had started out as a footpad, a lier-in-wait, but almost despite himself had slowly developed into a local legend. He'd lived alone in the Forest for almost nine years, living on its bounty and by what his wits could bring him. He developed an uncanny accord with the Forest and the creatures that lived in it, and every year the human world had less attractions that might call him back. And yet he never forgot his humanity. If anything, the harsh world of the Forest taught him the value of mercy and compassion.

He never robbed anyone who couldn't afford it, and would often poach fish and game to provide food for poor families unable to provide for themselves. He never let a tax collector pass unrobbed, and would help those who turned up lost or distressed in his part of the Forest. He had a way with birds and animals, and small children. Officially he was an outlaw, with a price on his head, but no local man or woman would turn him in. Scarecrow Jack was a part of the Forest and accepted as such. He kept apart from people, for he was by nature shy and ill at ease in company. Some said he was one of the wee folk, or a rogue goblin, or even the result of a mating between human and demon, but he was none of those things. He was just a man who loved the Forest.

Scarecrow Jack.

He got to his feet, still keeping carefully to the fort's shadows, and uncoiled a length of rope from across his shoulder. He checked the knot that held the grappling hook secure, and looked up at the battlements with a calculating eye. He hefted the rope a moment to get the feel of the weight, and then threw the hook up into the night sky with a swift, easy movement. Moonlight glinted on the steel hook as it arced over the battlements and disappeared from sight. Jack waited a moment to let the hook settle, and then pulled carefully on the rope until it went taut. He tugged hard a few times, to be sure the rope would bear his weight, and then climbed nimbly up the outer wall of the fort. His experienced feet found a good many footholds in the apparently smooth stone to help him on his way, and he soon reached the battlements and dropped lithely down onto the inner catwalk. He crouched motionless in the shadows for a long moment, but there was no sign of anyone watching.

Jack quickly made his way down into the courtyard, and padded silently over to the stables; the number of horses would tell him how many guards there were. But even as he approached the stable he knew something was horribly wrong. He stopped by the slightly open doors and sniffed cautiously. The thick, coppery

smell of blood was heavy on the night air. Jack eased
the doors open and crept slowly forward, one step at a
time, and then stopped dead as his excellent night vision showed him the wrecked stalls and the dark stains
on the floor and walls. Jack frowned. By their condition, the bloodstains had to be weeks old, but the smell
of blood in the stable was so fresh and strong as to be
almost overpowering. . . . He checked the floor for
tracks. Two people had come and gone recently, but
there was no sign to show what had attacked the
horses. Jack scowled and left the stables.

The air outside was clear and fresh, and he breathed
deeply to clear the stink of blood from his nostrils. Jack
looked thoughtfully around the empty courtyard. He'd
known something had to have gone wrong in the fort
for it to have seemed deserted for so long, but this . . .
worried him. It wasn't natural. It grated on his senses,
like a roll of thunder too faraway to hear. Jack couldn't
put his feelings into words, but that didn't bother him.
He lived as much by instincts as reason. He glared
warily about him and followed the guards' tracks across
the empty courtyard and into the main reception hall.

Four horses stood close together, fast asleep. Jack remembered the state of the stables and nodded under-
standingly. The four nooses hanging from the ceiling
were less easy to understand. Jack scowled. The bad
feeling he'd had in the courtyard was even stronger
here, and once again he could smell blood on the air.
It was cold too, unnaturally cold. Something bad had
happened here; he could feel it in his bones. He
checked the dusty floor for the guards' tracks, and
moved carefully past the sleeping horses. They seemed
disturbed in their sleep, as though bothered by bad

dreams, but they didn't wake as he passed. Jack followed the tracks out into the corridor, and then stopped and peered about him uncertainly. The gloom wasn't much of a problem to him, but he didn't like being inside buildings. They made him feel all trapped and nervous, and he kept thinking the walls were closing in on him. He shivered once, like a dog, and then put the thought out of his mind. He had a job to do.

He followed the guards' tracks through the narrow corridors, and came eventually to the main dining hall. He opened the door a crack and peered cautiously into the brightly lit hall. He froze where he was when he saw a woman sitting guard over her three sleeping companions, and he then relaxed a little as he saw she was also fast asleep. Jack frowned disappointedly. From the look of the party they had to be Rangers, but he'd always thought them to be more professional than this. Jack's frown deepened as he saw that all four of them were twitching and mumbling in their sleep. More bad dreams, by the look of it. He could understand that. This place gave him the creeps. And then one of the Rangers suddenly sat up and screamed, and all of them woke up.

Jack didn't dare move for fear of drawing attention to himself. He stood very still in the shadows of the door, and listened carefully as they discussed their dreams. And then one of them spotted him.

The dark figure was off and running before MacNeil could get to the door. He plunged down the corridor after the fleeing shape, sword in hand. For a moment the dim figure had looked disturbingly like one of the demons from his dream, but as his eyes adjusted to the gloom, MacNeil could see he was chasing a man dressed in rags. A stray memory tugged at him—Scarecrow Jack?

MacNeil smiled slightly. He'd heard about that outlaw, and the price on his head. He tried to force a little more speed out of his tired legs, but the outlaw could run like a startled deer and MacNeil was hard put even to keep him in sight. He ran on, vaguely aware the rest of his team were following some way behind. The chase continued, through rooms and corridors that blurred together in the darkness, until finally the outlaw charged between the sleeping horses in the reception hall and out into the courtyard. MacNeil had to spend a few moments calming the dismayed horses before he could follow, and when he finally got out into the courtyard, Scarecrow Jack was nowhere to be seen. The rest of the team arrived soon after, and they stood together by the hall door, looking around them at the courtyard's impenetrable shadows.

"This may seem a stupid question," said Constance finally, "but just who the hell are we looking for?"

"An outlaw," said MacNeil. "He was spying on us from the doorway."

"How long for?" said Flint.

"Too long," said the Dancer. "He's very good, whoever he is."

"Scarecrow Jack, I think," said MacNeil.

The Dancer raised an eyebrow. "I hadn't realized we were in his territory. I wonder what he wants with us."

"More importantly, how did he get in here, and where is he now?" MacNeil hefted his sword impatiently. "He couldn't have got in through the main doors; they're still locked and bolted. I saw to that before we turned in."

"He must have come over the wall," said Flint. "He's probably up on the catwalks somewhere."

They all looked up at the battlements, but there wasn't enough light to see them as anything more than darker shadows against the night.

"If he was up there, he's long gone by now," said MacNeil disgustedly. He hesitated and then slammed his sword back into its scabbard. Flint and the Dancer looked at each other and put away their swords. MacNeil turned to Constance.

"Can you use your Sight to find the outlaw?"

The witch shook her head. "My Sight is still clouded by whatever's here in the fort with us. If we were to go out into the Forest, I might be able to help you track him down."

MacNeil shook his head. "We'd never find Scarecrow Jack in the dark, and by morning he could be miles away." He looked thoughtfully up at the battlements. "If he could get over that wall, so could anyone else. We'd better keep our eyes and ears open."

"Perhaps I'm missing something," said Constance, "but why should a footpad like Scarecrow Jack want to break in here? What could he be looking for, in a border fort?"

"I was wondering that," said Flint. "This isn't the kind of thing he usually does, according to all the stories. It's not his style at all. Is there something here we don't know about, Duncan? Something we haven't been told?"

MacNeil smiled slightly. "Nothing much escapes you, does it, Jessica? All right, let's get back to the dining hall, and I'll tell you the whole story. I don't want to talk out here. You never know who might be listening."

Back in the dining hall, MacNeil pulled up a chair and gestured for the others to do the same. He waited patiently while they got settled, and then leaned forward.

"One of the reasons we're here," he said slowly, "is to find out what happened to the hundred thousand ducats of gold this fort was supposed to be guarding." He looked around at the others and smiled as he watched their jaws drop.

"A hundred thousand ducats," said Flint reverently. "That is one hell of a lot of gold."

"Damn right," said MacNeil. "It's the payroll for all the border forts in this sector. It was only supposed to stay here overnight, while arrangements were made for it to be broken up and distributed, but unfortunately that turned out to be the night the fort broke off all contact with the outside world. You can imagine the heart flutters that caused at Court. So, officially we're here to find out what happened to the fort's missing personnel, but we're also supposed to find the gold and make sure it's intact and secure. You can guess which of those orders has top priority."

"That's why you insisted we check every room earlier on," said Flint.

"Right," said MacNeil.

The Dancer looked at him steadily. "Why weren't we told any of this before?"

MacNeil smiled and shrugged. "They don't know you like I do. Anyway, I'm telling you now. If Scarecrow

Jack has somehow found out about the gold, you can bet he's not working on his own anymore. He couldn't even move that much gold without help."

"How do we know it hasn't already been moved?" said Flint.

"The odds are against it," said MacNeil. "All the signs would seem to suggest that we're the first people to have entered this fort since . . . whatever happened."

Constance frowned. "Scarecrow Jack usually works alone. And I've never heard of him being interested in gold."

"Everyone's interested in gold," said Flint.

"Not Jack," said Constance. "He's different."

MacNeil looked at her. "You know Scarecrow Jack?"

"I met him, once," said Constance. "A few years back I was searching for mandrake roots not far from here, and I got lost. Jack found me and showed me the way back to the main trail. He was very polite, very sweet, and extremely shy. I liked him. He's a simple enough soul, happy with the life he leads. The Forest gives him everything he needs. But . . . I suppose anyone can be tempted."

"Exactly," said MacNeil. "So, we've got to find the gold, or what happened to it, before Jack gets back here with his friends. For all we know, there could be a small army out there, just waiting for him to report back."

The Dancer looked at the ceiling thoughtfully. "We'd have a hard job defending this place against even a very small army."

MacNeil shrugged. "All we have to do is keep them away from the gold for a few days, and then the reinforcements will be here. But to do that, we've got to find the damned gold first."

"All right," said Flint. "Where do we start? We've already looked everywhere once."

"Yeah," said MacNeil. "Which means we must have overlooked something . . . some clue. So we'll just have to search every room and corridor and hidey-hole all over again, and keep on looking until we do find something."

"Now?" said Constance. "At night?"

MacNeil looked at her sardonically. "Still bothered by your dream, Constance? Afraid the nasty demons are going to jump out of the shadows at you?"

Constance looked at him steadily. "You can be very irritating at times, Duncan. Something here in this fort drove the people insane, so that they killed themselves and each other. It's still here, and it's still dangerous. And evil is at its strongest during the hours of darkness."

"I'm sorry, Constance," said MacNeil, "but there's no real evidence for any of that."

"My Sight—"

"Is clouded here. You said so yourself."

"You'd have believed Salamander!"

For a long moment no one said anything.

"The sooner we start this search, the sooner we'll be finished," said MacNeil quietly. "We'll make better time if we split into two teams. The first one to find anything sings out. Flint, you and the Dancer start at the entrance hall. Check it over thoroughly, even if you have to rip the walls apart to do it. Then start working your way back, room by room. Constance and I will start here and work our way out to meet you. Between us, we should cover every room in the fort."

"It's going to be a long job," said the Dancer.

"Then we'd better make a start, hadn't we?" said MacNeil.

3

Wolves in the Forest

Scarecrow Jack moved through the dark woods like a speckled ghost, his feet making no sound as they trod a path only he could see. Jack was a part of the Forest and knew its secret ways. Trees loomed over him like sleeping giants, their gnarled arms stirring uneasily in the gusting wind. Milky shafts of moonlight spilled through occasional gaps in the overhead canopy, and collected in shimmering pools on the forest floor. Jack stopped suddenly and dropped down to crouch motionless in the shadows. Something was wrong in the Forest. He sniffed cautiously at the air, but only familiar scents came to him: the sharp, taut smells of bark and leaf, and the rich smoky aroma of broken earth. Jack concentrated on his inner magic, the simple basic accord between him and the trees. There was a storm coming, a bad one by the feel of it, but he already knew that from the afternoon clouds and the closeness of the air. Something was *wrong* in the Forest ... something old and terrible had been disturbed from its ancient sleep. . . .

There were giants in the earth in those days.

Something evil was abroad in the night. The birds and the animals knew. The night should have been alive with the small, furtive sounds of hunters and their prey, but instead the darkness was still and silent, and animals and birds alike huddled together in their lairs and waited for the evil to pass.

Jack frowned, worried. How could such an evil have awakened in the Forest without him being aware of it before now? And then he smiled grimly as he realized he already knew the answer. He'd been so taken up with his new partners of late that he'd had no time for anything but them. Half the Forest could have burned down, and he wouldn't have noticed it till he smelled the smoke. Jack sighed regretfully. He wasn't happy with the way things were, but for the moment he was powerless to do anything about it. He'd just have to wait and keep his eyes open. His eyes . . . or someone else's. He grinned broadly as an answer came to him. He stood up and closed his eyes, cast his mind out among the tall trees, calling in a soundless shout. He opened his eyes and waited patiently, and a few minutes later a flurry of whiteness came sweeping through the night toward him like a silent ghost. Jack put up his arm at the last moment, and the owl landed heavily on his forearm and settled itself comfortably. The claws pricked his arm through the thin rags, but didn't penetrate his skin. The owl looked at him seriously, and Jack met its great golden eyes with his own. An understanding passed between them.

He was flying through the Forest, gliding on outstretched wings. The night was unnaturally quiet, and an evil presence beat in the darkness like a giant heart. He turned in the evil's direction and flew toward it, curious. The trees swayed by on either side of him and then fell suddenly away as he burst out of the Forest and into the clearing. Moonlight flared around him like a shout of thunder as he fluttered to a halt in midair. A great pile of stone and wood lay at the center of the clearing—the border fort. Once he would have used it as a resting place or a nesting ground. But not now. The evil was there, waiting. A great eye crawled slowly open deep in the darkness, and the owl turned and fled back to the safety of the tall trees and Jack was suddenly himself again, the contact broken.

He lifted his arm, and the owl flew back into the darkness and was gone. Jack frowned thoughtfully. While in the border fort his senses had been dulled by the unyielding presence of the human world, but now that he was back in the Forest all his instincts cried out against entering the fort again. Unfortunately, he no longer had a choice in the matter. Jack shrugged and padded off into the trees, accelerating slowly into a steady lope he could maintain for hours if he had to. He was already late, and Hammer hated to be kept waiting. Jack smiled widely. There were a lot of things about Jack that Hammer hated.

His smile vanished as he thought about Jonathon Hammer. The man might be a cold bastard, but he'd undoubtedly saved Jack's life, and Scarecrow Jack always paid his debts. He scowled briefly. It was his own damned fault for getting caught off guard in the first place. A simple little hole-in-the-ground trap, disguised and baited, and he fell for it. Literally. If Hammer hadn't come along at just the right time, the guards would have had him for sure, and Scarecrow Jack's head would have stood on a pike in the nearest market square as a warning to others.

Jack ran on through the night, brushing noiselessly

past the hanging branches of the close-set trees. Too many of them were dead and rotten, a legacy of the Darkwood. Jack felt their presence like an ache in his soul, a barely cauterized wound in the Forest. Normally he would have stopped and checked each one for signs of life or regrowth, but tonight he didn't have the time. A flickering light appeared in the darkness ahead, and he slowed to a walk. He moved silently forward and crouched motionless in the shadows at the edge of a clearing. Jack watched Hammer striding impatiently up and down beside a blazing camp fire, and tried to figure out how he was going to make Hammer understand about the fort.

Jonathon Hammer was a tall, muscular man with impressively broad shoulders. He was in his late thirties and looked it. He wore his dark hair short, brushed forward to hide a receding hairline. His eyes were deceptively warm, as was his smile, but for all his efforts there was a cold, vindictive quality to his face that never left it. He wore a simple leather vest over a white cotton shirt, and plain black trousers stuffed into the tops of his muddy boots. By his dress he could have been anything from a trader to a clerk to a bailiff, but the long sword hanging diagonally down his back marked him for the warrior he was. Hammer was a good six and a half feet tall, but the hilt of the sword stood up beside his head, while the tip of the scabbard was almost long enough to brush the ground behind him. It was the longest sword Jack had ever seen, and from the width of the scabbard it looked like a heavy sword as well, but Hammer moved easily with it on his back, as though unaware of its presence. He also carried another sword on his hip, but though he occasionally took that off, Jack had never seen him remove the longsword from his back. He even slept with it on.

In his time, Hammer had apparently been most kinds of soldier. He'd served as a mercenary for hire, a baron's man-at-arms, and as one of the king's guards, but he'd always been too ambitious and greedy for his own good. Wherever he went, sooner or later he'd start a still, or a crooked gambling school, or fight an officer he didn't like, and then he would be off on his travels again. It was on one of these that he'd found the longsword, but that was one part of his life he never talked about.

Most recently he'd been part of a company of guards escorting a wagon load of gold to the border fort. He'd never seen so much gold in one place before, and it had filled his dreams ever since. With that much gold he could raise his own army of mercenaries and take the Forest Kingdom by storm. King Jonathon the First . . . Jack smiled. Hammer never had believed in thinking small. He'd stayed with the guards just long enough to see the gold safely delivered and stored, and then he deserted and took to the Forest, lying low while he plotted some way to take the gold for himself. But that night something had happened in the fort.

Hammer had stood at the edge of the clearing, listening to the screams, but hadn't dared investigate alone. He watched the fort for the next few days, but there were no signs of life. It took him awhile to track down the archer called Wilde, and acquire the services of Scarecrow Jack, but he apparently regarded it as time well spent. With those two at his side, he'd been ready to face anything the fort could throw at him.

Unfortunately, the Rangers got there first.

Jack crouched in the shadows at the edge of the out-laws' clearing, and studied Hammer and Wilde with narrowed eyes. Delay was dangerous; the later he was, the more Hammer would make him suffer for it. And yet still Jack hesitated. He needed time to think about the two men he'd become allied with. Hammer was one thing. He owed Hammer. But Wilde . . .

Edmond Wilde was sitting on the other side of the fire, hungrily gnawing a greasy chicken leg. He was tall and lanky, somewhere in his late twenties, and dressed all in shabby black. He had a thin face with dark, close-set eyes, and in the darkness he looked not unlike an unsuccessful vulture. His black hair was long and greasy, and he was constantly tossing his head to clear the hair out of his eyes. His movements were awkward and furtive, as though he was ashamed to draw atten-tion to himself. But put a bow or a sword in his hand, and he was a different man. His back straightened, his eyes became cold and alert, and an aura of menace hung around him like a shroud. Wilde was almost as good with a bow as he thought he was, which meant he was a master bowman.

The bow lay on the ground at his side, unstrung so as not to stretch the cord. It was a Forest longbow, al-most seven feet in length. Jack had tried to pull it once when Wilde wasn't around, and found he could hardly bend the thing using all his strength. Since Wilde wasn't exactly muscle-bound, Jack assumed there had to be some trick to it. He would have liked to ask Wilde, but he didn't. Wilde wasn't the kind you could ask things of. He had been on the run when Hammer found him, though he'd never said from what. Given what Jack had seen of the man's tastes and attitudes,

Wilde was probably wanted for rape or murder. Or both.

The archer never talked about his background, but though his clothes were patched and filthy, they had originally been of a fairly high quality. His language was unfailingly coarse and vulgar, but the accent was often decidedly upper-class. Not that that proved anything. The only thing Jack was sure of where Wilde was concerned was that the man was a complete swine. The bowman all but worshiped Hammer as long as he was in earshot, but had all the loyalty of a starving weasel. Hammer kept him in line by fear and brutality. Wilde seemed to accept this as normal behavior where he was concerned. Jack smiled sourly. He could understand that. As far as he was concerned, there was nothing wrong with Wilde that hanging wouldn't cure. He was a loud-mouthed, hypocritical, vicious bastard—nasty when drunk and unbearable when sober. He'd steal the pennies off a dead man's eyes, and then complain because there weren't more of them. But still he was a master bowman, and Hammer said he has a use for him, so he stayed.

Jack sighed again. Of all the people in the world he could have become obligated to, it had to be Jonathon Hammer. He shrugged and padded out of the trees and into the clearing.

Wilde jumped, startled, and scrambled to his feet with his hand on his sword. He scowled shamefacedly when he saw who it was, and sank down beside the fire again.

"Our noble savage is back," he growled to Hammer.

Hammer ignored him and glared silently at Jack. He hadn't even stirred when Jack made his dramatic entrance, but his eyes were very cold. "You took your time," he said finally.

"It's a big fort," said Jack. "I looked everywhere, but there's no sign of any of the gold. There are no bodies either, just a lot of blood. It's been there some time. I got a good look at the Rangers who are staying there, but they spotted me, and I had to run for it."

Hammer frowned. "Did they see enough of you to recognize who you are?"

"I don't know. Maybe."

"That was careless of you," said Hammer. "Very careless."

He rose unhurriedly to his feet and lashed out with the back of his hand, sending Jack sprawling to the ground. He'd seen the blow coming but hadn't been able to dodge it in time. Hammer was fast for his size. Jack scrambled back out of range and watched Hammer warily. He could feel blood trickling out of his left nostril, and he wiped it with the back of his hand, leaving an uneven crimson stream across his knuckles. Wilde chuckled happily. Jack ignored him and stood up slowly, ignoring the pain in his face. He didn't say anything; he couldn't. He owed Hammer. But once he'd helped Hammer to get his precious gold, all debts would be paid, and then Scarecrow Jack would vanish into the woods so quickly it would make Hammer's head spin. . . .

Hammer sat down by the fire again, and after a moment Jack sat down opposite him.

"What did you learn at the fort?" said Hammer, his voice calm and relaxed, as though the sudden violence had never happened.

"Getting in and out of the fort is easy," said Jack, gingerly patting his nose with his sleeve. "There are only four Rangers in there, and they can't even mount a proper night watch. I don't think they know where the gold is, either."

"Maybe they've hidden it somewhere," said Wilde.

"I looked all over the fort," said Jack, still looking at Hammer. "There's no sign of the gold anywhere."

"Just four men," said Hammer thoughtfully.

"Two men, two women," said Jack. "One of the women is a witch."

Wilde stirred uneasily. "A witch. I don't like magic."

"Witches die just as easily as anyone else," said Hammer. "Providing you haven't lost your touch with a bow."

Wilde smiled lazily. He picked up his bow and strung it with a quick, practiced motion. He took an arrow from the quiver lying beside him and notched it to the string. He looked unhurriedly about him, his eyes searching the darkness beyond the firelight. And then he drew back the arrow, aimed, and let fly, all in a single fluid motion too fast for the eye to follow. A white owl fell out of the darkness and into the clearing, transfixed by Wilde's arrow. It wriggled feebly on the clearing floor, blood staining its snowy breast. Jack darted over to kneel beside it. The bird's struggles were already growing weaker. It looked reproachfully at Jack.

"You shouldn't have followed me, my friend," said Jack quietly. "I'm mixing with bad company these days."

He took hold of the shaft just below the flight and snapped the arrow in two before pulling out the pieces as smoothly as he could. The owl hooted once softly and then was quiet. Fresh blood welled out from the ugly wound. Jack placed his left palm over the wound and closed his eyes. His mind went out to the Forest, and the trees gave him their strength. He took that strength, channeled it through him, and let it flow gently into the injured owl. The blood stopped flowing, and the wound knitted itself together and was gone. Jack opened his eyes and leaned back on his haunches. Magic took a lot out of him. The owl struggled back to its feet. It swayed unsteadily a moment, getting used to not dying after all, gave Jack a hard look, and then spread its wings and flew back into the familiar darkness of the Forest night.

Jack sensed a movement behind him and spun around, knife in hand. Wilde hesitated, an arrow already in position for another shot at the owl.

"Go on," said Jack softly. "Give it a try. You might get lucky."

Wilde looked at him uncertainly. "You wouldn't kill a man over a bloody owl."

"Wouldn't I?"

Wilde felt a sudden chill run through him. A man with a dagger was no match for an archer, let alone a master bowman, and yet . . . this was Scarecrow Jack, and the power of the trees was in him. Wilde felt a presence in the darkness around him, as though countless unseen eyes were watching—the eyes of the Forest. . . . The wind whispered in the branches of the trees around the clearing, and surely it was only his imagination that made it sound like voices.

"That's enough, both of you," said Hammer. The moment was broken, and Wilde slowly relaxed. He put down his bow and slipped the arrow back into his quiver. Hammer looked at Jack, and the dagger disappeared into his sleeve. Hammer nodded slowly. "Get your things together. We're going back to the fort."

"Now?" said Wilde. "In the middle of the night?"

"What's the matter?" said Jack. "Afraid of the dark?"

Wilde shot him a venomous look. "I was thinking of the Rangers. They'll be on the alert now, thanks to you."

"They won't be expecting us to try again tonight," said Hammer. "And we can't afford to wait. If they're following regulation procedure, reinforcements for the fort will be here in a couple of days, and that means a full company of guards. We've got to get into the fort, find and remove the gold, and leave the vicinity, all in twenty-four hours or less, or we might as well forget it. Jack, what's the weather going to be like?"

Jack scowled. "Pretty bad. There's thunder on the way. I can feel it. And rain, lots of it. It's going to be a bad storm, Hammer, and it's going to break soon."

"That could work for us, as a distraction." Hammer's right hand rose absently to caress the long leather-wrapped sword hilt beside his head. Jack didn't like to watch when Hammer did that. It looked almost like patting an animal. The longsword worried Jack. Even through the silver scabbard, he could feel an unending hum of raw power. The sword had its own sorcery, and it wasn't a healthy magic. In all the time he'd been with Hammer, Jack had never seen him draw the sword. Deep down, he hoped he never would. Hammer's hand fell away from the sword hilt, and Jack relaxed a little.

"Wilde," said Hammer slowly, "when you see the witch, kill her. Magic-users are always unpredictable, and we can't afford to take any chances. Jack and I will take care of the other Rangers."

Wilde nodded silently. Jack started to say something and then stopped himself. He remembered the witch. She was young and very pretty. But he didn't owe her anything, and he did owe Hammer.

But not for always, Hammer. Not for always.

He waited patiently at the edge of the clearing while Hammer put out the camp fire, and Wilde checked over his bow and arrows with surprisingly gentle fingers. Jack sat down on a handy tree stump and let his mind drift while he waited. As it had so many times recently, it took him back to the trap from which Hammer had rescued him.

It had been a simple trap, as traps go. Jack had been following deer tracks when he suddenly heard a clatter of disturbed birds nearby. He immediately froze in place, his rags blending him into the dappled shadows. Something must have frightened the birds for them to react so sharply, and Jack hadn't survived nine years alone in the Forest by ignoring warning signs. After a while he eased silently through the trees in the direction the sound had come from, and ended up crouching motionless at the edge of a small clearing. A man was sitting on a tree stump in the middle of the glade, with his back to Jack. He wore a guard's uniform, and a hand ax leaned against the stump by his boot. Jack stayed where he was for some time, watching and waiting, but the guard didn't move. There was no sign of anyone else, so far. Jack frowned. They must be searching for him again. Maybe the price on his head had gone up. If so, the odds were the guard wasn't in the Forest on his own. He'd better get out of here while he still could.

And yet there was something odd about that guard. Very odd. He still hadn't moved a muscle, despite all the time Jack had spent watching him. His head was bent forward; maybe he was sleeping. Or ill. Or even dead. Jack scowled. He didn't like the direction his thoughts were leading him, but he couldn't ignore it. There weren't many predators in this part of the Forest that would take on an armed man, but there were always the wolves. . . .

Jack bit his lower lip and frowned indecisively. Approaching an armed guard in an open clearing was not something to be undertaken lightly, but if there was a man killer loose in the Forest, he wanted to know about it. And anyway, he was curious. He smiled and shook his head. One of these days his curiosity was going to get him into trouble.

He stole silently out of the trees and into the clearing, looking quickly about him, ready to turn and run at the first sign of danger. Everything seemed normal. The sun shone down from a cloudless sky, and the air was pleasantly warm. Insects buzzed drowsily on the still air, and birds sang undisturbed in the trees. The clearing was empty apart from the guard, who still hadn't moved. Jack drew the knife from his sleeve, just to be on the safe side, and crept forward one step at a time, his eyes fixed unwaveringly on the guard's back. He'd almost reached the seated figure when the ground suddenly gave way beneath his feet, and he fell into the concealed pit below.

He fell awkwardly and landed on the packed earth at the bottom of the pit with an impact that knocked all the breath out of him. He lay still for a time, gasping for air and then groaning quietly as the immediate pain died slowly away. After a while his breathing steadied, and he was able to think coherently again. He tried cautiously to move his arms and legs, and a wave of relief swept through him when they all responded normally. A broken limb would have meant his death, even if he had managed to escape from the pit. Staying alive in the Forest wasn't easy at the best of times, and the woods knew nothing of mercy. Jack sat up slowly, wincing at his various cuts and bruises. He looked at the circle of light above him, and saw he'd fallen a good nine or ten feet. He'd been lucky; he could have broken his neck. He scrambled to his feet and stood still, listening carefully. He couldn't hear anything. Whoever had set the trap might not be around. With just a little luck he could climb out of the pit and be gone before they came back. Jack searched the sides of the pit for hand- and footholds, and then cursed disgustedly. The walls were nothing but loose earth that crumbled away under his fingers. There was no way it could support his weight while he climbed.

Jack looked up at the bright circle of light. Nine or ten feet, and it might as well be nine or ten miles. He had no more hope of climbing out of the pit than he had of flying out. He tried anyway, just to be cussed, but it did no good. He retrieved the knife he'd dropped in his fall, and tried cutting handholds in the walls, but it was no use. He put the knife back in his sleeve, sat down on the bottom of the pit, and waited for his captors to show up. There was always the chance they wouldn't kill him straightaway. They might decide to take him to the nearest town for an official hanging, and that meant chances to escape, if he kept his wits about him. Jack smiled sadly. It was a nice thought, but that was all. He'd escaped too many times in the past for them to take any chances. If they had any sense at all, they'd just shoot an arrow into him while he was still in the pit, and then take in his head for the reward.

Jack leaned back against the earth wall and looked up at the sky. It was bright and clear and very blue. He was in his Forest. There were worse ways to die.

The light above him was suddenly blocked by a man's head and shoulders. Jack scrambled to his feet and reached for his knife. There was no real point in trying to dodge an arrow, but he'd go out fighting anyway, just to spite them. He was Scarecrow Jack.

"Hello, down there," said a man's voice.

"Hello, yourself," said Jack. His voice wanted to shake, but he wouldn't let it.

"Looks like you're in a spot of bother," said the man.

"Looks that way."

"I take it you're Scarecrow Jack?"

"Depends."

The man laughed easily. "Lucky for you I come along. I'll be back in a minute. Don't go away."

He disappeared, and Jack's spirits rose cautiously. Maybe he had got lucky after all. The man returned and threw down a coil of rope. Jack tugged on it a few times to be sure it would take his weight, and then climbed up the rope and out of the pit. He moved quickly away from the edge and stared warily at his rescuer. The man was clearly a soldier of some kind by his stance and his clothes and the sword on his hip, but he wore no insignia of rank or loyalty. He was a big man with an amiable enough face, but Jack's eyes were drawn to the long sword hilt that stood up behind the man's left shoulder. Even from a few feet away Jack could feel the power that lay dormant in the sword, waiting to be called into action. Jack began to wonder if he might not have been safer in the pit after all.

"Thanks," he said carefully. "You might just have saved my life."

"Could be," said the man. "How did you end up in a stupid trap like that?"

Jack shrugged. "I always was too curious for my own good." He looked around at the guard sitting on the tree stump, and wasn't surprised to see he was still sitting there, apparently uninterested in what was happening behind him. Jack walked over to the motionless figure and looked him in the face. It was a dummy— convincing enough from a distance, but still just a dummy. Jack laughed in spite of himself.

"Set a scarecrow to catch a Scarecrow. Neat. Almost elegant. And it would have worked, if you hadn't come along. My thanks."

"I want more than that," said the man calmly.

Jack looked at him warily, his right hand drifting casually toward the knife in his sleeve.

"Don't," said the man. "Don't even think about it. You wouldn't want me to draw my sword, would you?"

"No," said Jack. "I wouldn't."

"My name is Jonathon Hammer. If it wasn't for me, you'd be dead. You owe me your life, Scarecrow Jack. I'll accept a few months' service from you in payment for your debt. Is that acceptable?"

Jack thought about the pit, and Hammer's sword, and nodded slowly. "Yes. For the next two months, I'm your man."

"Good. I'd heard you were an honorable man, in your

way. Do what I tell you, when I tell you, and we'll get along fine. You might even get rich. But if you should ever consider betraying me . . ."

"My word is good," said Jack coldly. "I don't break it. Ever."

"Yes," said Jonathon Hammer, smiling slightly. "That's what I heard."

That had been two weeks ago, and they were shaping up to be the worst two weeks of Jack's life. More than once he contemplated just walking out on Hammer and Wilde, and disappearing back into the Forest, but he couldn't. Scarecrow Jack was an honorable man, and he always paid his debts.

Hammer and Wilde were finally ready to leave, and Jack led them back through the Forest to the border fort. The sooner this was over, the better he'd like it. And yet . . . in the end he hadn't said anything, because they'd only have laughed, but there was definitely something wrong about the border fort. Something unnatural. He could feel it in his water. He decided to say nothing for the time being, but keep his eyes and ears open.

He had a bad feeling his problems weren't anywhere near being over.

4

Dreams in the Waking World

The storm finally broke over the Forest. Thunder roared and lightning flared, and the rain came down in solid sheets, slamming through foliage and bouncing back from the Forest floor. Open trails quickly became a morass of mud and soaking mulch. Birds and animals shuddered in their lairs at the continuous pounding of the rain, and in all the Forest nothing moved save three determined outlaws, already soaked to the skin.

The thunder rolled on and on, barely pausing long enough for the intermittent flashes of lightning that lit the Forest in stark black and white. The outlaws moved slowly from cover to cover, wading through deep puddles and treacherous mud, slipping and sliding and falling painfully until only Hammer's will kept them moving. The moon was hidden behind dark clouds, and the party's lantern light couldn't travel far through the rain. Scarecrow Jack's woodcraft was tested to the limit as familiar landmarks became strange and unfamiliar, but finally he brought them back to the edge of the great clearing. The three outlaws sheltered under a tree and studied the dim silhouette of the border fort through the driving rain.

Jack ignored the cold and the wet; he was used to it.

The rain soaked his rags and dripped continuously from his face, but beyond a certain point he simply didn't feel it. He had an animal's indifference for conditions beyond his control. Besides, judging from the way Hammer and Wilde had been reacting whenever they got downwind of him, it was probably time his rags had a good wash. He glanced at Wilde, standing miserably beside him, huddled inside a thin cloak. The rain had slicked the archer's long hair down around his face, and in the dim light he looked not unlike a half-drowned river rat. He sniffed and shivered, and cursed continuously in a low monotone. He pulled up his cloak's high collar to keep out the rain. It formed a kind of funnel that guided the rain down his neck and back. Hammer ignored the sudden rise in cursing, and glowered through the rain at the border fort. Like Jack, he seemed unaffected by the cold and the wet.

"At least now we can be fairly sure there won't be any guards on the battlements," he said finally. "They won't be expecting anyone to be abroad in weather like this."

"No one with any sense would be," said Wilde. He sneezed dismally and wiped his nose on his sleeve. "How much longer do we have to stand around here? I'm catching my death in this rain."

Hammer looked at Jack. "Is this storm going to go off soon?"

Jack looked about him and considered for a moment. "Unlikely. It may even get worse. This storm's been building for a long time."

"All right," said Hammer, "we go now. Stick close together. Whatever happens, no one is to go off on their own."

He looked about him one last time, hooded his lantern, and then ran across the open clearing toward the border fort, followed closely by Wilde and Jack. Out in the open the rain was coming down so hard it drowned out every other sound, and even with the lantern and the lightning it was hard to see anything more than a few feet away. Wilde lurched and slid in the mud, and Jack was hard put to keep him moving. Hammer was soon only a vague shadow in front of them, and there was no sign of the fort. Jack shuddered violently as the driving rain chilled him to the bone. The clearing seemed much wider than he remembered, and he began to wonder if Hammer had lost his bearings and led them past the fort. And then, finally, a massive stone wall loomed out of the rain before them, and they had to stumble to a halt to avoid crashing into it. The wall gave some protection from the wind, but that was all. Jack shook himself like a dog, but it didn't help much. He couldn't recall having felt this wet in his life. The rain was so heavy now it even made breathing difficult.

Hammer gestured for him to unsling his coil of rope. It was no use trying to speak; the rain and the thunder made it impossible to hear. Jack unslung the rope and checked the grapnel was still secure. He looked up at the wall, and the rain beat harshly on his face until he had to turn away. He took a moment to compose himself, blinking rapidly to get the rain out of his eyes, and then he snatched one quick look and threw the grapnel up into the air, aiming as best he could. It just cleared the battlements and fell to lodge securely somewhere beyond them. Jack pulled the line taut and looked at Hammer, who nodded for him to go first. Jack took a firm grip on the rope, checked it would take his weight, and began to walk his way up the wall. The rain made both the rope and the wall horribly slippery, and more than once only quick reflexes and a death-like grip saved him from a nasty fall. When he finally reached the battlements he was almost too tired to pull himself over them. He sat on the catwalk, breathing harshly, and then climbed reluctantly to his feet and tugged twice on the rope to signal it was clear for the next man. Wilde made even more hard going of the climb, and Jack had to reach down and practically haul the man up the last few feet. Hammer came last, making it look easy.

They started along the narrow catwalk, heading for the steps that led down into the courtyard.

Duncan MacNeil led his team through the fort, heading for the cellar. The constant roar of the storm came dimly to them through the thick stone walls. MacNeil and Constance carried lanterns while Flint and the Dancer held their swords at the ready.

"I don't see why we have to look at the cellar again," said Constance. "We've already established the gold isn't there."

MacNeil shrugged. "It's got to be here somewhere. It occurred to me there might be a subcellar underneath the first, or even a hidden passageway."

"And if there isn't?" said Constance.

"Then we go through every damn room in this fort and take it apart brick by brick until we do find the gold. Are you sure you can't See where it is?"

The witch sighed audibly. "I'll try again, Duncan, but I can tell you now it's not going to work. Something nearby is still interfering with my magic."

She stopped, and the others stopped with her. Constance put her lantern down on the floor, massaged her temples with her fingertips, and closed her eyes. The low background mutter of the storm was a distraction, but she finally put it out of her mind. Darkness gathered, smothering her Sight. She shuddered as a bitter cold swept through her, and a feeling of unease grew and grew until it bordered on panic. Constance fought to control it, and as she did her Sight suddenly cleared and she Saw a single huge eye. It was staring in her direction, slowly becoming aware of her presence. Constance immediately broke off the contact and shielded her mind as thoroughly as she could. In that brief glimpse she'd sensed something she had no desire to See again. She huddled frightened in the darkness, but even inside her shield she could sense something awful prowling through the dark in search of her. It slowly moved away, and Constance sighed shakily and opened her eyes.

"Well?" said MacNeil impatiently.

"There's something here in the fort with us," said Constance directly. "I don't know what it is or where it is, but it's very old and very deadly."

"Don't start that again," said MacNeil. "There's no one in the fort but us. You're just feeling the strain a bit, that's all. We all are."

Constance looked at him coldly but said nothing. With her Sight still clouded, he might just be right. But she didn't think so. MacNeil started down the corridor again, and Flint and the Dancer followed him. Constance picked up her lantern and brought up the rear. Her hand trembled with suppressed anger, and shadows swayed menacingly around the team. MacNeil didn't look back at her. Truth to tell, he wasn't so sure Constance wasn't right. He remembered how strongly she'd reacted to the cellar before, and much as he wanted to, he couldn't ignore her warnings. She had the Sight.

You'd have believed Salamander. . . .

Yes, he would have. But Constance didn't have Salamander's experience, and unless she came up with something more concrete than a few upset feelings, he couldn't justify staying away from the cellar. Even if the place did give him the creeps.

Constance was trying hard not to sulk, or at least not visibly. She worked so hard, tried her best, and still he didn't trust her. When she'd first found out which Ranger team she was joining she'd been so thrilled she all but danced on the spot. She knew all about Sergeant Duncan MacNeil. She'd been following his career at a distance for years. Ever since he'd protected her from the demons when she was just a child, living in the small town of King's Deep.

She'd pulled as many strings as she dared to get herself assigned to his team, all so that she could repay him for what he'd done for her—by being the best damned witch he'd ever had. She had other dreams about him too, but she rarely allowed herself to think about them. And now here she was, on her first mission with him, and it was all going wrong. Because he wouldn't give her a chance. Constance's lower lip jutted rebelliously. She'd show him. She'd show them all.

It didn't take long to reach the cellar. It looked just as it had before, a mess. MacNeil sniffed and shook his head. Grief knew how long they'd been dumping rubbish there—every day since the fort was first occupied, by the look of it. Constance hung her lantern from a wall holder while Flint looked disgustedly around the cellar.

"Everything but gold," she said unenthusiastically. "You don't really want us to dig through this stuff, do you, Duncan?"

"Afraid so," said MacNeil.

Flint sniffed. "I just hope I don't catch anything contagious."

"That's not all we have to worry about," said Constance suddenly. "Have you noticed how cold it's got?"

The others stopped and looked at her. MacNeil frowned as he suddenly realized his breath was steaming in the air before him. All at once he was shivering, his bare face and hands seared by the biting cold. He pulled his cloak around him and tried to remember if it had been this cold when he first entered the cellar. He had a strong feeling it hadn't. He looked at the others, and their breath was steaming too. He looked around him, and his flesh began to creep as he noticed for the first time that a faint pearly haze of hoarfrost was forming on the cellar walls.

It can't be that cold down here. It can't. . . .

He forced himself to concentrate on the matter at hand, and stared determinedly at the junk covering the floor. "If there is a subcellar," he said roughly, "you probably get to it by a trapdoor in the floor. Start shifting this rubbish out of the way. Pile it up against the walls, and then we can get a clear look at the floor."

The others nodded and set to work. MacNeil put his lantern down safely out of the way and joined them. Shifting the assorted debris took some time and not a little effort, but eventually they uncovered a trapdoor. It lay in the exact middle of the cellar floor, a good six square feet of solid oak, held shut by two heavy steel bolts. MacNeil knelt down by the trapdoor and looked closely at the bolts, but felt strangely reluctant to touch them. He rubbed his hands together to drive out the cold and buy him some time to think. They were just ordinary, everyday steel bolts. There was no reason at all why he shouldn't touch them. Except that all the hairs on the back of his neck were standing up and both his arms were covered in goose flesh, and none of it came from the bitter cold in the cellar.

He looked at Constance, carefully keeping his voice calm and easy. "Try your Sight. See if you can sense anything about the trapdoor and what lies beneath it."

The witch nodded and stared at the trapdoor. Her eyes became vague and faraway.

Deep in the earth something stirred and strove to wake. The weight of earth and stone lay heavy upon it, and time gnawed at its blood and bones. A darkness came and went, too swiftly to disturb its slumber, but now at last the chains of sleep began to fall away as day by day it drifted closer to waking. It dreamed foul dreams and the world went mad. Soon its long sleep would end, and the world would tremble when the sleeper spoke its name.

Constance broke the contact, and once again her Sight became vague and clouded. She swayed sickly and almost fell, nauseated by the few faint traces of the thing she'd sensed. MacNeil took her arm, concerned at her sudden paleness, and she smiled weakly at him.

"I'll be all right in a moment, Duncan."

"What did you See?"

"The same thing I've Seen before, only this time I Saw it a little more clearly. There's something down there, Duncan—something old and evil and unspeakably powerful. It's sleeping for the moment, but it could wake any time. It sent the dreams that drove the people here insane."

MacNeil frowned. "All right, Constance, I believe you. I don't want to, but it doesn't look like I have any choice. What is it? A demon?"

"I don't think so. It's older than that. I couldn't get a fix on exactly where it is, but I don't think it's directly under the trapdoor. It's . . . somewhere deeper."

MacNeil nodded slowly. "We've got to take a look down there, Constance. Is it dangerous?"

"Yes," said the witch. "But don't ask me how."

"That's not good enough."

"It's the best I can do! Why do we have to go down there now, anyway? What's wrong with waiting till the reinforcements get here?"

"Think about it," said MacNeil. "I've been ordered to find the gold at any cost. How is it going to look on our records if they find out we knew about the trapdoor, but didn't investigate because we were too scared? No, Constance, I'm opening that trapdoor and we're going down, and that's all there is to it. Flint, Dancer, stand ready. Once that trapdoor's open, if anything comes out, kill it first and ask questions later, if at all."

"Got it," said Flint. The Dancer smiled.

MacNeil looked at Constance. "Keep your magic ready and help where you can, but don't get in our way. We're the fighters; that's our job."

The witch nodded, and MacNeil reached down and took hold of the first bolt on the trapdoor. It seemed to stir slowly under his fingertips, as though it were alive. He snatched back his hand and knelt down to study the bolt closely. It seemed perfectly normal. *Just nerves, that's all,* he thought determinedly. *Just nerves.* He wiped his fingers on his trousers and tried again. He held the bolt firmly and pulled hard. It slid smoothly back, with hardly a sound. MacNeil swallowed dryly and tried the second bolt. It was stiff, and he had to work it back with a series of quick jerks, but finally it came free. MacNeil took hold of the heavy steel ring in the center of the trapdoor and pulled firmly. The trapdoor didn't budge. He breathed deeply and tried again. The muscles in his back and shoulders swelled as he pitted all his strength against the stubborn wood, and then the trapdoor suddenly flew open with a ragged tearing sound.

And out of the trapdoor mouth gushed an endless fountain of thick, viscous blood. It roared up to splash against the ceiling, and fell back again in a stinking crimson rain. More and more blood came roaring up past the open trapdoor, gallon upon gallon, soaking everything in the cellar. MacNeil and the others scrambled back from the flying blood, but there was nowhere they could hide from it. The blood continued to gush up from under the cellar, forced out by some unimaginable pressure, and then stopped as suddenly as it had begun. MacNeil slowly raised his head and looked around him. Blood dripped from the scarlet ceiling and ran down the walls. It steamed slightly in the cold air. The floor and the trapdoor looked as though they'd been painted red. The stink of blood was almost overpowering. MacNeil moved cautiously forward to stare into the dripping opening, and the others came forward to join him. They were all liberally spattered with blood. Flint shook her head disgustedly.

"I've seen battlefields that were less bloody than this. Where the hell did it all come from?"

"Beats me," said MacNeil. He stared down into the darkness that lay below the cellar. Nothing moved in the impenetrable gloom, but the air was thick with the stench of freshly spilled blood. Constance handed him his lantern, and he lowered it carefully into the darkness. The amber light showed him a set of rough wooden steps, leading down into a narrow earth tunnel that fell away into the ground. The light didn't carry far, but for as far as MacNeil could see the steps and the tunnel walls were slick with blood. The others crowded in around him to take a look, and then all of them froze as from far below the cellar came the sound of something moving. It was a slow, dragging sound, but MacNeil couldn't tell whether it was drawing closer or moving away. He looked at the others, but it was clear they weren't sure either. The sound stopped. MacNeil put down his lantern beside the opening and drew his sword.

"Flint, you and Constance stay here to guard the opening. Dancer, you come with me. We're going to take a look at what's hiding down in that tunnel."

The Dancer smiled and drew his sword.

MacNeil looked at Flint. "If anything comes out of this trapdoor but us, kill it. If something goes wrong, shut the trapdoor and bolt it. Whether we're out or not. If there is something dangerous down in that tunnel, I don't want it running loose in the fort. When you're sure the trapdoor's secure, get out of here and report back to the reinforcements. They have to be warned."

"We can't just abandon you," said Constance.

"Yes, we can," said Flint. "He's right, Constance. Our

duty comes first, and Rangers are expendable. It's part of the job."

The witch looked away. MacNeil looked at her for a moment, and then picked up his lantern and stepped carefully down into the opening and onto the first of the wooden steps. The narrow slat creaked loudly as he put his weight on it, but after an uncertain moment it settled again. He slowly descended into the darkness, holding the lantern out before him. The Dancer followed behind him, sword at the ready. Shadows swayed menacingly around them as they descended into the earth.

MacNeil counted thirteen steps before he found himself facing the narrow tunnel that ran under the cellar. *Unlucky for some,* he thought wryly, and moved forward a little to give the Dancer room to join him. The circular tunnel was barely six feet in diameter, and MacNeil had to bend forward to avoid banging his head on the ceiling. There was sufficient room for MacNeil and the Dancer to walk side by side, but only just. The walls were smoothly rounded and bore no marks of human tools. The clay-like earth was tightly packed and slick with running blood. More blood lay in shallow pools on the tunnel floor. *Like walking through something's guts,* thought MacNeil, wrinkling his nose at the stench. He stood listening for a long moment, the Dancer waiting patiently at his side, but there was no trace of the sound they'd heard earlier. He started forward into the gloom, the Dancer padding quietly beside him. MacNeil found the man's presence reassuring. The darkness and the silence and the stench reminded him too much of his time in the Darkwood. He clutched his sword hilt tightly, aware his hand was sweating profusely despite the cold. It didn't matter what was waiting for him; he'd face it and kill it and that was all there was to it. He was a guard and a Ranger, and he'd never backed away from anything in his life.

But there was a time when you wanted to. The demons came out of the long night faster than you could kill them, and you wanted to turn and run. And you might have, too, if the dawn hadn't broken first. The sun rose and the long night fell and the demons retreated with the darkness. The dawn saved you. And now you'll never know whether or not you would have run.

MacNeil shut out the insistent whispering voice and concentrated on the darkness ahead. The tunnel seemed to be curving gradually downward, and he wondered uneasily just how deep it ran. His boots slid and skidded on the blood-soaked floor, and shadows ducked and weaved around him as the lantern rose and fell in his hand. He shot a quick glance at the Dancer, but he seemed entirely unperturbed, his face as calm and bland as it always was. And then the Dancer held up a hand and stopped suddenly. MacNeil stopped beside him.

"What is it?" he whispered.

The Dancer shook his head. "Listen."

MacNeil frowned, concentrating, and in the distance he heard again the soft dragging sound, coming from deep in the tunnel. As he listened, he realized the sound was drawing gradually nearer. It was a sliding, bumping sound, as though something heavy was being dragged along the tunnel floor toward them. MacNeil put the lantern down on the floor behind him, safely out of the way. He glanced quickly at the Dancer, and saw that he was smiling. The two men stood together, swords at the ready, and waited for whatever it was to come to them.

A huge form lurched out of the darkness ahead. At first it was only a pale gray shape filling the tunnel, but as it drew nearer MacNeil gradually realized he was facing a giant. Standing upright, it would have been twenty feet tall and more, but in the cramped confines of the tunnel it was forced to crawl on hands and knees like an animal. Its skin and hair were milky white, and its great staring eyes were blind. It was entirely naked, covered with dirt and foulness and fresh bloody smears from the tunnel. MacNeil wondered sickly how long it had lived underground, and what it had found to feed on, crawling through tunnels under the earth like a vast misshapen worm. Its hands were huge and broad, the stubby fingers tipped with long curving fingernails grown into claws. Its teeth were long and pointed, and the great wide face held no human emotions. Saliva dripped from the snarling mouth, and the giant sniffed at the air, as though searching for the scent that had brought it crawling up out of the depths of the earth. Its shoulders filled the narrow tunnel from side to side. Its back rubbed against the ceiling, and its hand and knees sank into the bloodstained floor.

Look at the size of it, thought MacNeil dazedly. *Look at the bloody size of it. . . .*

The crawling giant pulled itself slowly toward MacNeil and the Dancer, and they backed cautiously away as they realized it wasn't alone. Behind it came another giant, and another. From farther down the tunnel came the sound of still more giants, hidden in the darkness. The giant in the lead raised its great head and howled like a hound, a horrid choking roar that echoed and reverberated throughout the tunnel. MacNeil and the Dancer winced at the awful sound, and the giant hauled itself forward with unexpected speed, the long muscular arms reaching blindly out for them.

MacNeil stood his ground and lashed out at the nearest hand with his sword. The blade cut deep and grated on bone. The giant howled deafeningly and jerked its hand back. The sword stuck in the thick flesh, and MacNeil had to use both hands to pull it free. He staggered back, still dazed by the sheer size of his foe. The hand alone had to be a good two feet wide across the knuckles. He threw himself to the floor as the hand closed into a fist and swept ponderously through the air where he'd been standing. The fist slammed into the wall and the giant went berserk with rage, battering the walls with both fists as it tried to find its enemy. The Dancer moved in beside MacNeil as he scrambled backward out of range, his sword gleaming dully in the lantern light. The giant hauled itself forward, and the Dancer stepped inside its reach and cut both the creature's wrists. A thick purple blood spurted into the air, and the giant howled once before swinging one fist with unexpected speed. The Dancer threw himself backward but couldn't move fast enough. The giant hand just clipped his shoulder in passing, and the Dancer was thrown against the tunnel wall with numbing force.

The giant pulled itself forward, the great white form filling the tunnel, battering the bloody walls and ceiling. Behind it, another crawling giant fought blindly to get past the first. MacNeil staggered to his feet, grabbed the lantern, and hacked at the giant's arm. More blood flew into the air, but still the creature wouldn't stop. MacNeil tried to reach the giant's throat, but couldn't get past the hammering fists. The Dancer moved forward to stand beside MacNeil, but even he couldn't do more than slow the giant's advance. Slowly, step by step, they were forced back down the tunnel. The giants howled and roared, the horrid sounds deafening in the enclosed space. MacNeil and the Dancer had almost reached the steps when the giant suddenly lunged forward. The left hand caught hold of MacNeil's shoulder, and the right fastened onto the Dancer's sword arm. MacNeil groaned as the huge hand crushed his shoulder in a vise-like grip, and the sword fell from his numbed hand. The Dancer's face was white from the pressure on his arm, but somehow he still held onto his sword, though he hadn't the strength to use it. The giant pulled them slowly forward, its mouth stretching wide to reveal huge, jagged teeth.

There was a clatter of feet on the stairs behind them as Flint and Constance came charging down into the tunnel. Constance raised her hands and spoke a single Word of Power. A searing white light flashed down the tunnel from her upraised hands and struck the giant in the face. It screamed shrilly as the blazing heat burned away its face, leaving only charred bone and empty eye sockets. It dropped MacNeil and the Dancer and pawed feebly at its ruined head. The Dancer shifted his sword to his left hand, stepped forward, and cut the giant's throat. Thick purple blood gushed out onto the tunnel floor, and the giant collapsed and lay twitching in its own gore. Behind it, another crawling giant tore at its flesh and began to pull itself past the unmoving body, still searching for prey.

MacNeil snatched up his sword, and he and the Dancer retreated back to the steps. Constance still held the stance of summoning, a pure white force crackling between her hands. Flint stood at her side, sword at the ready. They stood guard as MacNeil and the Dancer pulled themselves exhaustedly up the stairs and out into the cellar. Flint went up next, and finally Constance lowered her hands and the fire went out. She scrambled up the steps and out into the cellar. MacNeil slammed the trapdoor shut after her and pushed home both the bolts. Barely a second later the trapdoor shuddered violently as a giant fist beat furiously against it from below. The hammering continued for several minutes while MacNeil and the others watched anxiously, and then it stopped, leaving only an echoing silence.

Constance sat down suddenly, as though all the strength had gone out of her. MacNeil leaned on his sword and concentrated on getting his breathing back to normal. He realized he was still clinging desperately to his lantern, and put it down on the floor beside him. His hands were trembling now that the action was over, and not only from fatigue. Giants in the earth . . . perhaps that was what had happened to all the bodies. His mind's eye showed him an army of crawling giants struggling up through the trapdoor, stealing the bodies and then dragging them back down to the secret places of the earth. He swallowed hard and shook his head to clear it. His hands and his breathing had steadied, and he looked cautiously at the others to see if they'd noticed his momentary weakness. Flint and the Dancer were sitting side by side. The Dancer was trying to clean his sword one-handed while Flint massaged some feeling back into the arm the giant had crushed. Constance was kneeling beside the trapdoor, staring at it worriedly.

"What's the matter?" asked MacNeil. "The trapdoor will keep the giants out. Won't it?"

"That's the point," said Constance slowly. "As far as I can See, the giants aren't there anymore. They've just . . . gone. Vanished."

MacNeil looked at the trapdoor and then at the witch. "Just how dependable is your Sight at the moment?"

"Not very. It comes and goes, and calling up balefire for you weakened my magic considerably. But I'm sure about this, Duncan. There's nothing down there now. Nothing at all."

"That's impossible," said MacNeil. "Those giants were flesh and blood, not ghosts."

"The one I hit was very much alive," said the Dancer. "I've still got most of its blood all over me."

Flint smiled fondly at him. "Your biggest bag yet. You should have brought the body back with you. We could have had it stuffed."

"I'll remember next time," said the Dancer.

"There's nothing down there now," insisted Constance. "There's no trace of the giants at all. Open the trapdoor and you'll see I'm right."

They all looked at one another, but nobody said anything. Finally MacNeil hefted his sword and shrugged unhappily.

"All right, dammit, let's take a look. Everyone stand ready. Same procedure as before; if it moves, kill it."

The Dancer rose to his feet in a single lithe movement, the cleaning rag gone from his hand and his sword at the ready. Flint got to her feet a little more slowly and gave him a wry smile.

"Show off."

Constance got up and moved back from the trapdoor, scowling worriedly. MacNeil hesitated and looked thoughtfully at the witch.

"Can you call up that balefire again?"

"No. Just using it once drained most of my strength. I'm a witch, not a sorceress, and I know my limitations."

MacNeil nodded and bent over the trapdoor. He stood listening for a moment, but couldn't hear anything moving down in the tunnel. He hefted his sword, took a deep breath, and pulled back the two bolts. Everything was quiet. He braced himself, heaved the trapdoor open, and stepped quickly away. The trapdoor fell back onto the floor with a crash, but the dark opening was still and silent. The Rangers waited tensely, but nothing stirred in the darkness. MacNeil took his lantern and lowered it cautiously into the opening. For as far as he could see, the tunnel was empty. He looked back at the others.

"Nothing. No sign they were ever there."

"I told you," said Constance. "They're gone."

"Looks like it," said MacNeil. "But I'm not going down into the tunnel to check." He started to close the trapdoor, and then stopped and looked closely at its underside. The heavy wood had been split and splintered by savage blows from giant fists. MacNeil shivered once, and then closed the trapdoor and bolted it. He thought for a moment and then looked at the others.

"Help me move some of those heavy barrels on top of the trapdoor. I want this opening blocked off completely."

Between the four of them, they were able to manhandle two great casks stuffed with rusting ironwork onto the trapdoor. The wood creaked loudly under the weight of them. The Rangers leaned two more barrels against them, just to be sure, and then stepped back and admired their handiwork while they got their breath back.

"That should hold them," said MacNeil.

"That would hold a rabid elephant," said the Dancer. "And I should like at this stage to point out that I am a swordsman, not a laborer."

"Would you rather the giants got out and we had to fight them again?" asked MacNeil.

The Dancer thought about it for a moment and then nodded eagerly.

The trouble is, he probably means it, thought MacNeil.

"We have a problem," said Flint suddenly.

"We have several," said MacNeil. "Which did you have in mind?"

"Well," said Flint, "what if the gold is down there in the tunnels somewhere? How the hell are we going to get it out?"

"We're not," said MacNeil firmly. "I'm damned if I'm going back down there armed only with a sword; they don't pay me enough to do that. In fact, they couldn't pay me enough. There isn't that much money in the world. We'll wait till the reinforcements get here, and let them figure out a way to get down there in force."

Flint and Dancer nodded soberly. Constance frowned

but said nothing. MacNeil sighed quietly and stretched his aching muscles. He never used to get this tired after a sword fight. He must be getting out of condition; it was time to start dieting again. MacNeil scowled. He hated diets.

"All right," he said wearily, "let's get out of here. You know, times are changing. I can remember when deserted forts just had rats in their cellars."

"Yeah," said Flint. "Next time, let's just put some poison down."

The Rangers laughed and left the cellar. In the darkness below, something stirred in its sleep.

Hammer, Wilde, and Scarecrow Jack crowded into the reception hall and pulled the door shut behind them. The roar of the rain died away to a loud murmur, and they could hear themselves think again. They stopped to shake off the worst of the rain and then looked around them in the pale glow from Hammer's lantern. Wilde produced flint and steel and lit a torch he took from a wall bracket. The flaring light filled the hall with an amber glow and unsteady shadows. Four horses regarded the newcomers with grave suspicion. The outlaws looked around them, taking in the blood-stained surroundings and the four empty nooses hanging from the overhead beam.

"What the hell happened here?" said Wilde. "Hammer, you never told us it would be like this."

"Everything was normal here when I delivered the gold," said Hammer slowly. "I knew something pretty bad must have happened when the fort fell out of contact, but this . . . I don't know. It doesn't matter anyway. Whatever happened here, it's over now; those bloodstains have been dry for some time. Unless it interferes with us, it's none of our business. Let's just get the gold and get the hell out of here."

Wilde glowered uncertainly about him. "I don't know, Hammer. I never banked on anything like this."

"Is that right?" said Hammer. "What did you think, that we could just walk in and out again, as easy as that? If you want to get rich, you have to be prepared to take a few risks."

"Calculated risks are one thing, Hammer. This is . . . different."

"Not going soft on me, are you, Edmond?" said Hammer. "I'd hate to think you were going soft on me."

Wilde met Hammer's gaze for a moment, and then his eyes faltered and he looked away. "Have I ever let you down?"

"Of course not, Edmond. You never let me down because you know that the first time you do, I'll kill you. You don't want to worry about what happened here, my friend, you want to worry about what I'll do to you if you don't stop wasting my time. Now then, we go that way to get down to the cellars. You go first."

Wilde looked at the door Hammer indicated. A wide, dark stain had soaked into the wood, and the heavy metal lock had been smashed apart from the other side. The bowman handed his torch to Jack without looking at him, and walked slowly over to the door. He drew his sword, hesitated for a long moment, and then suddenly pulled the door open and stepped quickly back, holding his sword out before him. There was only a dark corridor, silent and empty and daubed with old blood. Wilde hefted his sword but made no attempt to enter the darkness. Jack stepped forward and silently offered Wilde his torch back. Wilde took it and briefly nodded his thanks without looking around. He started down the corridor, and Jack followed him. Hammer brought up the rear, carrying his lantern in one hand and the sword from his hip in the other. The long sword hilt above his shoulder glowed very faintly in the dark.

Shadows swayed menacingly around the three out-laws as Wilde led them deeper into the border fort. Their footsteps echoed loudly in the quiet, and the air grew steadily colder. Scarecrow Jack looked warily about him, wishing he was back in the Forest. Ever since he'd entered the fort his instincts had seemed muffled and confused, but still he was sure that some-thing awful had happened here, and not that long ago. The bloodstains bothered him. With so much blood spilled, why weren't there any bodies? Maybe some-thing ate them. . . . Jack frowned and shook his head. Being indoors was getting to him. He hated being in-side any house or building, behind walls and under roofs. They made him feel trapped, hemmed in. That was partly why he'd left his village all those years ago and made his home in the Forest. The Forest was alive; the stone and timber buildings were dead and silent. He felt more alive among the great trees than he ever had among his people. He went back occasionally to visit his family, but he always slept out of doors and he never stayed long.

The border fort worried him in many ways. He found the thick stone walls oppressive. He kept feeling that they were crowding in around him. The ceiling was un-comfortably low, and he kept wanting to duck his head. It hadn't bothered him too much the first time he'd entered the fort; he'd been so involved in his mission he hadn't had time to think about where he was. But now he couldn't seem to think about anything else. And above all that, there was a feeling . . . a feeling of something terrible, somewhere close at hand. Even with his instincts clouded, Jack knew it was there, just as he always knew where the hidden trails were in the Forest or what the weather was going to be. He tried to get some kind of feel for what it was he found so threatening, but his mind couldn't seem to get it in focus. Whatever it was, it was very old and very deadly, and they were getting closer to it all the time.

Scarecrow Jack wiped at the cold sweat on his face, and wished he was somewhere else. Anywhere else.

Wilde led the way around a corner, and then stopped dead in his tracks. Jack and Hammer moved quickly forward to stand beside him. The corridor ahead was choked from wall to wall and from floor to ceiling with a thick, dirty gray webbing. At the edges it frayed into delicate individual strands, but the rest of the web was a sprawling, chaotic tangle that thickened at the center into a pulsing, solid mass. It was impossible to tell how far back the webbing went, but it looked to be several feet at least. Shadows moved in the web, dark shapes that came and went with unnerving speed. Some were small, barely a few inches wide, but others were easily the size of a man's head, and a few were larger still. Every now and again Jack thought he caught a glimpse of burning blood red eyes. He sniffed cautiously at the cold air. It smelled foul, as though something dead and unburied lay close at hand.

"Did you come this way earlier?" Hammer asked Jack quietly.

"I think so, but . . . I never saw anything like this."

"It's obviously been here some time," said Hammer. "No spider could weave a web that size in a few hours."

"It wasn't spiders that made this web," said Jack firmly. "No spider spins like that. There's no pattern to the strands. No pattern that makes any sense."

"Maybe a strange kind of web means a strange kind of spider," said Hammer.

"Is this what happened to the people here?" said Wilde.

"How the hell should I know?" said Hammer. "I suppose it's possible, but I'd bet against it. If they had been attacked by spiders, the bodies would still be here, wouldn't they?"

"Not necessarily," said Jack. "Some spiders drag their prey back to their webs and spin cocoons around them. Then they either store the bodies to eat later or use them to lay their eggs in. The larvae eat their way out of the body after they hatch."

The outlaws looked at one another, and then peered into the web to see if any of the unmoving shadows were human in shape.

"We'll have to go back and try another way," said Wilde.

"We can't," said Hammer flatly. "There's no other way that will get us down to the cellar. We'll just have to cut our way through this mess, that's all. Cut it . . . or burn it."

He gestured to Wilde, and he stepped warily forward and thrust his torch at the nearest clump of webbing. It blackened and steamed, but wouldn't break or shrivel. Wilde pulled the torch back and looked almost challengingly at Hammer, who scowled at Wilde and then at the web.

"All right, we do it the hard way. Wilde, you take the left, I'll take the right. Jack, hold the lantern and watch out for spiders."

Jack took the lantern from him, and Hammer stepped forward and hacked at the nearest clump of webbing with his sword. It parted reluctantly under the blow and clung stickily to the blade. Hammer had to use both hands to jerk the sword free. Wilde smiled mockingly as he placed his torch in a wall bracket, safely out of the way. Hammer lifted his sword to cut the web again, and then stopped as the two separated strands of webbing before him slowly wound themselves together again. Wilde backed away. Jack bit his lower lip uncertainly. He was starting to get a very bad feeling about the web.

Deep in the webbing, something moved. A shadow stirred in the middle of the milky haze. It was tall, like a man, and the three outlaws watched uneasily as it moved slowly toward them, walking through the thick strands of webbing like a man striding through mists. Jack and Wilde fell back a pace as it drew nearer, but Hammer held his ground, sword at the ready. The shadow loomed up against the boundary of the web, looking more and more like a man. Except it was thinner and bonier than any man should be. It reached out a hand toward Hammer, and the webbing bulged outward and split open. Milky strands parted stickily as the bony hand thrust forward. The fingers were nothing more than yellowed bone, crusted with old dried blood and rotting strings of meat. The web bulged out again, stretching and tearing, and like some obscene mockery of birth, the creature clawed its way out of the web and stood before the three outlaws, smiling a smile that would never end.

It was mostly bone, a living skeleton of a man who had died long ago. Scraps and strings of decaying meat still clung here and there, to bones stained with blood that had dried long before, but it was the web that held the grisly figure together and gave it shape and purpose. Where muscle and sinew should have been, thick milky strands glistened slickly in the dim light, curling and twisting slowly around the dead bones like dreaming snakes. The creature looked unhurriedly from one outlaw to another. Nothing moved in the empty eye sockets, but still it saw them, and its death's-head grin never wavered.

"Is it alive or dead?" said Jack.

"It's dead," said Hammer. "One way or another."

He stepped forward and cut at the creature's throat with his sword—a fast, vicious, professional blow that should have torn the creature's head from its bony shoulders. Instead it raised an arm with inhuman speed and blocked the blow easily. The blade jarred against the solid bone and glanced away harmlessly. Hammer quickly recovered his balance and cut deliberately at the raised arm, aiming for the strands of webbing that held it together. The sword tip sliced easily through the milky strands, cutting them in two, but the severed ends flowed back together in a second, as though they'd never been parted. Hammer froze, startled, and the creature lashed out with a bony fist. Hammer threw himself aside at the last moment, and the fist swept on to smash into the corridor wall with enough force to crack several of the smaller bones. The creature recovered its balance in a moment, and turned its endless grin on the outlaws again. It felt no pain. It had been dead a long time, and was beyond such human weaknesses as suffering or compassion or mercy.

"What the hell is this?" said Hammer. "Some kind of lich? Jack, you ever seen anything like this before?"

"No," said Scarecrow Jack. "There's never been anything like this in the Forest. It has no place among the living."

"That's where you're wrong, nature boy," said Wilde. "I've seen this before in the Forest. In the Tanglewood, to be exact, on the border of the Darkwood. The web is alive, a single living creature that devours its prey by enveloping it. And after it's sucked the meat off the bones, it puts them back together again and sends them out into the world to find new prey. Pretty smart, for a web. Hard to kill, too."

Hammer glanced briefly at Wilde. "What were you doing in a dangerous place like the Tanglewood?"

Wilde stiffened at the open contempt in Hammer's voice. "I used to be a hero," he said flatly. "Remember?"

"That was a long time ago," said Hammer.

The creature suddenly lunged forward, and the outlaws scattered. Wilde drew an arrow from his quiver and nocked it to his bow. The creature spun around to face him, and Wilde sneered into its unwavering grin. He aimed and let fly in a single smooth motion, and the arrow punched through the creature's skull and out the back, sending the creature staggering backward. It slammed up against a closed door, and Wilde fired three more arrows in quick succession. The heavy shafts smashed through the skull and sank deep into the wood of the door, pinning the skull to the door. It struggled to get free, but the deep-sunk arrows held it fast. Wilde looked at Hammer with all his old arrogance.

"I'm as good as I ever was, Hammer, and don't you forget it."

He broke off abruptly as the creature sagged back against the door and went limp. It hung lifelessly, supported only by the arrows through its skull. And then the strands of webbing that held the creature together writhed and coiled and fell away, dropping to the floor with soft pattering sounds. They humped and slithered across the floor with unnatural speed, and plunged back into the main mass of the web. Bloodstained bones collected in a heap on the floor, until all the webbing was gone and only the skull remained, pinned high up on the door. The jawbone was the last to fall, taking the endless grin with it.

Jack started to say something, and then stopped and looked at the web. Something new was happening in the seething milky heart; he could feel it. Wilde and Hammer followed Jack's gaze as the thick ropy strands writhed and twisted until the whole cloudy mass was boiling with slow, sluggish movements.

Wilde nocked an arrow to his bow and fired it into the writhing mass. The arrow disappeared without trace. A long strand of milky webbing raised itself into the air like a tentacle, and Jack had to throw himself to one side as it suddenly lashed out at him. Hammer stood his ground and sliced through the tentacle with his sword. The severed end fell writhing to the floor. What was left of the tentacle rose farther out of the main mass until it was the same length as before. More tentacles surged up out of the web, clawing at the air like so many searching fingers. Jack backed quickly away.

"We've got to get out of here, Hammer. There's no way we can fight something like that!"

"He's right," said Wilde quietly. "It can't be killed. We'll have to go back."

"No," said Hammer. "There is a way."

He sheathed his sword on his hip and reached up for the hilt of the longsword on his back. The long leather-wrapped hilt seemed almost to leap into his hand, and the great length of blade swept out of its scabbard in one swift movement. The sword was almost seven feet long and six inches wide at the crosspiece. The weight must have been immense, but Hammer hefted the blade one-handed as though it weighed nothing. The gleaming steel had a sickly yellow sheen that was subtly unpleasant to the eye. Jack winced at the sight of it. Even with his senses muffled, he could feel the power in the sword. Magic roared and raged in the long blade, barely contained by ancient spells, and without even knowing what the power was, Jack knew it was evil.

He also had a strong feeling that just possibly the sword was alive, and aware.

Hammer stepped forward, and the great sword leapt out and into the center of the web. Milky white streamers frayed out into the air as the trembling web tried to draw back from the glowing blade. The longsword burrowed deep into the heart of the webbing like a hound hot on a scent, dragging Hammer along behind it, and where the glowing blade touched the web, the thick milky stuff decayed and fell away as strands of rotting gossamer. The web boiled, heaving and bubbling, throwing out long arms and streamers as though it could run from what was destroying it.

Hammer moved slowly forward, his face twisted with distaste at the stench of rotting tissues, and the sword burned a bitter yellow. He swept the blade back and forth, and the web fell apart in rotting clumps. Dark creatures stumbled forward, lurching out of the milky heart of the web—patchwork things of bone and horror, obscene unliving puppets manipulated by the web. They threw themselves at Hammer, bony hands reaching out like yellowed claws, only to rot and fall apart as the glowing blade caressed them in passing, releasing the long dead bones from servitude to the web.

The corridor was nine feet high and eight feet wide, and the webbing had filled it for fifteen feet. When Hammer finally came to a halt and looked back, all that remained were a few blackened streamers hanging still and lifeless from the walls and ceiling, and a scattering of old bones on the bare flagstones, at peace at last. Hammer looked at his sword. The long blade was glowing brightly with the same yellow sheen as a corpse fire on a cairn.

"You damned fool," said Wilde quietly. "That's Wolfsbane, isn't it?"

"Yes," said Hammer. "It is." He thrust the longsword back into its scabbard. The sword slid slowly into place, as though reluctant to be sheathed.

Jack checked the candle in his lantern. Somehow he'd managed to hold onto it through all the excitement, and miraculously, the candle was still alight. Wilde retrieved his torch from the wall bracket, and then glared suddenly at Hammer.

"I thought that hellsword was lost in the Demon War," he said harshly.

"It was. I found it."

"Then keep away from me, Hammer. Keep well away."

"What's the matter, Wilde? Frightened?"

"Of that thing? Yes. So would you be, if that sword hadn't already got its hooks into you."

Jack didn't know what they were talking about, and decided that for the moment at least he really didn't give a damn. The web was dead, along with its creatures, but there were other dangers. And much as the longsword worried him, he was more concerned with finding the gold and getting the hell out of the fort before the Rangers found them. He said as much and Hammer nodded.

"You're right. Since you were stupid enough to let yourself be seen, the Rangers could still be searching the fort for you, and we can't afford to be found. If they're anywhere nearby, they couldn't have missed hearing us. We'd better find a secure place and lie low for an hour or so; give things a chance to settle down again."

"Are you crazy? I'm not staying in this godforsaken place one minute longer than I have to." Wilde glared unflinchingly at Hammer, his hand clenched into a fist around his bow. "You saw the web; those creatures are supposed to be extinct, ever since the Tanglewood was destroyed during the Demon War. If this fort is going to be full of things like that, things that shouldn't even exist, then I say we get the hell out of here right now, before something really nasty comes crawling out of the woodwork."

"You disappoint me, Edmond," said Hammer. "You really do. Look at you. I can remember when you were part of the Royal Guard itself. You killed the rebel Bladesmaster, Sir Guillam, and stood with the king in the last great battle of the Demon War. And now all you can do is flap that stupid mouth of yours and jump out of your skin every time you see a shadow move."

"I remember those times too," said Wilde steadily. "I was younger then, and believed all the lies they told me about honor and duty. I know better now. I don't put my neck on the line for anyone but me."

"You'll do whatever I tell you to do," said Hammer softly. "Won't you, Edmond?"

Their eyes met for a long moment. Wilde looked away first.

"All right, we'll hole up for an hour. But I don't like it."

"You don't have to," said Hammer. He turned his back on Wilde and stalked off down the corridor. The bowman watched him go, his face very cold, and then moved off after Hammer. Jack brought up the rear, watching Wilde's back thoughtfully. He hadn't known Wilde possessed such a heroic past. Out of the five thousand and more men and women who'd fought in the last great battle of the Demon War outside the Forest Castle, less than two hundred had survived, the bravest of the brave. That didn't sound much like the Edmond Wilde that Jack knew. The bowman was an outlaw and a murderer, who shot most of his victims in the back. He looted and stole, fought for whoever would hire him, and there were at least three rape charges against him. Jack shook his head. He'd never understood people anyway.

Hammer hurried down the corridor, checking each door he passed. The first two turned out to be a cupboard and a crowded storeroom, but the third led off into a small annex. Hammer gave it a quick look over and nodded, satisfied. "This will do. No windows and only the one door. Easy enough to defend, and small enough to be overlooked. Get some rest, both of you. We'll give it an hour or so, and then see how the land lies."

He waved the outlaws in, closed the door, and jammed a chair up against the doorknob. Then while Jack and Wilde were still looking around, he commandeered the only other chair and sat down with a contented sigh, stretching his legs out before him. Wilde glared at him, and turned away and thrust his torch into a wall holder with unnecessary violence. He sat down in a corner where he could watch the door, his back to the wall and his bow in his lap. Jack sat down in the opposite corner, wincing at the feel of the cold stone floor through his damp rags. He set his lantern down beside him, looked unenthusiastically around the annex, and sighed quietly. It was dark, stuffy, and far too small for his liking. And he was feeling the start of a cold. Some days you just can't win. He wriggled uncomfortably, searching in vain for a position that would let him relax. It seemed ages since he'd last laid down on a mossy riverbank, warmed by the summer sun. He sniffed resignedly and settled himself as best he could. He was tired, and a short rest would do him good. Just a short rest.

On his chair facing the door, Hammer slept soundly, his chin on his chest. The longsword hung quietly in its scabbard, waiting and watching.

* * *

Duncan MacNeil plunged down one corridor after another, working his way determinedly through the warren of interconnecting corridors and passageways. Flint and the Dancer hurried after him, with Constance bringing up the rear. MacNeil glared angrily about him into the gloom. He was sure he'd heard the sound of fighting somewhere nearby, but so far he'd found no evidence to suggest there was anyone in the fort but the Rangers.

Outside, the storm still raged. The driving rain was almost as loud as the thunder, and occasionally lightning would flare through one of the narrow embrasures, dazzling the Rangers. The rest of the fort was pitch dark. MacNeil held his lantern out before him, and did his best not to trip over anything. And then he rounded a corner and stopped dead in his tracks as he saw before him the remains of the huge web. The others crowded in beside him. Decaying strands of webbing still hung from the walls and ceiling, and the air was thick with the stench of corruption. Yellow bones stained with old blood lay scattered across the floor, and MacNeil didn't need to examine them to know they were human.

"What the hell happened here?" said Flint softly. No one answered her.

MacNeil knelt down and looked closely at the floor. There were a few vague footprints, but not enough to track whoever made them. He didn't touch the bones or what remained of the webbing. He got to his feet and looked unhappily around him. None of it made any sense. He'd already been through this corridor once less than three hours ago, and there'd been no trace of anything then. MacNeil shook his head and smiled wryly. He should be used to things not making sense by now.

He turned to Constance. "Can you See what happened here?"

Constance frowned and closed her eyes. "There were three men here. Outlaws. One of them was Scarecrow Jack. Another was one of the guards who brought the gold here. They were fighting something, but I can't See what."

"Whatever made the web, presumably," said Mac-Neil. "What else can you See?"

Constance's brow furrowed as she concentrated. "There was something else here," she said slowly. "Something apart from the outlaws and the web . . . Duncan, they've brought something evil into this fort. Something old, and powerful." She shuddered suddenly and opened her eyes. "I can't See anything else. The three outlaws are gone. I could try tracking them with a spell, but calling up the magic needed would knock me out for several hours."

"It's not worth it," said MacNeil. "Three outlaws aren't going to be much of a threat, no matter what they've brought with them, and I might need your abilities yet. No, we'll track them down the hard way, by checking every room till we find them. It'll take a while, but what with one thing and another, I doubt we'd be getting much sleep tonight anyway."

Constance looked at him but didn't say anything. The outlaws had brought something awful into the fort, something that endangered them all, but her Sight hadn't given her a clear picture of what it was. And until she was sure, she couldn't say anything more to MacNeil. He wouldn't just take her word for it.

Even though he would have taken Salamander's word . . .

"Strange coincidence," said Flint suddenly.

"What is?" said MacNeil.

"We fought monsters down below, and now it seems the outlaws have been fighting something nasty here in the corridor. And we all dreamed of monsters. Maybe there's a connection."

"Such as?"

Flint shrugged. "Beats me."

The Rangers stood together a while, thinking about the new turn of events, and MacNeil frowned as an idea came to him.

"I don't know about the rest of you, but it seems to me that if the outlaws were heading for anywhere in particular, it's almost bound to be the cellar. That's where the gold was supposed to have been stored, after all."

He paused, and the others looked at him expectantly.

"So?" said Constance.

"So, I think we ought to get back down to the cellar first, so we can wait for them."

Flint and the Dancer looked at each other. Constance looked at the floor. MacNeil smiled suddenly.

"It beats the hell out of a room-by-room search, doesn't it?"

"Good point," said the Dancer.

There was a pause, and then Flint looked directly at MacNeil. "Why are you telling us all this? You lead this team; you make the decisions, and we back you up. That's the way it's always been."

"This is different," said MacNeil evenly. "This isn't the usual kind of case that Rangers have to face. There are dangers here that are way outside our usual scope. I don't think I have the right to just order you to just follow me into danger. So I'm giving you all the chance to say no if you want to."

Flint shook her head slowly. "I thought you'd got over Salamander's death by now. It wasn't your fault; you had no way of knowing that ambush was there. All right, Salamander had Seen a danger in that town, but she couldn't See what it was. She died there because *she* made a mistake, when she decided to trust her sword instead of her magic. Giles and I trust your decisions. We always have. Are you going down into the cellar again?"

"Yes," said MacNeil. "I am."

"Then the Dancer and I are coming with you. We've been part of your team for eight years now, and we've no mind to join another. Wherever you go, we go. Right, Giles?"

"Right," said the Dancer.

MacNeil looked at Constance, who smiled back at him. "Same here," she said calmly. "After all, where would you be without me to look after you? I'm a part of this team too."

"Let's go," said MacNeil. "We don't want the outlaws to get there first."

He turned and led the way back down the corridor, so they wouldn't see how moved he was by their loyalty. Flint and the Dancer exchanged grins and moved off after him. Constance brought up the rear, humming tunelessly to herself.

"More monsters, do you think?" said Flint to the Dancer.

"Seems likely," said the Dancer.

"Good," said Flint. "You can use the exercise. You've been getting slow and sloppy lately."

"Right," said the Dancer. "Over the hill and past it, that's me."

They chuckled quietly together. Behind them, Constance was smiling too, but her eyes were faraway. More than once she'd sensed a presence in the fort, and it was at its strongest in the cellar. And now they were going back there. Constance's smile widened slightly. She'd never faced a real challenge to her powers before. She'd make MacNeil proud of her yet.

5

Dangers Seen
and Unseen

Hammer and Wilde were already sound asleep. The noise of the storm was a long way off, and the small annex was warm and dry and peaceful. Jack leaned back against the rough stone wall and fought back a yawn. He knew it was asking for trouble for all three of them to fall asleep, but it had been a long, hard day, and his eyes were closing in spite of himself. Sleep settled slowly about him like an old familiar blanket. The torch crackled quietly in its wall holder, and the gold and amber light was pleasantly peaceful. Jack stretched slowly, easing his tired muscles. For the first time since he'd entered the border fort he felt comfortable and at peace. If he'd been a little less sleepy he would have found that worrying, but as it was the thought passed briefly through his mind without disturbing him. Hammer murmured something and shifted in his chair, but didn't waken. Wilde breathed noisily through his mouth. Jack's eyes closed, and his chin sank forward onto his chest. The three outlaws sank slowly deeper into sleep.

And dreamed.

Jonathon Hammer ran through the Forest, sword in hand. His boots thudded loudly on the packed earth of the beaten trail as he forced himself on despite his heaving chest and aching legs. He wasn't sure how long he'd been running, but he knew he couldn't keep going much longer. He looked quickly about him, blinking furiously as sweat ran down his forehead and into his eyes. The tall trees stretched away in every direction, blending into a featureless mass of shadow and greenery and dappled light. He stumbled to a halt, gasping for breath, and leaned against a wide tree trunk for support. Being chased by half a dozen guards was bad enough, but having to run in full chain mail was adding insult to injury.

He considered taking it off and dumping it, but reluctantly decided he didn't have the time. The guards couldn't be more than a few minutes behind him, rot their souls. He'd been careful to stick to the narrow and more obscure Forest trails so that they couldn't come after him on horseback, but even so he hadn't been able to lose his pursuers. Someone among them must know this part of the Forest as well as he did.

Hammer shook his head disgustedly and waited impatiently for his breathing to settle. He wiped the sweat from his face with his sleeve, and flexed his aching muscles. He couldn't afford to stiffen up; a cramp or a stitch at the wrong moment could get him killed. Hammer held his breath and listened carefully. He couldn't hold it for long in his exhausted state, but as far as he could tell he was safe for the moment. The only sounds he could hear were the normal Forest sounds of wind and bird and animal. Hammer glared about him, and wondered what to do next.

In the beginning, it had all seemed so simple. The

guard Commanders had watched everyone like a hawk during the border patrol, but once that was finished they relaxed a little, and for any man with an eye to the main chance, it was the perfect time to organize a friendly little poker school. Everything had been going fine, until that fat fool Norris had accused him of cheating. Before he knew what he was doing, Hammer had drawn his sword and cut Norris down. After that, he'd had to break and run for it, cursing his own hot temper all the way. He should have waited till he and Norris next had guard duty together, and then stabbed the bastard in the back. Now he'd have to change his name again. Luckily he only called himself Hammer when he was fighting as a mercenary.

Hammer had always known he had a great destiny ahead of him. He'd always known he was special, set apart from other men. He'd tried pretty much everything in his time, searching for his true vocation, the one that would lead him to greatness, but his only real skill was as a soldier. He'd served as a mercenary, as a man at arms, and finally as a guard. He didn't care whom he fought for or against, as long as the money was good. He honed his fighting skills in practice and in battle, and waited for his chance, the great chance to become what he had always been meant to be: a ruler of men. He had greatness in him. He could feel it. And with the right chance, he'd prove it.

Assuming, of course, that he survived long enough. He still didn't know what had gone wrong, but the guards had been on his heels since first light. Maybe he hadn't disguised his trail carefully enough. More than once his pursuers had drawn close enough for him to see them in the distance, and on each occasion it had taken every ounce of his cunning and woodcraft for him to draw ahead again. Six guards, armed with swords and axes. He supposed he should be grateful there weren't any bowmen among them.

He stiffened suddenly as the first faint murmur of approaching footsteps reached him. He swore softly, and hefted his sword uncertainly. The guards were closer than he'd thought. He pushed himself away from the tree and stumbled on down the beaten trail. He tried to break into a run, and found he couldn't. His legs were too tired, and he just didn't have the breath for it. Like any professional fighting man, Hammer knew his body's limits, and he knew how close he was to them. He glared quickly about him, and lurched off the trail and into the shadows between the trees. Leaving the trail was a calculated risk, but it was the only chance he had. His progress slowed to a crawl as he forced his way through dense patches of hedge and briar, but his chain mail protected him from the worst of the thorns. The sunlight gradually faded away as the overhead canopy grew thicker, cutting out the light. Hammer stumbled to a halt in the gloom, and listened for any sign that the guards had followed him off the trail, but all he could hear was his own harsh breathing and the pounding of his heart. He swallowed thickly, and wiped again at the sweat that ran down to sting his eyes. He had to keep moving, put more ground between him and the guards. Hammer forced himself through another patch of briar, and the earth suddenly shifted and fell away beneath his feet. He lurched to one side, flailing wildly about him for the balance, and then the ground gave way and he went screaming down into darkness.

After a heartstopping pause, he slammed into a hard unyielding surface, and slid helplessly down an uneven earth slope that seemed to go on forever. Jutting stones bruised him painfully as he shot past them, but his scrabbling hands couldn't find anything to hang on to in the darkness. Finally the slope spilled him out onto a flat cavern floor, and Hammer rolled and skidded to a halt. He lay still awhile, getting his breath back, and then checked cautiously for broken bones. For once, luck seemed to be with him. His armor had saved him from anything worse than a few dozen bruises. He sat up slowly, wincing, and looked around him.

He was in a cavern, a hundred yards across and more, hewn countless centuries ago from the bare rock by who knew what human or inhuman hands. The walls of the vast cave were laced with hundreds of tiny glowing crystals. They shed a pale silver light across the scene, like strange, disembodied moonlight. Great twisted stalagmites rose up from the cavern floor, straining to reach the hanging stalactites far above. An underground stream ran through the cave, the still waters dark and uninviting. Hammer got to his feet, and was surprised and rather impressed to discover he was still hanging on to his sword. If nothing else, it proved his instincts were still sound. He stumbled over to the stream, and sank painfully down beside it. He was starting to really feel his bruises now that the shock was passing. He dipped his hand into the freezing water and splashed it across his face. The shock of the cold was refreshing, and helped to clear his head and settle his nerves. He did it again, just for the pleasure of it, and then shook his head briskly and rose to his feet. He looked around for a way out, and his heart sank.

The earth slope was hopeless. It was far too steep, and anyway the soil was too crumbly to bear his weight when climbing. The stream presumably had its entrance and exit points, but they appeared to be hidden somewhere under water. Hammer scowled about him into the gloom, and as his eyes grew used to the pale, diffused light, he spotted a tall crack in one of the walls, a good ten feet high and almost a yard wide. He started toward it, and then stopped as a bright, shining glimmer caught his eye. He hefted his sword thoughtfully and moved slowly forward. Somebody had made his cavern long ago, that was clear from the tool markings on the walls, and who was to say their descendants might not still be around, and armed. . . .

As Hammer drew nearer, the bright glimmer gradually resolved itself into a long silver scabbard, resting on the ground beside the crack in the wall. Hammer looked carefully around him, ears pricked for the slightest sound, but there was no sign of the sword's owner anywhere in the cave. Hammer lowered himself on one knee, and looked the sheathed sword over without making any attempt to touch it. Sword and sheath were a good seven feet long, and from the width of the scabbard the blade had to be impressively broad. The scabbard itself appeared to be solid silver and was covered with ancient runes, etched deeply into the metal. Hammer didn't recognize any of them, but they looked to be very old . . . and disturbing. If he didn't look right at them, the runes seemed almost to be moving, writhing. . . . Hammer swallowed sickly and turned his head away for a moment. For the first time he realized what he'd stumbled upon.

Long, long ago—well past the point where history fades into legend—there were six swords of power: the Infernal Devices. No one knew who made them, or why. All anyone knew for sure was that they proved to be inherently evil, and their use nearly destroyed the world and all who lived in it. Three of the swords disappeared. Three remained; Rockbreaker, Flarebright, and Wolfsbane. The Forest Kings locked them away in the castle armory, and swore they would never be used again. And there the Damned swords remained for hundreds of years, until in the deepest despair of the Demon War, King John called them forth one last time. One sword, Rockbreaker, was destroyed. The other two were lost in battle, disappearing into a great crack in the earth.

And now Jonathon Hammer had found one of the Infernal Devices.

He stared unblinkingly at the greath length of the scabbard. Ancient sigils had been graven into the cross-piece of the sword, forming a single word: *Wolfsbane*. There was power here, just waiting for him to pick it up and use it. It was a dangerous power; the Infernal Devices were believed by some to be alive, and able to possess the minds and souls of their owners. But Hammer had never believed such stories. He reached out a hand to the long, leather-wrapped hilt. And then it came to him that this was his destiny, the marvelous future for which he had been searching all his life. This was what all his days had been leading toward, the greatness that would inevitably be his once he wielded an Infernal Device. At last he would become what he had always been meant to be: a ruler of men. Hammer picked up the scabbard with his left hand. Despite its great size it seemed to weigh almost nothing. Hammer slung the scabbard over his left shoulder and buckled it securely into place. It felt comfortable on his back, as though it had always belonged there.

There was a clattering of falling stones as six guards came stumbling and sliding down the steep earth slope into the cavern. Hammer spun around, his hand falling automatically to the sword at his hip. For a moment all he could think was *They've found me,* and then his mind calmed and his hand fell away from the sword at his side. He didn't need that anymore. He had something better.

The six guards assembled at the base of the earth slope and looked quickly about them before fixing on Hammer. They grinned coldly and fanned out to form a semicircle before him. The pale light from the cavern walls gleamed dully on their swords. The guards didn't waste time speaking to Hammer, and he had nothing to say to them. There was nothing to say. He had murdered a fellow guard. He had put himself outside the law, and every man's hand would be turned against him. That was why the guards had followed him so determinedly; they shared some of his shame. When one guard went bad, it reflected on the honor of every other guard. Of course, if he was to die before news of his actions got out ... Hammer smiled slowly. The guards wouldn't rest until he was dead, he knew that, but he no longer feared their anger. Nothing could harm him now. The guards moved purposefully forward, and Hammer went to meet them, still smiling. He waited until the last moment and then raised his right hand and drew Wolfsbane from its scabbard.

The sword came free in a rush, the great length of blade glowing a bitter yellow in the gloom. The guards stopped their advance and stirred uneasily. Even without knowing what the sword was, they could feel a presence in the cavern that hadn't been there before. Something had awakened that should have been left to sleep forever, and it was hungry. Hammer chuckled softly, and the hunger was reflected in his laughter. He stepped forward, sword at the ready, and the guards dropped automatically into their fighting positions. They were six to one, six fully armed guards against a proven traitor and coward. They raised their swords, and the slaughter began.

Hammer gutted the first guard with a sideways sweep of the longsword, and spun to decapitate a second guard before the first hit the ground. The headless body managed another couple of steps before it realized it was dead and fell limply to the ground. Blood gushed across the cavern floor. Two guards leapt at Hammer together, their swords seeking his heart. Wolfsbane twisted in Hammer's hands, and he blocked both blows with almost contemptuous ease. He swung the sword up and down again in a movement almost too fast to follow. The nearest guard lifted his blade to parry the blow. Wolfsbane sheared clean through the steel blade and buried itself in the guard's head, cleaving his skull to the jawbone. Hammer jerked the longsword clear of the falling body and spun around to face the three remaining guards. For a moment they stood very still, shocked at the sudden easy deaths of their companions, and then, as one, they threw themselves at Hammer. Wolfsbane's sickly light glowed brightly as it cut through flesh and bone and steel alike, and as quickly as that the last three guards were dead.

Hammer stood over the dead bodies, and watched expressionlessly as they quickly decayed and fell apart into dust. Within seconds, nothing remained but a few pieces of rusting armor and a slowly dispersing stench of corruption. Hammer tried to swallow, but his mouth was too dry. *Wolf's Bane. Bane, that which causes ruin and decay.* It was just as he remembered from the Demon War, when Wolfsbane had cut a deadly path through the demon horde, and left nothing to show of its passing save a few moldering bones. Hammer looked down at the longsword glowing in the air before him. The hilt felt unpleasantly warm in his hand, and there was something sickening about the horrid yellow light that pulsed within the blade. It was like looking at the source of all the death and corruption in the world, and knowing it to be alive and aware and hungry. And then Hammer looked at the hand holding the sword, and felt a scream build in his throat.

The flesh of his hand was diseased and rotten. Dark patches spread across his skin, which cracked and fell apart to reveal the wet red muscles beneath. Maggots writhed in his flesh as the decay spread, fraying the blackening muscles and tendons and uncovering the discolored bones. Hammer shook his head slowly, watching in horror as the corruption spread remorselessly up his arm.

No! This didn't happen!

Hammer tried to throw the Infernal Device away, and found he couldn't. The rotting claw wrapped around the sword hilt wouldn't release its grip. Hammer staggered unsteadily over to the stream, some inane thought about washing himself clean jerking unsteadily through his mind. At the water's edge he looked down and saw his reflection staring back. A rotting corpse stood at the water's edge, holding a sword that shone like the sun. The lich had no face left, and the gleaming teeth were bared in a mocking grin. The bony jaw gaped wide as Hammer finally screamed.

They're still watching me. They look excited but embarrassed, like someone caught watching a freak in a carnival sideshow. Not so surprising, really. That's all I am to them. A genuine hero, on display. Watch him walk and talk, almost like a normal human being. See him perform his entertaining little tricks with a bow and arrow. See him hit the target again and again, and pretend you can see excitement in his eyes instead of boredom. Come and see the hero, but don't get too close. After all, he's not a normal man, not really. Just another freak in the sideshow.

Edmond Wilde filled his mug and gulped the thick, sugary wine. It was far too sweet for his taste, but it was potent, and he'd settle for that. He looked around him, smiling slightly as people looked quickly away rather than meet his eyes. Peasants. Stupid, grubby peasants in faded clothes from stinking little towns and villages, come to gawk at the county fair, the one patch of light and color in their miserable, squalid lives. The same kind of life he'd left to join the guards . . .

The county fair was always the same, year after year. A handful of scruffy tents full of second-rate jugglers and acrobats, animals tamed to placidity, and games of chance rigged till the dice screamed. And a freak show, of course, hidden away around the back, so as not to disturb those with more sensitive natures. A gloomy little tent where you could pay to see a calf with two heads, a winged lizard in a bottle, and a wild man in a cage biting the head off a live chicken. There was even a skin show, for those whose tastes ran that way. Half a dozen aging fan dancers with bright smiles and dyed hair who might be persuaded to do more than dance if the price was right.

All the fun of the fair.

And then there was the archery competition. That was why he was here, of course. Edmond Wilde, the master bowman. Come and see the man who stood beside the king in the last great battle of the Demon War. See the man who became a hero simply by surviving when so many better men died. Test your skill against the master bowman, and win a purse of fifty gold ducats if you can beat his score! Wilde smiled sourly. No one had beaten him, and no one ever would. He was the best. Wilde drank more wine and wiped his mouth on his sleeve. He was the best bowman there was, and he made a living fleecing peasants in a traveling carnival. Being a hero was all well and good, but it didn't put money in your pocket. When the Demon War was over, he was still nothing but a guard, living in a guards' barracks and drawing a guard's pay. He wanted more than that. After everything he'd been through, he deserved more than that. So he left the guards and struck out on his own, and little good it did him. His only skill was with the bow and the sword. He had no gift for business, and his savings didn't last long. He lost it all in one tavern after another, and never missed it till it was gone.

And then the carnival found him, and they needed a main attraction as much as he needed a job. As far as Wilde was concerned, it was better than nothing, but only just. The towns and villages came and went, and he lost track of their names just as he lost track of the days and weeks and months that slid past unnoticed. He used his bow when he had to, feeling the joy of bow and arrow and target coming together in a pattern of certainty of which he was only a part, knowing all the time he was wasting his talent but unable to think of anything better. He drank whatever wine was available, and never complained at the taste or the quality. Wherever he went there were always women, awed by his name and reputation, and so starry-eyed they never saw the contempt in his smile. He didn't value himself and despised those who did. And so the days went on, becoming weeks and months and finally years. Wilde knew his life was drifting away but didn't know what to do about it, or even if he cared much anyway. There was always another town, another bottle, another woman.

Wilde emptied his mug, went to fill it again, and scowled as he saw the bottle was empty too. It was a good hour or more before the archery contest was due to start, and he was bored. He was also fed up with being stared at. He dropped the empty bottle and mug onto the ground, slung his bow over his shoulder, and wandered aimlessly through the fair. The sunny afternoon was full of the cries of the stall holders and the hawkers, loudly proclaiming the virtues of their wares, and the chatter of the bustling crowds. Women shrilled excitedly over brightly colored cloths and wool, and all but fought each other for new patterns and recipes and spices. Children ran screaming and yelling between the stalls, almost bursting with the excitement of it all, stopping now and again to stare wide-eyed at simple luxuries that were often far beyond the purses of their parents. The open-air bars did a good trade, and knife grinders and pot menders filled the air around them with flying sparks. And everywhere Wilde went the crowds parted before him, falling back to let him pass, mostly because they were awed at his presence among them, but occasionally because they could sense the directionless anger that burned within him, so close to the surface.

He walked on through the crowds, not knowing where he was going or what he was looking for, and not really caring. He just felt better when he was moving. At least then he had the illusion he was doing something. His feet finally led him past the last of the stalls and out into the edge of the fair. A few small tents stood huddled together, a dumping ground for carnival costumes and properties not in use. A girl was standing by one of the tents. She wore a low-cut dress of black and scarlet, and wore it well. She had a fine head of night-dark hair, and her eyes were a startling blue. She couldn't have been more than fifteen, but she already moved like a woman. Peasants grew up fast. They had to, or like as not they didn't grow up at all. A girl her age was usually married and starting a family of her own.

She looked away when Wilde met her gaze, but he didn't miss the slight smile or the spark in her eyes. He'd seen them often enough before. He strolled un-

hurriedly toward her. She didn't look to be wearing a
wedding ring, but that didn't mean much in the poorer
towns, and the last thing he needed was trouble with a
jealous husband. But he was bored, and angry with
himself and the world, and anyway, he had an hour to
kill. He just hoped this one didn't have fleas. He stood
before her, and they smiled at each other and said
pleasant things neither of them really meant, and then
they went into the tent together. It was cool and pleasantly dim inside. The girl kissed him once, lingeringly,
and then turned away and began to unbutton her dress.
Wilde removed his bow and his quiver and his sword
belt and put them carefully to one side, and then
pulled off his shirt and dropped it on the floor. The girl
waited until his trousers were down around his ankles
and then spun suddenly around and pushed him over
backward. Wilde fell awkwardly, the wine singing in his
head. There was a brief flash of steel as the girl produced a knife from somewhere and cut the purse from
his belt, and then she was running for the tent flaps.

Wilde roared with anger and threw himself after her.
One flailing hand caught her around the ankle, and the
girl lurched to a halt. She snarled back at him, her
pretty face ugly with hatred, and stamped down hard
on his hand with her free foot. Wilde didn't let go. His
fingers were screaming with pain, but he was too angry
and too drunk to give a damn. He grabbed hold of her
leg with his other hand and hauled her down beside
him. She cut at him with her knife, but he caught her
wrist and made her drop it. Her wrist was very small in
his hand. She fought him silently, her face twisted with
pain and fury, but he soon forced her onto her back
and knelt over her, grinning harshly. Nobody robbed

Edmond Wilde without paying for it one way or another. The girl cursed and spat at him, and he slapped
her face to teach her some manners. She screamed
loudly. Wilde put his hand over her mouth, and she bit
it. He snatched his hand away, and she screamed again.

The tent flaps burst open as a man charged in with
a sword in his hand. Wilde swore quickly and threw
himself away from the girl, clawing for his sword belt.
Bastard must be the girl's protector . . . her sort always
had a protector. . . . Wilde drew his sword and regained
his feet while the newcomer's eyes were still adjusting
to the gloom, and he thrust out his sword in a perfect
lunge. The sword grated briefly against the newcomer's
ribs as the blade slammed home. He groaned once and
fell limply to the floor. The girl made a run for the tent
flaps, and Wilde cut her down without thinking.

He looked at the two bodies lying twisted and bloody
on the tent floor, and the last of the drink burned out
of his mind, leaving him sober at last. He bent down
and reclaimed his purse, and thought frantically on
what to do. The girl and her would-be rescuer were
bound to be locals, and their fellow villagers would
hang him for a murderer without even bothering to
hear his side of the story. He was a carnival man, an
outsider. . . . Already he could hear feet running toward
the tent as people came to investigate the girl's
screams. He pulled up his trousers and grabbed his
bow and quiver. He kicked the dead girl in the side.
Bitch. All your fault. He moved quickly over to the tent
flaps and looked out. Half the county fair were heading
toward him. He ducked back into the tent, ran to the
rear, and cut himself an exit in the thick canvas wall.

The edge of the Forest wasn't too faraway. If he was

quick on his feet he could lose himself in the trees before the villagers could catch him, and then they'd never find him. The cry went up as they spotted him again, and he ran for the trees. It didn't take him long to realize he wasn't going to make it. He was out of shape, and the villagers were gaining on him. He stumbled to a halt and glared back at his pursuers. It took only a moment to draw his bow and nock an arrow to the string. The pursuers were being led by a guard. Wilde hesitated. *I can't shoot a fellow guard. I can't . . .* He cursed calmly. He couldn't let them take him. He shot the guard in the throat, and the impact of the arrow threw the man backward off his feet. The running crowd began to stumble to a halt. Wilde shot two more of them, just to be safe, and then turned and headed for the trees again. He'd almost got there when his foot caught in a concealed hole, and he fell heavily to the ground. He heard as much as felt the bone snap in his leg.

He tried to get to his feet again and couldn't. It was an effort just to get air into his lungs. He looked dazedly around for his bow, but it had fallen out of reach. And then the villagers arrived. The first to get there kicked Wilde in the ribs, and the bowman fell backward, too short of breath even to cry out. The villagers crowded around him, screaming *Rape* and *Murder* until their voices merged into a single harsh rhythm ugly with bloodlust. They took turns kicking Wilde and beating him with sticks, until they grew tired and he no longer had the strength to do anything more than moan. And then one of them produced a rope.

No. . . .

They dragged Wilde over to the nearest tree, laughing and cheering. Nothing like a good hanging to liven up a fair. Someone threw the rope over a high branch, and the noose dangled before Wilde's face. He fought then, lashing out at the grinning faces with desperate strength, but there were more than enough men there to hold him securely while they tied his hands behind his back. Someone put the noose around his neck and pulled it tight. The coarse rope bit into his skin.

No . . . This isn't what happened. I got away. I ran off into the Forest and became an outlaw, and everyone feared me and my bow.

A dozen men took hold of the rope and slowly hauled Wilde off the ground until his dangling feet were a good yard above the grass. He wriggled and twisted as he choked, and the crowd cheered every kick of his feet. Wilde knew he was dying, and suddenly realized he didn't really give a damn after all. It wasn't much of a life he was leaving. He'd been a hero once, and it had spoiled him for everything else. Even death was better than a life of boredom and emptiness based around a fleeting moment of glory. And besides, he had fouled his own legend and deserved to die. His breathing grew ragged as the rope tightened, and the darkness gathered around him in welcome.

Scarecrow Jack lay on his back on a low mossy bank at the edge of a Forest glade. Sunlight fell between the great trees in shafts of golden light, thick with swirling dust motes. From all around came the rich, familiar scents of earth and tree and leaf and flower. A butterfly lurched through the air before him, and Jack watched entranced as it fluttered confusedly on its way like a scrap of animated whimsey. Birds were singing all around—everything from simple stabbing rhythms to long and complex full-blooded songs. Jack stretched lazily. The grass and the mosses were firm and dry, and the late summer day was pleasantly warm.

Scarecrow Jack smiled sleepily and was content. He was home.

The birds fell silent. Jack raised himself on one elbow and looked sharply around. A sudden silence usually meant an intruder, a stranger in the Forest. And yet though the silence lengthened, Jack heard no one approaching, and for all his senses could tell, the nearby Forest was empty of any man save him. Jack frowned. The Forest was too silent. There were no birds, or flies buzzing on the air; even the butterfly had vanished. Jack got quickly to his feet, suddenly disturbed. Something was wrong in the Forest. Very wrong.

Dark clouds covered the sun, and the golden shafts of light disappeared. Jack shivered uncontrollably as the warmth of the day died away. The air grew heavy and oppressive with the vague pressure of an approaching storm. Jack glared about him, searching for the source of his unease. Nothing moved in the glade or among the trees, but the surrounding shadows were very dark. Jack reached out for the communion of the Forest, but his inner sense was ominously silent. Something had come between him and the trees. It was out there somewhere, watching him. He could feel it. Something slow and determined was stirring in the darkness, gathering its strength. It watched with a predator's eyes and bided its time. Jack drew the knife from his boot. And then, finally, he looked up.

The clear blue of the sky was darkening into night. The sun grew dim and red and faded away. Night fell.

Jack whimpered softly. Day couldn't turn so quickly into night; it was impossible, unnatural. . . . A new light fell across the Forest, heavy and foul, as the full Blue Moon rose on a starless night sky. Jack shook his head dumbly, trying to deny the evidence of his own eyes, but already he could feel the Wild Magic beating on the air like a never ending roll of thunder, free and awful and potent once again.

Jack shrank in on himself. The Forest he knew was suddenly gone, corrupted into Darkwood. The life he had loved was gone forever, and he was nothing more than a man named Jack—an outlaw and lier-in-wait. He swallowed hard, fighting down the panic that threatened to unman him. He clutched the hilt of his knife tightly, and drew comfort from the simple familiar weight of it. The Forest might be dead and gone, but it could still be avenged. He was Scarecrow Jack, and nothing and nobody could ever take that from him.

He looked away from the Blue Moon. The open glade seemed suddenly bleak and menacing. It was too open, too vulnerable to attack. There was nowhere to hide if . . . if he needed to. He started to run and head for the trees, and then discovered that he couldn't. He looked down and found that the grass had grown up over his feet and ankles, wrapping its long, wiry strands into unyielding grassy chains. Jack tugged at his feet with all his strength, but the grass wouldn't break or give. He bent down and slashed the verdant chains with his knife, and they parted reluctantly under the sharp edge. Panic was gnawing at his mind again, and it was getting harder all the time to hold it off. He finally pulled his feet free and ran for the trees. The grass was growing taller all around him, throwing bright green streamers up into the night sky. They swayed constantly, though no wind blew, and the thicker strands reached out to snatch at his legs as he ran through them. The trees loomed up before him, and Jack felt his heart leap. He would be safe among the trees, as he always had.

It was dark beyond the glade. Out in the open, the air danced and shimmered with the Blue Moon's unhealthy light, but in the Darkwood there was only the eerie light of the phosphorescent lichens that spotted the tree trunks. Jack stumbled to a halt and searched with his inner sense for the source of his magic, but the trees were silent. He leaned against the nearest tree for support, and the bark sagged inward under his weight. He stepped quickly back from the tree, and on looking at it closely discovered it was already dead and rotten, eaten away from within. The ever present stench of corruption lay heavily on the air, thick and suffocating. The tree's gnarled and twisted branches suddenly writhed like twitching fingers and reached out for him. He jumped back, and the tree behind him wrapped its branches around him in a deadly embrace. Jack struggled fiercely, but the branches closed ever more tightly around him, crushing the air from his lungs. He tried to cut the branches with his knife, but couldn't apply enough leverage to do more than notch the bark. The branches lifted him up into the stinking air, and his feet kicked helplessly as the ground fell away beneath him.

No. This isn't right.

Jack stopped struggling and concentrated on that thought. The Darkwood was destroyed, the Blue Moon long gone. He knew this. He remembered their passing. It was impossible that they should have returned, and therefore they hadn't. Jack concentrated on clearing his mind of everything but that one simple thought, and the tree's branches loosened and fell away from him. Jack dropped to the ground and slipped his knife back into his sleeve before straightening up. He didn't need it anymore. He made his way back toward the open glade, and a pool of sunlight formed around him, pushing back the gloom. Far away, hidden in the darkness of the unending night, something screamed with rage. Jack didn't look around to see what it was. It didn't matter. He was Scarecrow Jack, and the strength of the trees was his. He was a part of the Forest, its agent and protector, and he would not allow this corruption to continue.

The dead and rotting trees stirred uneasily as he walked unhurriedly among them, but their thrashing branches couldn't cross the pool of light to reach him. Jack moved out into the glade and stood waiting. The Blue Moon glared down, but its light couldn't touch him. The Wild Magic raged powerlessly around him. Jack looked up at the night sky. *There ought to be stars.* One by one the stars came out, pale and insignificant at first when seen against the Blue Moon, but gradually growing in strength as they spread across the night sky. There was a sudden flutter of wings as an owl swooped down out of the darkness, its wicked claws outstretched before it. Jack didn't flinch, and at the last moment the owl veered aside rather than enter the pool of sunlight. The flapping of wings grew to a roar as hundreds of birds of all species came flying out of the night to swoop and soar around him. All the animals, small and large, every beast that had ever walked the Forest, came surging out of the darkness, snarling and clawing. Jack stood still and confident, and none of them could touch him. Scarecrow Jack felt the strength of the trees grow in him again. The birds and the animals disappeared. The light from the Blue Moon faded away and was gone, and night broke as the day returned. Jack stood alone in the open Forest glade on a bright summer's day. He looked unhurriedly about him. Everything was as it should be. He nodded slowly and laid down on the mossy bank again.

I have been dreaming. I will wake up now.

He closed his eyes and let go.

Hammer jerked awake, thrashing wildly about him, and then slowly relaxed as he realized where he was. He was safe in the border fort annex, and everything else had been a dream. Just a dream. He sighed shakily and sat up in his chair, his heartbeat slowly returning to normal. He ran his fingers through his hair, and mopped the cold sweat from his face with his sleeve. He stopped suddenly to look at his hands, turning them over and over before him, searching for signs of the decay he remembered, but they were fine. He was fine. It was nothing but a dream, a memory of the past that had been distorted in his sleep.

He looked across at the others. Jack was sleeping peacefully, but Wilde was moaning and writhing in his sleep. He suddenly started to choke, spittle flying from his lips as he fought for breath. Jack woke up and looked quickly about him. Hammer moved over to Wilde and shook him fiercely by the shoulders, calling his name. Wilde's eyes flew open and he stared up horrified at Hammer before realizing where he was. And then he relaxed with a great shuddering sigh, and his breathing slowed and eased. He felt at his throat with a trembling hand and swallowed dryly. Hammer straightened up and stood back a pace to give him room.

"Bad dream?" said Jack. Wilde nodded shakily. Jack frowned. "Same here. What about you, Hammer?"

"I had a nightmare," said Hammer, carefully keeping his voice calm and even. "So what? Maybe we've all got guilty consciences."

"I think there's more to it than that," said Jack. "This place is full of nightmares."

Hammer looked at him sharply. "How do you mean?"

"The first time I was here," said Jack, "I spent some time studying the Rangers. They were all asleep, even the one on guard duty. They were dreaming, and it didn't look like pleasant dreams. What did you dream about, Hammer?"

Hammer looked at him suspiciously for a moment, and then shrugged casually. "A bad time in my past. How about you?"

"I dreamed the Forest turned back into the Darkwood. Wilde?"

"My sins finally caught up with me," said the bowman quietly. "Let's get out of here, Hammer. I hate this place. It's evil."

"Places aren't evil," said Hammer impatiently. "Only people are evil."

"That isn't always true," said Jack. "There are places in the Forest it's wise to stay away from. Dark places. They were there before the coming of the long night, and they're still there now it's passed. You can feel the evil there, soaked into the wood and earth and stone like a dark stain that will never wash clean. This fort is just such a place. I can feel it. It's no coincidence that everyone here is having bad dreams."

"Evil," said Wilde doggedly. "This whole place stinks of blood and death. We've got to get out of here, Hammer."

"When we're so close?" said Hammer. "Have you lost your wits?"

"I will if I stay here much longer. So will you. This fort is a killer. It looks like just another fort, but it's alive and it wants us dead. Everything's crazy here. Bad dreams, creatures that shouldn't exist anymore, blood-stains and nooses and everybody gone—"

Wilde's voice rose hysterically. Hammer slapped him contemptuously across the face. Wilde's voice broke off, and his hand dropped to the sword at his side. Hammer stood very still, his eyes locked on Wilde's. The bowman's face had suddenly come alive again, the frightened vagueness gone like a bad memory. His mouth was flat and hard, and his eyes were very dark.

"Well?" said Hammer softly. "What are you going to do, Edmond? Hit me? Kill me? Don't be a fool. You might have been a hero once, but that was a long time ago. You raise a hand against me and I'll take it off at the wrist."

"I'm as good with a bow now as I ever was," said Wilde. His voice was flat and firm, his gaze unwavering. "And I'm still pretty good with a sword."

"Yes," said Hammer. "You are. But I've got Wolfsbane."

They stood looking at each other for a long moment. Jack looked uncertainly from one to the other. This was a new Wilde, a man he hadn't seen before. There was strength and anger in Wilde's face, and something that might have been dignity.

"You're my man now, Edmond," said Hammer finally, "because without me you're nothing. I'm the only chance you have to be somebody again, and you know it."

Wilde took a deep breath and let it out slowly. His hand fell away from his sword hilt. "Yes," he said softly, bitterly. "I'm your man, Hammer."

Hammer smiled and nodded slowly. "Good. I'm glad that's settled. There's a hundred thousand ducats worth of gold hidden somewhere in this fort, just waiting for us to find it, and it's going to take more than a few bad dreams to scare me away. I'm staying, and so are you. Is that clear, Edmond?"

"Yes."

"I didn't hear you, Edmond. Is that clear?"

"Yes! It's clear!" Wilde turned his back on Hammer and walked quickly away to stand by the closed door. Anger still burned in his face, but the strength and the dignity were already fading away.

"That's better," said Hammer. He turned to look at Jack, who shrugged.

"I'm your man too, Hammer. For the time being."

"You're my man until I say otherwise." Hammer yawned and stretched slowly. "The Rangers should have had enough time to settle down by now. I think we'll go down and take a look at the cellar, and see what there is to see."

He headed for the door, and Wilde opened it for him. They looked up and down the corridor, but it was empty for as far as they could see into the gloom. Everything was still and silent. Hammer looked back into the annex, and nodded for Jack to bring the torch and the lantern. Jack brought them over to the doorway. Hammer took the lantern and held it out into the corridor. Shadows swayed around the new light, but the corridor remained empty. Hammer led the way down the corridor, and the three outlaws headed for the cellar.

MacNeil led his team down the narrow passageway that led to the cellar. Flint and the Dancer followed close behind him, their quiet footsteps barely loud enough to raise an echo. Constance brought up the rear, muttering constantly under her breath. MacNeil assumed she was rehearsing spells. It was either that, or she was still mad at him for not trusting her Sight. He decided not to ask. He didn't think he really wanted to know.

MacNeil started to shiver as he stood at the top of the long series of stone steps that led down to the cellar door. His breath had begun to steam on the air again, and the walls ahead of him were patterned with white flurries of hoarfrost. MacNeil frowned. The cold spots worried him. They were becoming more frequent, appearing in places they'd never been before. He looked back at the others, and saw that they'd noticed the changes too. There didn't seem much point in saying anything, so MacNeil just held his lantern higher to give more light, and started down the steps that led to the cellar.

The door at the bottom of the steps was still closed. MacNeil looked at it carefully. It didn't look any different from the last time he'd seen it, and yet something felt . . . wrong. He reached out with his free hand to touch the door, and then snatched his fingers away. The wood was freezing cold—cold enough to burn the skin from his fingertips if he'd left them there a moment longer. He pulled a length of rag from his pocket, wrapped it around his hand, and turned the door handle as quickly as he could. The door swung open a few inches as he pushed it with his boot, and then stuck fast. Flint moved in beside MacNeil as he put his piece of rag away, and then they both put their shoulders to the door. They got it halfway open before it stuck solid. The four Rangers filed into the cellar, and then stopped by the door and looked around them in silence.

The floor and all four walls were thickly coated with ice, tinged pink by the bloodstains beneath, and long, jagged icicles hung down from the ceiling. The untidy heaps of junk that had been piled against the walls had disappeared under smooth coverings of frost, and the barrels weighing down the trapdoor had fused into a single huge mound of ice. The air was bitterly cold, searing the Rangers' lungs and numbing their bare flesh.

"Where's the cold coming from?" said Flint quietly. "It's still summer outside."

"It's coming from below," said Constance. "Something down in the tunnels doesn't like the warmth of day."

MacNeil looked at her sharply. "You mean it's woken up?"

"I don't think so. It's just dreaming. Dreaming about how the world was when it last walked the earth."

MacNeil made his way carefully across to the iced-over barrels. The other Rangers spread out behind him, moving slowly and cautiously. The icy floor made for treacherous footing. MacNeil put down his lantern, drew his sword, reversed it, and struck down hard. The solid steel hilt chipped the ice, and fragments flew into the air, but there were still inches more between him and the barrels. MacNeil scowled and looked at the witch.

"Use your magic, Constance. What's under the trapdoor now?"

The witch closed her eyes, and the Sight came strongly to her.

The trapdoor was closed and bolted. The wood was oak from the Forest, newly fashioned when the fort was made. It still remembered leaf and sap and tree. The bolts were steel, cold iron, and closed to her mind. Beyond the trapdoor was darkness. It was very deep and very cold, and far below something stirred in its sleep. It dreamed constantly now, its power growing as it rose from the sleep of ages, and the dreams grew strong in the waking world. Even in its sleep the Beast knew that it was being watched, and Constance drew back as a single great eye slowly began to open. She shut down her Sight and opened her eyes, gasping for air. Her Sight had shown her some of the mind of the Beast and its intentions, and she knew beyond any shadow of doubt that to stare into its waking eye was death and worse than death.

"Well?" said MacNeil. "What did you See?"

Constance shook her head feebly. "The tunnels are empty. Whatever's down there is much deeper in the earth."

"Any sign of the gold?"

"None at all. But I think I know now what's been happening here in the fort." She had to stop and swallow hard. Her mouth was dry, and she felt sick. Even a fleeting contact with the Beast's mind had left her feeling soiled and tainted. Flint and the Dancer looked at each other. MacNeil waited patiently. Constance took a deep breath and let it go slowly. It steadied her a little, and when she finally began to speak her voice was calm and even. Only her eyes still held some of the horror she felt at what she'd discovered.

"I thought at first it was a demon, but it's much older than that. It has slept here, deep in the earth, for centuries beyond count. Even the coming of the Darkwood did little more than disturb its dreams. But then men came and built a fort over it, and the clamor of their minds was too loud to be ignored. The creature stirred in its sleep, and its dreams went forth and found waking minds to feed on. The dreams drove everyone here out of their minds, and they killed each other in their madness. Their deaths fed the creature's power, and it took their bodies down to itself. I don't know why. Perhaps they're food for when it wakes. Or bait . . . I don't know. It's very close to waking now. Its dreams have shape and power in the real world. And when the creature wakes . . . the world as we know it will come to an end."

She stopped and looked at MacNeil. "You have to kill it, Duncan. Now, before it wakes and comes into its full power. Go down into the dark and kill the Beast. If you can."

MacNeil stared back at her, and the silence lengthened. He didn't want to believe her, but he had to. There was something in her face and in her eyes, something fey and knowing, that left no room for doubt.

"If it's that old and that powerful," he said finally, "how the hell am I supposed to kill it? I'd need something really powerful, like the Infernal Devices, and those damned hellswords are lost and gone."

"No," said Constance evenly. "One still remains. It's here in the fort with us, carried by a man called Jonathon Hammer."

"Hammer?" said the Dancer. "He's here?"

MacNeil looked at him. "You know this man?"

"Of him," said Flint. "He's a mercenary and proud of it. Sells his sword to the highest bidder and never asks questions. He'd kill his own mother if the money was right."

"He thinks he's good with a sword," said the Dancer.

"Is he?" said MacNeil.

The Dancer shrugged. "He's good. But I'm better."

MacNeil turned back to Constance. "How did a man like that end up with one of the Infernal Devices?"

"I don't know," said Constance. "The power in the sword shields it from my Sight. But it's somewhere in the fort, and Hammer will bring it here. And then you and he will go down into the dark and slay the Beast. Or we will all die, horribly."

She turned away and stared fixedly at the heavy barrels covering the trapdoor, still buried in their cocoon of ice. The fey gleam in her eyes was very strong now. MacNeil looked at her unyielding back and moved away, nodding for Flint and the Dancer to join him. They did so, and the three Rangers stood together by the far wall, murmuring in hushed voices.

"Just how much can we depend on her Sight?" asked Flint.

"Hard to say," said MacNeil. "She hasn't Salamander's experience, but there's no doubting the strength of her magic. If she says there's a creature buried in the earth, I'm inclined to believe her."

"But all that nonsense about dreams coming true," said the Dancer. "Do you believe that?"

"It would explain a lot of what's been happening," said MacNeil.

"I don't believe her," said Flint. "I saw some pretty nasty things come up out of the earth in the Demon War. I was there when Prince Harald and the Princess Julia took on one of those creatures with two of the Infernal Devices, and even those hellswords were barely enough to kill it."

"There's another thing," said MacNeil, frowning. "I can't believe this mercenary Hammer has actually got hold of one of the Infernal Devices. I mean, Flarebright and Wolfsbane were both lost in the Demon War. Weren't they?"

"Definitely," said Flint. "I saw it happen. They fell into a great crack in the earth and were lost."

"And Rockbreaker was supposed to have been destroyed by the Dark Prince," said the Dancer.

"There were six Devices originally," said MacNeil. "According to all the legends. Maybe one of the three missing blades has finally turned up."

"If it has, Hammer could well have it," said Flint. "From what I've heard, he's always had more than his fair share of luck. But if half the things I've heard about the Infernal Devices are true, I don't envy him. Those swords were supposed to be utterly evil and corrupt."

"Yeah," said the Dancer. "Just like Hammer."

"Ah, hell," said MacNeil. "We'll worry about that

when he gets here. If he gets here. In the meantime, we're still no nearer finding the gold. If it's down in the tunnels with the creature . . ."

"If," said Flint. "The witch never said she Saw the gold. And there's always the chance the creature's using the possibility of gold as bait."

"That sounds a bit too deliberate for me," said the Dancer. "The creature's supposed to still be asleep, remember?"

"Believe me, I hadn't forgotten," said MacNeil dryly. He looked at the huge mass of ice squatting over the trapdoor, the barrels inside it only visible as shadows, and frowned unhappily. "If Hammer is on his way down here, we've got to get that trapdoor open before he gets here. I want to be one step ahead of him all the way. If he really has got an Infernal Device, we're going to need every bit of an advantage we can scrape together."

"It'll take hours to break through that much ice," said Flint. "And there's no guarantee the ice is confined to this room alone. The tunnels could be full of ice for all we know."

"No," said MacNeil. "Constance would have said." An idea struck him, and he looked quickly across at the witch. "Constance, can you use your magic to clear away this ice?"

"Yes," said Constance steadily, "I can. But a spell of that magnitude will take pretty much everything I've got. All magic has its limits, and I'm close to the edge of mine. I might not even be able to use the Sight anymore."

"Cast the spell," said MacNeil.

Constance nodded, closed her eyes, and concentrated all her strength and power into one potent spell.

Magic stirred sluggishly within her and then flared up, assuming shape and form. Constance spoke a single Word of Power, and the mound of ice over the trapdoor exploded. Icy splinters flew into the air like grapeshot, but none came anywhere near the four Rangers. Several icicles fell from the ceiling, dislodged by the force of the explosion, and crashed to the floor. Great cracks appeared in the ice covering the floor and walls. The Rangers slowly lowered the arms they'd raised to protect their heads, and looked over at the trapdoor. The four heavy barrels had been blasted into kindling, and the trapdoor itself lay bare and defenseless in the middle of the icy floor.

MacNeil nodded approvingly to Constance. "Very impressive."

"It ought to be. It cost me enough."

"How much magic do you have left?"

"Some. The rest will return in time."

"How much time?"

The witch shrugged. "A few hours, a few days. It depends on how much of a strain I'm under."

"All right," said MacNeil. "Take it easy for a while."

"Chance would be a fine thing," muttered Flint behind him. "I haven't had a moment to myself since we got here."

MacNeil pretended not to hear that and moved over to the trapdoor. He squatted on his haunches beside it and ran his fingertips lightly over the two steel bolts. They were uncomfortably cold, but there was no trace of the unnatural sliminess he'd felt earlier. MacNeil glanced back at Flint and the Dancer, and smiled slightly as he saw that they were both standing well back with their swords drawn and at the ready. Constance was standing beside them. Her face was calm, but her eyes were worried. MacNeil looked back at the trapdoor. He remembered the crawling giants pulling themselves through the dark tunnels, and shuddered briefly in spite of himself. He took a deep breath and then pulled back the first bolt. It slid easily into place, with hardly a sound. The second bolt came free just as easily. MacNeil pursed his lips. Maybe Constance's magic had loosened them. And maybe whatever was waiting under the tunnels wanted the trapdoor opened. . . . MacNeil's palms were wet with sweat despite the cold, and he stopped to wipe them dry on his trousers before taking hold of the great steel ring in the center of the trapdoor. He took a firm grip and pulled hard, and the trapdoor swung up and back with a muffled squeal. The opening was full of darkness.

MacNeil looked at the underside of the trapdoor, and his lips thinned away from his teeth in disgust. The dented and battered wood was soaked with fresh, dripping blood. Maggots writhed and squirmed in the wood in the hundreds. A gust of air wafted out of the opening, thick with the stench of rotting meat. Flint swore harshly, and the Dancer swept his sword back and forth before him. Constance stood and watched, impassive as a statue. MacNeil leaned over the opening and looked down into the darkness. He couldn't make out a damn thing. He knew there was a flight of wooden steps just below the edge of the opening, but the darkness turned aside his gaze with contemptuous ease. It was like looking up into a starless night sky; the dark just seemed to fall away forever. MacNeil felt suddenly dizzy, as though he was staring down from a great height, and he tore his eyes away from the darkness.

And then he froze, as from far below came a single great roar of sound, like the insane neighing of some monstrous horse. The sound rose and rose until it seemed to echo and reverberate in MacNeil's bones, and then it suddenly stopped. The silence seemed very loud. MacNeil slammed the trapdoor shut, pushed home both the bolts, and backed quickly away.

"What the hell was that?" said the Dancer softly.

"The Beast," said Constance. "It sleeps very lightly now."

"Are you sure you want to go down there, Duncan?" said Flint, looking dubiously at the closed trapdoor.

"No, I'm not sure," said MacNeil. "But that's the only way we're going to find out what happened to the gold and the missing bodies."

"Personally, I'm mostly interested in the gold," said Hammer.

The Rangers spun around to find Hammer, Wilde, and Scarecrow Jack standing together by the open cellar door. Wilde had an arrow nocked to his bow, aimed impartially at all the Rangers. Constance smiled slightly.

"Come in," she said easily. "We've been expecting you."

Hammer raised an eyebrow at the Rangers' blood-stained appearance, and then looked calmly at MacNeil. "Put down your swords. Wilde here is a master bowman. He's very quick, and he never misses."

The Dancer chuckled quietly. "I'm a Bladesmaster. Tell him to put his bow away, or I'll make him eat it."

Wilde studied him coldly. "I've already killed one Bladesmaster in my time. He died just as easily as any other man."

The Dancer's eyes narrowed. "So that was you. From what I've heard, the situation was very different then. Still, you never know. Go ahead, Wilde. Give it a try. Who knows, you might get lucky."

Wilde grinned slowly, and his eyes were very cold.

"Don't, Edmond," said Flint quickly. She stepped forward a pace so that Wilde could see her clearly. He looked at her for a long moment, and then lowered his bow.

"Hello, Jessica. It's been a while, hasn't it?"

"Nine, ten years."

"Yes. It must be all of that. You're looking good, Jess."

"Wait a minute." The Dancer looked from Flint to Wilde and back again. "You two know each other?"

"Oh, we know each other very well," said Wilde, grinning. "Don't we, Jess?"

"That was a long time ago," said Flint. "Things have changed since then. You've changed a lot, Edmond. What the hell are you doing, traveling with scum like Hammer?"

Wilde shrugged. "I'm his man. For the time being."

"You used to be a hero," said Flint. "What happened to you?"

"The world changed," said Wilde, "and I lost my way."

"Reluctant as I am to interrupt such a tender reunion," said Hammer, "I do have some business to take care of here."

"Are you sure this is a good idea?" said Jack quietly. "Four Rangers, and one of them a Bladesmaster? The odds stink, Hammer. I'm all for a swift retreat, myself."

"Shut up," said Hammer. "Sergeant MacNeil, I think

perhaps you and I had better have a little talk. Just the two of us."

"Yes," said MacNeil. "I think that's probably a good idea. We can talk over there, by the trapdoor, well away from both our people."

Hammer nodded. "A truce. For the time being."

"Agreed," said MacNeil. He slid his sword back into its scabbard, and after a moment Hammer did the same. The foot-long hilt of the longsword strapped to Hammer's back seemed to peer mockingly at MacNeil as Hammer handed Jack his lantern and walked over to the trapdoor. Flint tapped MacNeil lightly on the arm, and he bent his head forward slightly so that she could whisper to him unobtrusively.

"Don't trust him, Duncan. Word is, he's loyal only to himself. His word's worthless, even when backed with guarantees."

"Thanks," said MacNeil quietly. "Unfortunately, we need all the help we can get if we're going to take on whatever's waiting down there in the tunnels. And Jessica, while we're talking . . . keep Wilde occupied. All right?"

"Sure," said Flint. "No problem."

MacNeil moved casually over to join Hammer by the trapdoor. They stood in silence a while, sizing each other up. They were both big men, hard and muscular, and each of them recognized in the other the strength of spirit that comes from constant testing in adversity.

Hammer was quietly impressed by the calm, confident strength he sensed in the Ranger Sergeant, but he had no doubt he could bend MacNeil to his will. Everyone bowed to him eventually. In the meantime, best to play the gentleman and throw the Ranger off guard with honeyed words. They needed each other. For now.

MacNeil wasn't sure how he felt about Hammer, but he had no doubts about the longsword on Hammer's back. Even without Constance to tell him, he felt sure he would have recognized the Infernal Device for what it was. This close, the sword grated on his nerves like an unending shriek in the still of the night. MacNeil wondered if Hammer really knew what he carried on his back.

"You want the gold," said MacNeil bluntly. "I'm more interested in the creature that's down there with it."

"Creature?" said Hammer. "What creature?"

MacNeil nodded at Constance. "Our witch has the Sight. She says there's something old and nasty buried deep in the earth below us. It's sleeping very lightly. She calls it the Beast. It's responsible for everything that's happened here."

"I take it you've already had some contact with this Beast," said Hammer, nodding at the blood that soaked MacNeil's clothing.

"When we first opened the trapdoor, a fountain of blood came flying out. Gallons of the stuff. The tunnels under the cellar are dripping with blood."

Hammer frowned. "Where's it all coming from?"

"The Beast," said MacNeil. "It knows what scares us."

Hammer nodded slowly. "So, a merger between your people and mine, to destroy the Beast. Right?"

"Right."

"I see. And what exactly do I get out of this deal?"

"For helping to recover the missing gold, you'd be entitled to a reward," said MacNeil.

Hammer smiled easily. "Why should I settle for a fraction of the gold when I could take all of it?"

"Because you'd have to fight your way past both us and the Beast to get it, and the odds aren't nearly as much in your favor as you like to think. Wilde's good with a bow, but we've got the Dancer. And whilst your sword is undoubtedly impressive, you don't have the faintest idea of what's waiting for you in the tunnels under this cellar."

Hammer's eyes narrowed. "What do you know about my sword?"

"It's an Infernal Device."

Hammer nodded slowly. "Yes. Wolfsbane."

"I thought that was lost in the Demon War."

"It was. I found it. Or it found me." He shivered suddenly, and for a moment his eyes held a desperate, haunted look that vanished almost as soon as MacNeil recognized it. "All right, MacNeil, a joint venture. You seem to have the most experience with this Beast. What do we do first?"

"First," said MacNeil, "you and I go down through the trapdoor and see how the land lies."

Hammer gave him a hard look. "Just the two of us."

MacNeil smiled. "Where's your sense of adventure, Hammer? Our witch says the Beast is sleeping. The two of us on our own might be able to creep up on it undetected. Besides . . . I don't trust this fort. Strange things have been happening here. There's always the possibility the Beast is using the gold as bait to lure us down to it. If that's so, I don't want us all down in the tunnels. It's far too convenient a place for an ambush. I'll feel a lot better knowing there's someone up here guarding our backs."

"All right," said Hammer. "Let's do it."

MacNeil looked over to where Flint and the Dancer and Wilde were talking. They seemed to be getting on well enough. At least Wilde and the Dancer weren't actually trying to kill each other.

When MacNeil had first moved away to talk with Hammer, Flint found herself facing Wilde without any idea of what to say to him. *Keep him occupied*, MacNeil had said. But what the hell was there to say? This wasn't the man she remembered from the last great battle of the Demon War. That man had been coarse and vulgar, even brutal on occasion, but he had also been brave and forthright and obsessively honest in his dealings with people. This new Wilde had a face grown tired and hard, with lines of practiced brutality etched clearly around the eyes and mouth.

"You're looking well, Jess," said Wilde. "How long have you been a Ranger?"

"Eight years. Maybe a little more. How long have you been an outlaw?"

Wilde shrugged. "I've lost track. The years tend to fade into each other after a while."

"You never told me you knew Edmond Wilde," said the Dancer to Flint.

Wilde grinned. "Times change, eh, Jess? There was a time when people used to boast they knew me, even when they didn't. Now even my friends disown me. Harsh old world, isn't it?"

Flint met his gaze steadily. "You're not the man I knew. The Edmond Wilde I remember wasn't a rapist and a murderer."

"You never did know me that well," said Wilde.

"I'm relieved to hear it," said the Dancer. "I'd hate to think she spent her time mixing with bad company."

"What's the matter, Dancer?" asked Wilde. "Afraid it might be contagious?"

"Don't push your luck," said the Dancer, very softly. "And stay away from Jessica."

Wilde laughed. "If I want her, I'll take her. And there's nothing you or anybody else can do to stop me. I'm better with a bow than you'll ever be with a sword. I'm the best there is."

Flint dropped a hand onto the Dancer's arm as he reached for his sword. "No, Giles! We need him!"

The Dancer looked at her, his face cold and impassive. "All right, Jessica. He's safe. For now."

Deliberately he turned his back on Wilde and walked away to be by himself. Wilde watched him go, grinning.

"You're a fool to taunt the Dancer like that," said Flint dispassionately.

"I can deal with him."

"No, you can't," said Flint. "He'd kill you."

"Would that matter to you?" said Wilde slowly. "It's been a long time since my death mattered to anyone."

"Friends are rare enough in this world. I wouldn't want to lose any of them."

"Even an outlaw like me?"

"Even you, Edmond. I still remember the way you fought outside the castle walls, standing back to back with me against all the demons in the long night. They even wrote a song about you."

"Bet they don't sing it anymore." Wilde smiled gently at Flint, and some of the harsh lines faded from his face. "I loved you once, Jess. And you said you loved me."

"That was a long time ago," said Flint. "We were different people then."

"Were we?" said Wilde, but Flint had already walked away to join the Dancer.

Scarecrow Jack and the witch called Constance had passed the time chatting pleasantly. She helped him find a secure place for his torch and the lantern Hammer had given him, and he thanked her shyly. Constance brought him up to date on what she'd discovered about the Beast, and he was able to confirm some of her guesses through his own Forest magic. Constance found his magic intensely fascinating and not a little disturbing. Jack's communion with the Forest owed nothing to the High Magic she'd spent her life studying; his power came from the Wild Magic, the old, mercurial force that linked man with reality itself. She was also rather worried to discover that Jack seemed just as scared of the Beast as she was. If a legend like Scarecrow Jack didn't know what to do for the best, what hope did she have? Constance put the thought firmly to one side. She'd worry about facing the Beast when she had to, and not before. And so she and Jack talked quietly together, and never once looked across at the trapdoor.

MacNeil slid back the two bolts and hauled the trapdoor open. Once again a vile stench issued from the dark opening, filling the cellar. MacNeil let the trapdoor fall backward onto the floor, and stepped back a pace. Jack batted a hand feebly before his face, as though searching for fresher air. Hammer looked warily into the opening, his hand resting on the hilt of the sword at his hip.

"It smells like something died down there," he said finally.

"Wouldn't surprise me in the least," said MacNeil. He retrieved his lantern from where he'd left it, got down on one knee beside the opening, and gingerly lowered the lantern into the darkness. The pale light showed the first steps leading down into the darkness, all of them caked with dried blood. MacNeil moved the lantern about, showing Hammer glimpses of the blood-stained walls. Hammer looked at MacNeil.

"This is a setup," he said flatly. "Whatever's down there has to know we're coming. It's waiting for us."

"Seems likely," said MacNeil. "But I'm still going down. Unless you've got a better idea."

Hammer started to say something and then stopped, staring silently at the dark opening. MacNeil got unhurriedly to his feet again.

"I'm going with you," said Jack suddenly.

MacNeil and Hammer looked quickly around to find Jack standing behind them. They exchanged a glance as they realized neither of them had heard him approach. Jack said nothing more. He just stood there, smiling gently, waiting for them to make their decision. MacNeil looked at him thoughtfully. So this was the legendary Scarecrow Jack, the wild free spirit of the Forest. He didn't look as impressive as MacNeil had thought he would. His clothes were little more than rags, and though he'd apparently been through a recent drenching, he still looked and smelled as though he hadn't bathed since he was baptised. And yet there was something about him ... something in the calm face and steady gaze that made MacNeil want to trust him. Even if he was Hammer's man. MacNeil shrugged mentally. If Scarecrow Jack was half the man his legend made him out to be, he'd be a useful ally in the tunnels under the cellar, and right now he could use an ally he could safely turn his back on.

"I've heard a lot about you, Jack," he said finally. "I wouldn't have thought this was your kind of fight."

"This is everybody's fight," said Jack evenly. "The Beast will destroy the Forest and everything that lives in it if we allow it to wake. You're going to need me down there, Sergeant. I can feel it."

"He's right," said Constance. "I can't go with you. My magic makes me especially vulnerable to the Beast. It might be able to use me against you. Jack's part of the Wild Magic; he can guide and guard you when I can't."

MacNeil looked at Hammer, who shrugged indifferently. "All right," said MacNeil briskly, "but, Jack, if we have to use our swords, get out of the way fast and stay out of the way. Is that clear?"

"Sure," said Jack. He stared unmoved into the dark opening in the floor. "Who goes first?"

"I do," said MacNeil. "That's my job." He checked the amount of candle left in his lantern, hefted his sword once, and then stepped gingerly down onto the first of the bloodstained steps inside the opening. The wooden step groaned loudly and gave under his foot. MacNeil waited a moment, and the step steadied itself. He made his way carefully down the stairs, and the light from his lantern moved slowly ahead of him, revealing more steps falling down into the darkness. Hammer drew the sword on his hip and followed MacNeil down the stairs. Jack retrieved his torch from the wall holder, and followed Hammer down into the darkness. Halfway down the steps, MacNeil glanced back over his shoulder at Hammer.

"I would draw your other sword, Hammer. You're going to need it down here."

"No. Not yet."

"I've seen what lives in these tunnels. There are great crawling giants—"

"I said not yet! I'll draw the Device when I have to, and not before. The Beast isn't the only thing here that sleeps lightly."

MacNeil remembered some of the whispers he'd heard about the Infernal Devices during the Demon War, and shuddered despite himself. There were those who said the Damned swords were more of a threat than the demons could ever be. MacNeil squared his shoulders and carried on down the stairs, and he and Hammer and Jack quickly disappeared into the gloom, until even the glow of the lantern and the torch was gone, smothered in darkness.

Flint and the Dancer shut the trapdoor after them, grunting in surprise at the weight of the great slab of solid oak. They looked at the two steel bolts, glanced at each other, and then stepped back from the trapdoor.

"Bolt it," said Wilde. "You never know."

The Dancer shook his head. "If they have to retreat in a hurry, they're going to need a quick exit."

"What if they bring something back with them?"

The Dancer smiled. "That's what we're here for."

Wilde looked at him coldly. "Confident, aren't you, little man? When this is over, I'm going to enjoy tearing your reputation into shreds, Bladesmaster."

"Dream on," said the Dancer. "Dream on." He looked

thoughtfully at the closed trapdoor. "We'll give them an hour, and then we'll go down looking for them."

"Right," said Flint.

"It would make more sense for us to get away and pass on the word to your reinforcements," said Wilde.

"You can do that," said the Dancer. "The rest of us are Rangers. Rangers don't run, and we don't leave cases half finished. We know our duty."

"Besides," said Flint, "Duncan's our friend. We can't abandon him. And if he dies, we'll avenge him."

"If we can," said Constance.

6

The Beast

The stairs seemed to fall away forever. Darkness pressed closely around the narrow pool of light as MacNeil led Hammer and Scarecrow Jack down into the earth. MacNeil held his lantern out before him, but its light didn't travel far. Jack's torch made hardly any impression at all on the gloom, but the constant crackling of the flame was a familiar, comforting sound. MacNeil moved carefully from step to step, refusing to be hurried by Hammer's crowding presence at his back. The blood that stained the wooden steps had frozen into scarlet ice, and the going was treacherously slippery.

MacNeil counted the steps off silently as he went, looking forward to the moment when he could leave them behind for the relative safety of the earth tunnel. Thirteen steps. Unlucky for some. But on reaching the thirteenth step he discovered there was another step beneath it. MacNeil's pulse quickened, and he made himself breath slowly and evenly. There was nothing to worry about; he must have miscounted the first time, that was all. Thirteen, fourteen; it was an easy mistake to make. But there was another step beyond the fourteenth, and another after that. MacNeil counted twenty steps and then stopped. He leaned forward and held his lantern out as far as he could. The steps stretched away before him, disappearing down into darkness, and there was no sign of the tunnel.

"What's the matter?" said Hammer quietly. "Why have we stopped?"

"The stairway's . . . different," said MacNeil. "There are too many steps. The Beast must be dreaming again."

"So what do we do?" said Jack. "Just keep going, and hope the stairs will lead us somewhere eventually?"

"There's nothing else we can do," said MacNeil. "There's no other way down. Let's go. It's cold here."

"Cold as the grave," said Jack.

MacNeil pretended he hadn't heard that, and started down the stairs again. After a while he stopped counting; he found the rising number too disturbing. They were already far below the cellar, and still the steps led on down into the dark. It was bitterly cold and growing colder all the time. MacNeil's breath steamed thickly in the air before him, and frost had begun to form on his hair and clothes. His bare face and hands were growing numb, and he had to clutch his lantern and his sword tightly to be sure he wouldn't drop them. The continuing stench of decay and corruption seemed to be changing subtly. The sickly sweet smell was just as strong, but it had slowly acquired a new, alien taint that MacNeil found strangely unsettling. It was unlike anything he'd ever smelled before, and he hoped fervently that he'd never have to smell it again. It grated on his nerves like an itch he couldn't scratch, until he felt like hacking at the air with his sword.

It had slept here, deep in the earth, for centuries beyond count....

MacNeil clutched his sword hilt tightly until his fingers ached. The smell and the darkness and the constant unease reminded him of his time in the Darkwood, and for a moment an old fear moved within him. He pushed it firmly away and continued down the steps. And then his foot jarred on an uneven surface, and the lantern's golden light showed him the mouth of an earth tunnel. He moved cautiously forward into the opening and waited for the others to join him. It wasn't the tunnel he remembered. This larger passage was easily seven to eight feet in diameter. The rough earth ceiling was cracked and broken, and the crumbling walls looked as though they might collapse at any moment.

"Not much room to fight," said Hammer suddenly, and MacNeil gave a start. Hammer grinned as the Ranger turned to glare at him. "Jumpy, aren't you?"

"I've good reason to be," growled MacNeil. "The last time I came down here, I found something nasty waiting for me." He looked about him, frowning. "But that was in a different tunnel. It was smaller than this, and the walls were slick with blood.... Maybe this time we'll find some sign of the missing bodies."

"Or the gold," said Hammer. "Let's not forget about the gold." He reached out and prodded one of the walls, and the loose earth broke apart under his fingers. "Shoddy workmanship. They could at least have shored it up."

MacNeil looked at him. "Men didn't build this tunnel, Hammer, any more than they built that stairway.

The Beast is stirring in its sleep, and we're walking in one of its dreams."

Hammer snorted and stamped hard on the packed earth of the tunnel floor. "Pretty realistic dream."

"Yes," said Jack quietly. "Let's just hope the Beast isn't having a nightmare."

The three men looked uncertainly at one another for a moment. Hammer's hand rose halfway to the hilt of the longsword on his back, and then fell away. MacNeil swallowed dryly and coughed to clear his throat. He didn't want the others to think his voice was unsteady through fear.

"Let's get moving. There's no telling how long we've got before the Beast wakes, and we're still no nearer finding the bodies or the gold."

"I've just had an unpleasant thought," said Jack. "If we're walking inside the Beast's dream, what happens to this tunnel when the Beast wakes up?"

MacNeil glared at him. "The next time you have an unpleasant thought, do us all a favor and keep it to yourself. How the hell am I supposed to know what will happen? The tunnel's real enough for the moment, and that's what matters. Now let's go. We're wasting time."

He strode off down the tunnel, and the others moved quickly after him. MacNeil held his lantern out before him, and the gentle glow showed him the tunnel stretching away into the gloom, sinking gradually deeper into the earth.

MacNeil had always looked on fear as a weakness, and his own fear as a hidden shame. Fear was something you acknowledged but never gave in to. If there was a problem, you faced it, with force if necessary. If you couldn't beat it, you retreated and tried again later. And went on trying until you did beat it. But real fear, the sheer, overwhelming terror that paralyzes you with dread . . . MacNeil had never felt that, and had nothing but contempt for those who had. But deep down he knew that wasn't true. He had felt such a fear once, long ago during the long night when the demons came swarming out of the darkness in a never ending flood, throwing themselves against his sword again and again and again. He'd wanted to run then. And perhaps he would have if the dawn hadn't come in time to save him. The Blue Moon had passed and the sun had risen and the demons had fallen back. But he had wanted to run. . . .

Now he was back in the darkness again, surrounded by the stench of death and corruption, on his way to fight a creature older and more powerful than the demons had ever been. And this time, buried in the depths of the earth, there was no hope of any dawn to save him.

Fear curled and writhed within him, twisting his gut and bringing a hot sweat to his face and hands despite the freezing cold. He could feel his hands shaking, and his breath was coming fast and jerkily. He was afraid, and all his experience and pride weren't strong enough to drive that fear away. He wanted to turn and run, run back down the tunnel and up the stairs and into the fort and just keep on running until he'd left the border fort far behind him. He could do it. He could. No one would reprimand him if he chose to just report the situation to his superior officers and let them deal with it. There were those who'd say he'd done the only sensible thing. But he wouldn't be one of them. He knew differently. Constance had said the Beast must be slain before it woke or it might be too late, and MacNeil believed her. He couldn't run away. He had his duty and his honor, and as long as he had a sword and strength of arm to swing it, he would do what he knew to be right. No matter how scared he was.

The tunnel's descent gradually became more evident as the floor fell steadily away. MacNeil tried not to think about how deep under the fort they'd come. The thought of all that weight over his head was disturbing.

"How deep does this go?" muttered Hammer. "We've been following this tunnel for ages."

"It's not much farther," said Jack. "We're getting very close now."

MacNeil stopped suddenly, and the others stopped with him. He looked thoughtfully at Scarecrow Jack, an idea tugging at his mind.

"Constance said you had . . . qualities that might help us. What kind of magic have you got, Jack? Do you have the Sight?"

Jack shrugged. "I don't think so. I just get feelings about things—about the Forest and what lives in it. And sometimes the trees give me some of their strength, to help me do what needs to be done. But only sometimes."

MacNeil looked at him steadily. "Do you have any feelings about this place? About the Beast?"

"There's something not far ahead of us," said Jack, his eyes vague and thoughtful. "It's sleeping, but it knows we're coming. It's very cold. And very hungry . . ."

As if in response there came again a shrill neighing scream from deep in the earth, the vast, monstrous sound of an insane horse. The scream was brutally loud, and the three men clapped their hands to their ears in pain. The scream continued on and on and on, far beyond the point where any normal lungs could have sustained it, and then cut off as suddenly as it had begun. The echoes seemed to linger in the air for some time, but in the end even they fell silent. The three men slowly took their hands away from their ears. MacNeil looked at Hammer.

"It's time to draw the sword. The Device."

"No," said Hammer. "Not yet."

"We need it!"

"You don't understand," said Hammer tiredly. "You don't understand at all."

In the cellar, Wilde sat on one of the piles of rubbish and swung his legs back and forth impatiently. He hated waiting. As long as he was doing something, anything, he was fine, but waiting gave his nerves the chance to work on him. He fiddled aimlessly with his longbow, checked the string was taut for the hundredth time, and let his hand drop again to the sword at his side.

He looked across at Flint and the Dancer, sitting casually beside the trapdoor. The wait didn't seem to be bothering them. They just sat together, talking quietly, their faces calm and easy. Wilde smiled slightly. Jessica never had been one for getting rattled. He remembered her standing on her own in a corner of the castle courtyard, waiting for the huge gates to open on the last great battle of the Demon War. She'd looked tall and splendid in her shining chain mail, her night-dark hair pulled back in an elaborately tied ponytail. Her face had been calm then, too, as she slowly and methodically sharpened the edge of her sword. He'd been pacing up and down and sweating buckets, half out of his mind with fear, but her poise and calm had shamed him into cooling down and recovering his composure. Her confidence had helped him find his. He'd never forgotten that.

Now they were together once again, getting ready for another battle. The situation hadn't changed much, but the people had. Him most of all. He sighed quietly and shrugged the memories from him. What was gone was gone, and best forgotten. He looked carefully at the Dancer. He'd always thought the man would be . . . bigger. After all, he was a Bladesmaster, one of the legendary perfect killers. No one knew exactly how many men the Dancer had killed in his time, there'd been so many, and yet seen up close he didn't look much at all. Throw a stick into any tavern and you'd hit a dozen just like him. Wilde smiled slowly. Sir Guillam hadn't looked like much either, but all the king's guards hadn't been enough to stop that Bladesmaster when he went berserk. They'd needed Wilde to do that. His smile died away as he stared at the Dancer. Ten years ago, he would have been sitting where the Dancer was now, smiling and talking with Jessica. Ten years ago, he'd had it all. He'd been a hero, and Jess had been proud to stand at his side. Now he was just another outlaw and the Dancer had taken his place with Jess.

Wilde plucked the taut bowstring, feeling it thrum under his fingertips. There was power there, power to maim and kill and make the world go the way it ought to go. The odds were he'd be going into some kind of battle soon, and in all the excitement, who could possibly blame Wilde if one of his arrows happened to go just a little astray and shoot the damned Bladesmaster in the back? And with the Dancer out of the way, getting the gold away from the Rangers would be relatively easy. Wilde grinned happily. At the end of the day he would have it all again; a fortune in gold, his freedom from Hammer, and Jess back at his side where she belonged. He'd talk her into it; he'd always been able to talk her into anything.

Constance leaned back against the cold stone wall and watched Wilde unobtrusively. Of all the three outlaws, Wilde worried her the most. Hammer was dangerous, but she could understand what drove him, even if he didn't. Scarecrow Jack was obviously there only because he was under Hammer's thumb. But Wilde . . . there was something disturbing about the quiet, scowling bowman. When he'd first spoken with Flint, there had been something almost sad and tragic about him, but now all Constance could see in his face was a harsh, pitiless brutality that made her wish for a sword with which to defend herself. Not that she was scared of him, of course. If he was stupid enough to try anything with her, he'd soon discover she had more than enough magic left to take care of the likes of him. And yet there was something about Wilde that both attracted and repelled her, as though she could see the tragedy of what he'd been as well as the brute he'd become.

The witch shook her head uncertainly, and turned her attention to the closed trapdoor in the middle of the floor. She wished she could have gone with Duncan, but she'd known she had to be sensible. She was vulnerable to the Beast and it knew that, even in its sleep. Her presence would only have endangered Duncan, and he was in enough danger down there as it was. At least partly from himself. Duncan never bent with the wind, never allowed himself to be weak, but even the strongest steel will break if it can't bend a little under pressure.

Duncan, watch your back. And come back safely.

Flint and the Dancer sat side by side, waiting patiently for the call to action, as they had so many times before. Flint polished her sword blade with a piece of rag. It didn't need polishing, but the simple repetitive action soothed and calmed her. The Dancer just sat where he was, relaxed and ready, his sword resting casually across his thighs. He showed no sign of nerves or excitement, but then he never did. His eyes were faraway, and Flint wondered what he was thinking about. They'd been partners and lovers for almost eight years now, but she still had only the vaguest notions of what went on in his mind when he removed himself from the world like that.

The Dancer wasn't like other people. Half the time he was off in a world of his own. Flint never doubted that he loved her, but he wasn't an easy man to get to know. He didn't say much, and for a long time now had been content to let Flint do the talking for both of them. He wasn't slow-witted, or even shy; he just didn't have much to say. If he wanted to make a point, he usually made it with his sword.

"Dancer . . ."

"Yes?"

"Do you really think they're going to be able to kill the Beast?"

The Dancer shrugged. "Maybe. Hammer's got the In-

fernal Device. Those swords are pretty damned powerful."

"But . . . if it isn't powerful enough, what are our
chances of killing the Beast?"

"Pretty bad, I should think. But we have to try. A lot
of people are depending on us."

"They usually are. But this time we could very easily
get killed."

"Comes with the job."

"Are you afraid, Giles?"

"No. Fear just gets in the way. Are you worried?"

"Yes."

"Don't be. I'm here with you. I won't let anything
happen to you, Jessica."

She held his hand tightly. They looked at each other
for a long moment, and then a shrill neighing scream
forced its way past the closed trapdoor and filled the
cellar. The ice on the floor and walls cracked and shattered, and icicles fell from the ceiling. Flint and the
Dancer leapt to their feet, swords at the ready. Constance and Wilde looked quickly about them, searching
for a foe they could face. The scream went on and on,
deafeningly loud and piercing, and then cut off suddenly.

"They've found the Beast," said Wilde.

"Or it's found them," said Constance. She raised her
head sharply and listened, sensing something moving
not far away. "Listen, can you hear anything?"

They all stood very still, straining their ears against
the silence. From far off in the distance, somewhere
above the cellar, there came a series of faint, uneven
sounds. Flint and the Dancer exchanged a glance and
hefted their swords. Wilde got to his feet and nocked

an arrow to his bow. Flint looked at him and shook her head.

"No, Edmond. You and the witch stay here and guard the trapdoor, while Giles and I take a look at what's happening upstairs."

For a moment she thought Wilde might argue, but the moment passed, and he just shrugged and sat down again. Flint hesitated, wanting to explain that it wasn't that she didn't trust him, but in the end she said nothing. He wouldn't have believed her anyway. She strode over to the cellar door and swung it open. The sounds seemed to have stopped for the moment. The Dancer came up behind her and offered her one of the torches from the wall brackets. She took it and started up the steps that led back to the ground floor. The Dancer stayed close behind her, sword at the ready. Constance shut the door behind them.

Flint and the Dancer made their way up the stairs, moved cautiously out into the narrow passageway at the top, and looked about them, listening carefully. The torch light seemed to carry a lot farther now that it was out of the cellar, and the flickering flame showed an empty corridor stretching away before them. Flint frowned unhappily. The sounds were louder and closer now, but she still couldn't work out what they were or where they were coming from. They were mostly soft scuffing noises, and they came from everywhere and nowhere, from ahead of them and behind them. The only thing Flint was sure of was that they weren't natural sounds.

"Could be rats," said the Dancer quietly. "Rats in the walls."

"I've heard rats before," said Flint. "This is different. Can you tell where the sounds are coming from?"

"No." The Dancer hefted his sword once. "But whatever it is, it's getting closer."

Flint scowled and started down the passage. Shadows swayed around her, lunging menacingly forward when she shifted her hold on the torch. At first it hadn't seemed as cold in the corridor as it had in the cellar, but that was beginning to change. The temperature was dropping rapidly. The whorls of hoarfrost patterning the walls were growing discernibly thicker, and a pale mist was forming on the still air. Flint stopped dead, and the Dancer stopped beside her. He looked at her inquiringly, but her mind was working furiously. Mist? *Inside* the fort? That wasn't possible. That just wasn't possible. Not this deep in the fort, so far away from the outside air. . . .

The Beast is dreaming . . . dreaming about how the world was when it last walked the earth.

Flint thought about what the witch had said and shuddered suddenly. How long had the Beast slept, if all it remembered of the world was fog and ice and cold? Flint clutched her sword and shook her head determinedly. She'd worry about the why of things later, when she had the time. Right now, all that mattered was finding out what was making the damned noises, and how dangerous it was. She gestured for the Dancer to stay put, and then walked slowly down the passage, listening carefully between each step. The noises were becoming clearer and louder, as though drawing steadily closer from somewhere indescribably faraway. There were sounds that might have been snarls or hisses or growls. They seemed to be coming from all around her, from the floor and the ceiling as much as the walls. Long strands of mist curled and twisted on the corridor air, growing thicker as they blended into a pearly haze. Flint realized she was getting too separated from the Dancer, and stopped where she was. She looked back and saw that the mist had thickened into fog behind her. The Dancer was only a dark shadow in the grayness, and the cellar door was lost to sight. Flint moved quickly back down the corridor to join the Dancer, and without exchanging a word they stood back to back, swords at the ready.

"Those noises are getting louder," said the Dancer evenly.

"Yeah," said Flint. "I don't like this, Giles. It's too . . . planned."

"So what do you think? A cautious retreat back to the cellar?"

"Yeah. We're too cut off here. And they're too cut off down there. Let's go."

They moved cautiously back down the corridor, searching the thickening gray haze for any sign of attack. The noises were becoming louder and more openly menacing, as though they didn't need to hide their true nature anymore. Flint began to think she saw something moving in the mists. The Dancer stayed close to her as they drew near the cellar door. Whatever was in the corridor with them, neither of them wanted to turn their backs on it. Flint was glad the Dancer was there with her. His quiet presence was infinitely comforting. The mist suddenly thickened into an enveloping fog: a great milky white mass that seemed to glow with its own eerie light. Shadows moved in the fog, tall and thin and only vaguely human in shape. They faded in and out of visibility as they moved, and Flint couldn't even be sure how many there were. She glanced at the Dancer, to make sure he saw them, too, and drew confidence from his grim smile and ready sword.

The shadows were drawing steadily closer, but Flint didn't dare back away any faster. They might think she was running from them. One of the shadows stepped suddenly out of the mists to face her, and Flint stared at it in shocked silence. The creature was easily eight feet tall, bent and hunched over in the low-roofed passageway. It was a dirty white in color and horribly thin, so that it looked more like a collection of bones than a living being. Its narrow frame was held together by long, ropy muscles that stirred and writhed like restless worms under the coarse skin. Its arms were almost four feet long, the bony hands dangling well past its knees, and the twig-like fingers ended in long, curving claws. The elongated head ended in a ferociously grinning mouth with dozens of dagger-like teeth. Its eyes were scarlet slits, without pupil or retina. The bony feet clacked loudly on the stone floor as the creature advanced slowly on the two Rangers. Its horrid grin widened slightly as it snorted hungrily.

"What the hell is that?" whispered the Dancer. "Some kind of demon?"

"I don't think so," said Flint, fighting to regain her composure. "I think it lived at the same time as the Beast. I once saw pictures of something like this in a book that came from the Northern Ice Steppes. They called such creatures trolls. They're supposed to be extinct."

"Then what are they doing here?"

"The Beast is . . . remembering them."

"It's got too good a memory for my liking. What do we do, Jessica?"

"Get ready. On the count of three, I'm going to turn and run for the cellar door. You hold them off until I've got the door open, and then get the hell away from those things and join me. Got it?"

"Got it."

"Watch your back, Giles."

"Count on it."

Flint flashed him a quick grin, counted three under her breath, and then turned and ran down the corridor. The troll started to go after her, and the Dancer moved quickly forward to block its way. The creature lifted its clawed hands to strike him, and the Dancer's sword flashed through a short, vicious arc. The troll tried to throw itself backward, but couldn't react quickly enough. The sword slammed into its prominent rib cage, punched through the sternum and out again in a flurry of blood. The troll screamed and sank to its knees, clutching the gaping wound with both hands. Blood ran between its fingers in a steady stream, and collected in a steaming pool on the cold stone floor. More trolls suddenly appeared out of the mists and moved toward the Dancer with murder in their crimson eyes. Behind them, more shadows stirred in the fog, waiting to be born again into the world of men. Smiling, the Dancer swept his sword back and forth before him.

Flint ran for the door at the end of the corridor. The sounds of battle came clearly from behind her; the roaring and screaming of the trolls, and the flat chopping sound of the Dancer's sword cutting through flesh.

The cellar door loomed up out of the fog before her, and she had to skid to a halt to avoid crashing into it. She slammed her sword into its scabbard, and fumbled at the doorknob with cold-numbed fingers. She could barely feel it. She cursed desperately and held her hand close to the dancing flame of her torch. Feeling slowly returned to her fingers, and she grimaced at the stabbing pain. She tried the doorknob again, and finally succeeded in opening the door. She yelled for the Dancer to join her, and the sounds of battle broke off, replaced by the sound of running feet and the cheated howls of the trolls as they gave chase. The Dancer came flying out of the fog toward her with the trolls close behind. There were too many of them to count, and their rage echoed deafeningly in the narrow corridor. The Dancer shot through the open doorway, and Flint followed him. She spun around, slammed the door shut in the trolls' grinning faces, and looked frantically for the bolts. There was only one, and she pushed it home. Something slammed into the door on the other side, and Flint and the Dancer fell back a step as the door shuddered in its frame. They leaned against the cold stone wall a moment as they got their breath back, while on the other side of the door the trolls howled and shrieked and pounded on the solid oak.

"That bolt isn't going to hold for long," said Flint. "We'd be better off in the cellar. We can barricade that door."

"Right," said the Dancer.

"How many of those things are there altogether?"

"Too many."

Flint decided not to think about that for the moment, and hurried down the steps toward the relative safety of the cellar. The Dancer took one last look at the shuddering door, and hurried after her. Narrow wisps of mist had already begun to trickle past the closed door. Flint threw open the door at the bottom, charged through, and waited impatiently for the Dancer to join her. The moment he did, she thrust her torch into his hand, slammed the door shut, locked it, and pushed home both the bolts. She then leaned back against the door and let out her breath in a long, slow sigh. The Dancer calmly slipped the flaring torch into the nearest wall holder. Constance and Wilde looked at them blankly.

"What the hell is going on?" said the bowman. "What did you run into up there?"

"Creatures that were supposed to have become extinct centuries ago," said the Dancer. "Tall bony things with teeth and claws. Trolls."

"They're only legends," said Constance.

"Will you all shut the hell up and help me barricade this door!" snapped Flint. "There are at least a dozen of those legends on their way down here right now, and this door isn't going to keep them out for long."

Together the four of them dragged some of the heavier rubbish over against the door and heaved it into position. The slippery ice on the floor helped. They were just manhandling the last of the junk into place when they heard muffled footsteps on the other side of the door. The Rangers and the outlaw backed quickly away and braced themselves. Something hammered on the door, and something else joined it. The sound rose and rose until it sounded like thunder in the enclosed space. Unseen claws dug into the wood, rending and tearing, and the bolts rattled ominously in their sockets. Flint looked at Constance.

"Can't your magic do anything to keep them out?"

The witch shrugged unhappily. "I don't have much magic left, but I can try." She raised her left hand and a soft blue flame formed around her fingers, jumping and spitting. The witch muttered something under her breath, and the sputtering flame flew away from her hand to sink into the wood of the door. The banging and clawing stopped immediately, and the trolls raised their voices in cries of pain and anguish. For a few seconds there was silence. A frown burrowed between Constance's eyebrows, and then the hammering suddenly started again. Constance shook her head.

"They're too strong for me. I'm a witch, not a sorceress. They'll be through that door in a matter of minutes, and what magic I have left isn't going to stop them."

"Isn't there anything you can do?" said Flint.

"Well, perhaps a little something to make life easier for us," said the witch. She glared at the thick layer of ice covering the floor, and it cracked and shattered and fell apart into tiny pieces. Constance smiled slightly. "That should help our footing when we have to face the creatures."

Wilde looked at her. "What makes you so sure we'll have to face them? The door's solid oak, and that barricade looks pretty good to me."

"It won't even slow them down," said the witch quietly. "These trolls aren't real, so they can be as strong as they need to be. The Beast is very near to waking now, and it senses we are a danger to it."

The hammering grew louder, and the door began to

shake. The barricade shuddered in sympathy, and then toppled away from the door as it split suddenly from top to bottom. The four defenders backed quickly away. The jagged crack in the wood grew wider as they watched, and then the two halves of the door were torn away, and the doorway was full of grinning trolls. The defenders stood their ground, and the trolls hissed and growled, snapping their huge teeth in anticipation. Their bony hands twitched constantly, and the lantern light shone dully on the long claws.

Flint and the Dancer stepped forward to put themselves between the trolls and the witch. Wilde nocked an arrow to his bow. The trolls surged forward into the cellar. Wilde's bow thrummed, and the first troll was thrown back by an arrow jutting from its eye. Two more of the creatures fell to Wilde's bow, and then he had to fall back as the first rush of trolls broke against Flint and the Dancer. The two Rangers stood unflinchingly together, their swords flashing brightly in the dim light. They cut through the massed trolls with deceptive ease, as though the bony creatures were no more substantial than the mists they came from. The trolls' blood flew through the air like a ghastly rain, smoking and sizzling where it collected on the broken ice covering the floor.

The Dancer swore calmly when some of the blood splashed his wrist and burned the bare skin, but he didn't let it distract him from his work. The trolls could only get through the doorway a few at a time, and despite their frenzied attack, the Dancer wouldn't retreat a step. He was a Bladesmaster, and now he had a chance to show what that really meant. His sword swept back and forth faster than the eye could follow,

leaving a trail of blood in its wake. He lunged and recovered and swung again, all in a single breath, his
blade scything through the howling trolls. Their clawed
hands reached for him with an unrelenting fury, their
great jaws snapping at his unprotected face, but always
he was that extra inch out of reach, and the dying trolls
fell before him to scream and writhe on the gore-
soaked floor.

Flint fought at his side, grinning fiercely as she
swung her blood-soaked blade. Trolls lay dead and
dying to either side of her, cluttering up the doorway.
She might not be as fast or as skillful as the Dancer,
but she'd been a guard all her adult life, and she knew
more about swordsmanship than most men ever would.
She had fought in the last great battle of the Demon
War in ill-fitting chain mail with a borrowed sword, and
after that there wasn't much that could daunt her. She
cut and hacked at the grinning bony faces before her,
and refused to feel the growing ache in her arms and
back. She was a Ranger, and she would fight till she
fell.

Wilde fired arrow after arrow past the two Rangers,
striking down the trolls as they tried to claw their way
past Flint and the Dancer by sheer force of numbers.
He lost track of how many of the creatures he'd killed,
and still they came surging through the narrow doorway. And all too soon Wilde ran out of arrows. He
placed his longbow and his empty quiver carefully to
one side, out of the way, and drew his sword. He
hefted it once and then looked at the two Rangers,
struggling against the endless tide of inhuman creatures.

Just like old times, eh, Jess?

He looked quickly about him, just in case there was another exit he hadn't noticed before, but there was only the trapdoor, and Wilde had decided very early on that wild horses weren't going to drag him down there. No, bad as it was, his only hope lay with the Rangers. He shrugged and, choosing his moment carefully, slipped in beside Flint and added his sword to hers. The trolls roared and screamed as they fell before him, and their death cries were a comfort to him. It had been a long time since he'd fought in a situation where the odds weren't stacked heavily in his favor, and it only took him a few seconds to remember why. A man could get killed sticking his neck out like this. . . . But still he fought on, because there was no other choice open to him. After a while, some of his old skills came back to him, and his sword sliced through the air in shining, deadly arcs. If Flint could have found the time to look at him, she might have seen echoes in the bowman's face of the Edmond Wilde she had once known so many years ago.

The witch called Constance raised her hands in the stance of summoning, and drew the remains of her power about her. Most of her magic was gone, but she drew on what little was left to her for one last effort. She spoke a Word of Power, and a blinding glare gathered around her upraised hands. The trolls nearest her screamed and fell back as their bones cracked and splintered within their bodies. A slow headache began to beat in Constance's left temple, and a steady trickle of blood seeped from her left nostril. Constance ignored it. Her body would stand up to the strain for as long as it had to, or it wouldn't. There was nothing she could do about it.

The four defenders fought on, blocking the entrance to the cellar with their bodies and their skill and their courage. Trolls fell and died before them, but there were always more to take their places. There were always more.

Deep in the earth below the fort, the tunnel finally began to level out. MacNeil stumbled to a halt, and Hammer and Jack crowded in beside him, staring into the pitch black opening that ended the tunnel. MacNeil frowned. He could tell there was some kind of drop immediately ahead of him, but that was all. Maybe the tunnel led into some kind of cave. . . . He moved cautiously forward until he was standing right on the edge of the tunnel floor, and then held his lantern out before him. The pale golden light reflected back from thousands of tiny crystals embedded in the cavern walls. They shone brightly in the darkness, like so many distant stars on a moonless night, illuminating a cavern so huge it took MacNeil's breath away. There wasn't enough light to fill all the cavern. It had to be at least half a mile in diameter, and possibly even more in height. The tunnel opened out high up on a wall, with the cavern floor hundreds of yards below. A narrow ledge ran along the wall, leading from the tunnel mouth to another opening some fifty feet away and perhaps ten feet lower down. MacNeil didn't like the look of the ledge. It was barely two feet wide, and the dark stone was cracked and uneven, as though it had only recently been cut from the bare stone wall. MacNeil looked down into the darkness and felt a sudden surge of vertigo. He turned his head away and breathed deeply until it settled.

Jack and Hammer stood on either side of him, staring out into the cavern. The glowing crystals stared back like so many knowing eyes. Hammer caught his breath for a moment, and then quickly let it go in case anyone had noticed. The cavern made him feel small and insignificant, and he didn't like that. Jack studied the narrow ledge cut into the cavern wall, and chewed his lower lip dubiously. It looked to be a long way down if someone lost their footing.

"How far down is that, do you think?" he said finally.

"I don't know," said MacNeil. "A hell of a long way, whatever it is."

"Do you think the Beast's down there?"

"Has to be," said Hammer. "But is the gold down there with it, or could it be in that other opening?"

MacNeil frowned. Anyone out on that narrow ledge would be very vulnerable to a surprise attack. They'd have to go in single file, hugging the cavern wall all the way. . . . But when all was said and done, he couldn't ignore the opening. Hammer was right; there were only two places down here the gold could be, and the second opening was the easiest to get to. He nodded slowly.

"All right, Hammer, it's worth a try. I'll go first."

He stepped out onto the ledge, testing it carefully before committing all his weight to it. The cracked stone seemed solid enough, and he moved farther along the ledge, pressing his shoulder against the cavern wall. He looked down once and immediately wished he hadn't. Heights didn't normally bother him, but this was different. Very different. He looked resolutely at the second opening ahead, only some ten feet below him and fifty feet away. It hadn't looked very far from

the tunnel mouth, but out on the ledge it seemed a hell
of a long way to go. He leaned even more against the
cavern wall and kept going. The solid rock face was a
comforting presence. Hammer moved out onto the
ledge after him, once he was sure it was safe, and Jack
brought up the rear. Of all of them, Jack was the only
one unaffected by the long drop. In the Forest he
climbed the tallest trees for fun. On the other hand, he
hadn't liked the enclosed space of the tunnel at all, so
the much larger space of the cavern actually helped to
put him at his ease. He moved confidently along behind Hammer, holding his torch high and staring happily about him with easy curiosity.

The second opening in the cavern wall proved to be
the entrance to another tunnel. MacNeil crouched
down on the ledge before it and studied the circular
tunnel in the light of his lantern. It was roughly seven
feet in diameter and appeared to have been bored
through solid rock. Its walls were unnaturally smooth.
MacNeil's imagination conjured up a picture of some
monstrous worm wriggling blindly through the solid
stone, and he scowled thoughtfully. For as far as he
could see in the lantern light, the tunnel appeared to
be deserted. And when all was said and done, he wasn't
going to discover anything more just squatting there on
the ledge. He sighed regretfully and moved forward
into the tunnel. Hammer and Jack followed close behind him.

After some twenty or thirty feet, the tunnel opened
out into a cave. And in that cave, piled carelessly one
upon the other, lay hundreds of stout leather sacks,
each bearing the royal imprint of the Forest Treasury.
Hammer pushed past MacNeil and ran forward to

kneel before the sacks. He grabbed the first that came to hand and opened it, clawing impatiently at the drawstrings. He thrust his hand into the sack and pulled out a handful of gleaming gold coins. He stared at them for a long moment, and then opened his hand and let the coins trickle slowly through his fingers and back into the sack. He smiled gently as he listened to the musical clatter of gold on gold.

"A hundred thousand ducats," he said softly.

"Don't get any ideas, Hammer," said MacNeil calmly. "That gold belongs to the king, and that's the way it's going to stay. You're entitled to a reward, and I'll see that you get it, but that's all."

Hammer smiled at him, and then pulled the sack's drawstrings tight and placed it down by the others. Scarecrow Jack sniffed dismissively and looked around him. He had no use for gold in the Forest. He frowned suddenly and held his torch close to the right-hand wall. The extra light revealed a narrow opening, low down on the cave wall and almost obscured by the shadows of the piled-up sacks. He drew MacNeil's attention to it, and the two of them crouched down before the opening. It was barely three feet in diameter and led into yet another tunnel. Once again the tunnel walls were unnaturally smooth and even. Jack looked at MacNeil.

"What do you think? Shall we take a look?"

MacNeil shrugged. "Might as well while we're here. But, Jack . . . keep your eyes open. That gold must have been brought down here for a reason, and I'm starting to get the feeling that so far we've just been led around by the nose. Constance thought the Beast could be using the gold as bait, to lure us down here."

Jack looked at him uncertainly. "What would the Beast want with us?"

"That's a good question, and I've a strong feeling we're not going to like the answer when we find it. Hammer!"

Hammer looked around sharply. "What is it?"

"There's another tunnel here. Jack and I are going to take a quick look; you want to come along?"

Hammer smiled and shook his head. "Somebody had better stay here to look after the gold."

"Somehow I just knew you were going to say that," said MacNeil. "All right, suit yourself. Jack, leave your torch here. We'll make do with the lantern."

He got down on his hands and knees and crawled into the tunnel. Jack handed his torch to Hammer and followed after MacNeil. Hammer watched him go, then turned his attention back to the sacks of gold, his lips moving silently as he counted.

The narrow tunnel was cramped and slippery, and MacNeil crawled along it as quickly as he could. He pushed the lantern along in front of him, and its unsteady light shone dully back from the smooth tunnel walls. The pale golden light made the tunnel seem even smaller than it was, and MacNeil could feel a shivering claustrophobia gnawing at the edges of his self-control. He shuffled stubbornly onward on all fours, peering ahead into the darkness beyond the lantern light. He could hear Jack struggling along behind him, and the quiet grunts and scuffling sounds reminded him suddenly of the crawling giants, moving blindly through the tunnels under the earth. He shook his head quickly to clear it, and then his hands slid off the smooth floor and onto rough stone, and he realized the tunnel had

opened out into another cave. He crawled out of the
tunnel, straightened up painfully, and held his lantern
out before him. Jack emerged from the tunnel mouth
and got up to stand beside MacNeil. They stood together for a while, and stared in silence at what they'd
found.

Every man, woman, and child who'd died in the border fort lay piled in one great heap at the back of the
cave. They seemed to have just been dumped there
and left to rot. The cave had to be a hundred feet
across, and the bodies filled half of it, stacked from
wall to wall and from floor to ceiling. Every body
showed signs of a violent death, and most were caked
with dried blood. MacNeil stared grimly at the piled-up
bodies, and felt painfully helpless. They were dead and
gone, and there was nothing he could do about it. The
children got to him most. The small bodies, torn and
mutilated and discarded. No child should have to die
like that. His hand dropped to the sword at his side,
and silently he promised them vengeance, whatever it
cost.

Jack moved closer to the bodies and looked them
over carefully, checking the exact cause of death where
he could. He didn't find their presence disturbing in
the way that MacNeil did. Living in the Forest had ac-
customed him to the presence of death in all its forms,
and it no longer affected him on an emotional level. It
was just a part of the world. And then something very
disturbing occurred to him, and he crouched to study
the floor of the cave.

MacNeil tore his gaze away from the great mound of
bodies, and tried to think with his mind instead of his
gut. There was something about both the gold and the

bodies that worried him. How did they get down here? Somebody must have brought them. Perhaps the crawling giants . . . MacNeil frowned and shook his head. The giants were little more than animals. Besides, they were too large to have managed the ledge on the cavern wall, never mind the last tunnel.

"Bring your lantern over here," said Jack suddenly. "I've found something interesting."

MacNeil moved back and crouched down beside him, and looked at the cave floor that Jack was studying so intently. It was bare rock, with a faint pattern of dust. There were a few vague traces that might have been tracks, but they were too faint for MacNeil to read them.

"Well?" he said after a while. "What do you see, Jack?"

"Footprints," said the outlaw quietly. "Human footprints. Men, women, and children—so many they overlap each other again and again. There's no other tracks at all. Nobody brought these bodies down here, Sergeant. They walked here."

MacNeil gaped at him, and then snapped his head around as something stirred on the edge of his vision. One of the corpses opened its eyes and looked at him. Another drew back its blackened lips in something that might have been a smile. Jack and MacNeil straightened up from their crouch, and the dead eyes followed them. There was a slow stirring in the mound of bodies, and all the hundreds of corpses opened their eyes and turned their blood-smeared faces to look at the living interlopers who had stumbled upon them. MacNeil felt a cold hand clutch his heart as his imagination showed him how it must have been: an endless line of walking dead, making their way through the dark tunnels and along the narrow ledge, and finally filing into this cave to drop and lie still. And then more coming, to fall on top of the first, and on and on until the mound of bodies was complete. The last few would have had to climb the mound to reach the top. . . . MacNeil swore dazedly and backed away. Jack moved with him. The corpses followed them with their unblinking eyes.

"Bait," said MacNeil hoarsely. "The gold and the missing bodies . . . just bait, to lure us down here and destroy us."

"But why go to so much trouble?" said Jack. "What makes us so important? Why didn't the Beast just drive us mad as it did the others?"

"I don't know!" said MacNeil. "There must be something the Beast wants from us; maybe we've got something that could harm it. . . ." His eyes widened suddenly. "Of course! The Infernal Device! It doesn't want all of us, just Hammer and his damned sword!"

"Wait a minute," said Jack, glancing nervously at the watching liches. "This can't be the Beast's doing; it's still asleep, remember?"

"It's not human," said MacNeil shortly. "Its mind doesn't work like ours. It must have recognized Wolfsbane when Hammer first came to the border fort to deliver the gold. The Beast knew how powerful the sword was, and saw it as a threat. So it sent its dreams out to destroy the people in the fort, to gather some bait that would lure the Device back . . . so that the Beast could destroy it.

"Get into the tunnel, Jack. We've got to collect Hammer and then get the hell out of here. If the Device is the key, we can't risk losing it to these creatures. Go on, move it! I'll be right behind you with the lantern!"

Jack nodded quickly and divided into the narrow tunnel. MacNeil gave him a count of five and then hurried after him, scrambling along the tunnel as fast as he could on hands and knees. But even as he struggled through the tunnel in his little pool of light, his imagination replayed the last thing he'd seen as he turned to the tunnel mouth: the great pile of bodies shifting and stirring like so many seething maggots. The dead were rising to walk again. Jack and MacNeil scrambled desperately through the tunnel. It seemed much longer than it had on the first trip through, and they'd barely reached the halfway stage when they heard something else enter the tunnel behind them. Somehow they found a little more strength and speed, and a few moments later the tunnel mouth fell away behind them as they threw themselves out into the outer cave. Hammer spun around, startled by their sudden entrances. He took one look at their shocked faces, and his hand fell automatically to the sword at his side.

"What is it? What have you found?"

"Walking dead men," said Jack breathlessly. "We've got to get out of here!"

"And leave the gold?"

"The gold will keep!" snapped MacNeil. "Those liches want your sword, Hammer! The Device! The Beast must be frightened of it. That's why it had the gold brought down here, to lure you into its clutches."

He stopped suddenly and looked back at the tunnel, and as he did a bare dead white arm snaked out of the tunnel mouth. MacNeil put his lantern down on the floor and drew his sword. The tunnel was full of soft, slow, scrambling noises. MacNeil swung his sword with both hands and cut cleanly through the lich's wrist. The sword rang dully on the stone floor, and the severed hand flew away across the cave. It scrabbled briefly on the floor, and then pulled itself back toward MacNeil like a huge pale spider. Jack kicked it away. The lich burst out of the tunnel mouth and threw itself at MacNeil. Its pallid skin was flecked with long-dried blood, but no blood pumped from the handless stump. Hammer handed Jack his torch and drew the sword at his hip. MacNeil cut at the dead man's neck with his sword, but the lich blocked the blow with its bare arm. The blade jarred on bone, but the lich just smiled. MacNeil backed away as the lich reached for his throat, and the dead man went after him. Another lich crawled out of the tunnel. MacNeil cut again at the advancing lich, but still it kept coming. Hammer moved in beside MacNeil and cut at the lich's legs. It finally fell to the ground as a half-severed leg collapsed under it, but already the second lich was moving toward MacNeil, and more of the dead were emerging from the tunnel mouth.

Hammer and MacNeil tried to stand their ground, but faced with an endless stream of opponents that wouldn't stay dead, they were forced back step by step. The only way to stop the liches was to hamstring or behead them, and even then the crippled bodies would drag themselves along the floor to try to pull down the living that dared stand against them. Most of the liches had once been men, but there were also women and even children. MacNeil found it almost impossible to cut down the first child, but then he looked into the dead child's eyes and saw there a blind, unreasoning malevolence that had nothing human in it. After that, he dealt with the dead children as methodically as he took on the adults, and with every child lich he faced he renewed his promise of vengeance against the Beast that used them in this way. Hammer didn't seem to care whom he was fighting. He swung his sword with grim competency, his only expression a slight, satisfied smile.

Jack stood to one side, holding his torch out before him and waiting for any lich that managed to get past the other two. He'd already guessed his knife wouldn't be much use against the dead, but he'd had some success with the torch. Their cold flesh felt no pain from the blazing brand, but their hair and clothing were bone dry and burned fiercely. Already the cave was brightly lit by half a dozen burning corpses that thrashed weakly on the floor as the fire slowly consumed them.

And still the dead crowded into the cave from the narrow tunnel, forcing the three defenders back. The cave floor was strewn with mutilated liches that still crawled determinedly after their prey. MacNeil felt an old fear stir within him again, threatening to unman him—the same fear he'd felt when the demons came swarming out of the endless night in a nightmarish assault that seemed to go on forever. Fear and panic tore at his courage until he wanted to scream at the liches, but somehow he held on to his self-control and continued his slow, cautious retreat to the tunnel behind him. Hammer moved back with him, and Jack guarded their rear with his flaring torch.

And still the dead came crowding into the cave, their

pale faces contorted by the dark dreams of the Beast that controlled them.

"We can't hold them off much longer," said MacNeil tightly. "Draw your other sword, Hammer. Drawn the damned sword."

"Yes," said Hammer. "I don't seem to have any choice anymore, do I?"

He cut viciously at a lich as it reached for him with clawing hands, and decapitated it. The head rolled away across the floor, its mouth working silently. The headless body staggered back and forth, groping blindly about it for its enemy, until the other liches jostled it out of the way. Hammer seized the few moments the confusion gave him, and sheathed his sword. He breathed deeply once, and then reached up and grasped the long sword hilt behind his left shoulder. His mouth twisted, as though tasting something infinitely bitter. The sword hilt seemed to fit itself into his hand as though it belonged there. He drew the longsword from its silver scabbard with one supple movement, and held the six feet of gleaming steel out before him as though it was weightless. The long blade glowed brightly with a sick yellow light.

"Wolfsbane," said Hammer softly. "Wolfsbane is loose in the world again."

The liches stopped their advance. Their empty eyes fastened on the glowing longsword in silent fascination, as something else studied the Infernal Device through their dead eyes, and knew it for what it was. The hellsword had been brought down into the depths of the earth, and now they would take it and bury it so that the Beast need never fear it again. The liches surged forward, hands outstretched, and Hammer met

them with Wolfsbane. The glowing blade swept back
and forth with inhuman speed, cutting through the
liches as though they were nothing more than wisps of
smoke. They fell helplessly before Hammer's attack,
screaming silently as the sword cut through flesh and
bone alike. Their dead flesh decayed and fell away into
corruption at Wolfsbane's touch, and soon the cave
floor was littered with fragments of rotting flesh and
discolored bone. But still the liches came swarming out
of the narrow tunnel, their numbers growing faster than
Hammer could destroy them. Hammer and MacNeil
and Scarecrow Jack continued to back away, fighting
desperately all the while, knowing that if they gave the
dead an opening, even for a moment, the liches would
tear them apart. Hammer lunged back and forth like a
man possessed, Wolfsbane glowing more and more
brightly as the dead fell before it and did not rise again.
Jack and MacNeil defended his blind sides as best they
could, for Hammer seemed to have no thought for anything but attack.

And still the dead came on, driven by the Beast's
dark dreams. Hundreds of men and women and children had died in the border fort, and Hammer and
MacNeil and Jack couldn't destroy them fast enough to
stem the tide. Step by step they were forced back out
of the cave and down the tunnel, and finally out onto
the narrow ledge itself, looking out over the long drop
to the cavern floor. Jack went first along the ledge,
carrying the torch, then MacNeil with his lantern, and
finally Hammer, blocking the liches' way with Wolfsbane. The Infernal Device glowed blindingly against
the darkness, its bitter yellow light reflecting from the
thousands of crystals embedded in the cavern walls.

The three men backed slowly away along the narrow ledge, and the dead came after them.

Down below, deep in the earth, something stirred in its sleep.

Flint and Wilde and the Dancer swung their swords with aching arms, fighting on long after most would have collapsed from sheer exhaustion. Their swords grew heavier every time they raised them, but they wouldn't give up. The trolls came swarming through the doorway in a never ending stream, their blood red eyes glowing hungrily. Tall, bony cadavers lay scattered across the bloody floor, but as yet none of the creatures had got past the defenders to reach the trapdoor. Only a few trolls could get through the door at a time, and so far Flint and Wilde and the Dancer had managed to keep the trolls bottled up by the doorway. But they all knew it was only a matter of time before one of them fell, and then they would be unable to hold the trolls back.

The Dancer was having the time of his life. His sword was everywhere, a bright, shining blur that mowed through the crowding trolls like a newly sharpened scythe through wheat. He was grinning broadly, and his eyes blazed with a dark and deadly joy. He was doing what he was best at, doing what he was born to do, and loving every minute of it. The overwhelming odds just gave a spice to the occasion. He was the Dancer, and he was content.

Flint fought at his side, substituting strength and stubbornness to match his skill and speed. She kept turning the situation over and over in her mind as she fought, searching for a solution, an answer that would give them victory over the trolls, knowing all the while that this time there was no answer, no way out. They were doing all they could, and the odds were that wasn't going to be enough. Tough. That was the way it went sometimes, especially if you were a Ranger. She fought on, ignoring the pain and blood from a dozen minor wounds. It wasn't over till it was over, and just maybe MacNeil would get lucky and kill the Beast. Yeah. Maybe.

Wilde fought on Flint's other side, wishing he hadn't run out of arrows so early. He was good with a sword, but he was much better with a bow. Besides, using a bow was a damn sight less dangerous than fighting at close quarters with a sword. He hacked at a troll and clove its skull from brow to jaw. The creature collapsed with a startled expression on its bony face, and Wilde grinned nastily. Stupid-looking things. He'd teach them to get between him and his share of the gold. He fought on, wishing he'd kept at least one arrow for the Dancer. Still, he needed the Dancer's fighting skills for the moment. Maybe later, when the trolls had been taken care of . . . yeah. Maybe later. He swung his sword, and the trolls surged about him, trying to drag him down. Blood soaked his shirt, only some of it from dead trolls.

Constance chanted one spell after another, her voice grown harsh and indistinct. Her throat was raw, and her aching head swam as she fought to make the last few remnants of her magic do far more than it was ever meant to. The few trolls that got past the fighters at the door shriveled up like moths in a flame as they drew near the witch. One troll kept on coming anyway, even while its flesh ran like wax down a candle. Constance gestured sharply, and the troll exploded in a shower of blood and guts. Constance moaned as a stabbing pain began in her forehead, just above her left eye. Blood spurted from her nose. She was pushing her magic to its limits, and she was paying the toll. She'd once seen a witch overstrain herself and die of a cerebral hemorrhage. It hadn't been pretty.

She swayed unsteadily on her feet, gripped by hot and cold flushes, and fought to remain conscious. If she passed out now, the trolls would make short work of her. Besides, the others needed her. Some of the dizziness passed, and she drew her magic about her again. The trolls weren't the only danger that had to be faced. Thin strands of mist had begun to form in the cellar. The trolls used the fog as a gateway into the real world, and if it established itself in the cellar, the trolls would be able to appear from anywhere in the room. The defenders would be overrun in seconds. Constance wrapped herself in her power, and concentrated on a single spell to keep the mists from forming. The trolls recognized her sudden vulnerability, and threw themselves at the three fighters in a flurry of teeth and claws. One of the creatures broke through and leapt at the witch with gaping jaws. Constance hit it in the throat with her fist. The collection of heavy rings on her fingers made an effective knuckle-duster, and the troll fell choking to the floor. Constance stamped down hard and broke the creature's neck. The witch smiled briefly and went back to concentrating on her magic.

The four defenders fought on, long past the point where anyone else would have given up and been destroyed, but in the end there were just too many trolls.

The Dancer found himself hard pressed by three trolls who came at him at once and refused to die no matter how much he hacked at them. In that moment when he was preoccupied, two more trolls forced their way in and attacked Flint. She killed one, but couldn't react fast enough to stop the other. It knocked her to the ground and stooped over her. Wilde cut down the troll before him, and looked up to see the troll bending over Flint. She tried to lift her sword, dazed by the fall, and the troll slapped it out of her hand. Flint reached after the sword, and the troll cut at her face with its claws. She turned her head aside at the last moment, saving her face, but the long claws ripped off her left ear. She screamed and fell back, blood running thickly down her neck as pain blazed in her head. The troll grinned and took her throat in its heavy hands. Flint tried to break its hold and couldn't.

Wilde screamed her name and leapt at the troll. His weight tore the creature away from Flint, and the two of them crashed to the floor. Wilde landed awkwardly, and his elbow jarred painfully on the solid stone. His hand instantly went numb, and he watched despairingly as the sword flew from his unfeeling fingers. The troll reared over him, huge and hideous, and Wilde slammed a punch into its gut. The creature laughed hissingly. Wilde heaved to one side to try to throw it off, but the troll moved with him, one clawed hand wrapped tightly around Wilde's throat. And then its other hand ripped into his belly and out again in a flurry of blood and guts, and Wilde screamed shrilly. Blood spurted from his mouth. The troll left him shuddering on the floor, curled around the awful wound.

Blood poured past his clutching hands and pooled around him.

Flint snatched up her sword from the floor and ran the troll through from behind. It died trying to clutch the blade as she jerked it free. Flint spared Wilde a single glance, and then had to turn back to take her place at the Dancer's side again. He'd disposed of the three trolls that were bothering him, but even he was having a hard time holding the doorway single-handed. Flint could feel blood trickling down her neck, and her head screamed in pain with every move that jarred it, but she couldn't stop and rest, even for a moment. The Dancer needed her. She cut savagely at the nearest troll, and smiled coldly as it fell to the floor, clutching its torn throat. Another troll took its place. The Dancer backed away from the door a single step, and Flint fell back with him.

Constance stood very still, battling the forming mists with the last of her magic. Flint and the Dancer fell back another step. More trolls forced their way into the cellar. The three Rangers fought on, knowing it was hopeless but fighting anyway, because there was nothing else they could do.

Deep in the earth below the fort, the Beast stirred. The great cavern above it shook violently. Massive slabs of stone cracked and groaned as they moved against each other, disturbed from their resting places for the first time in uncounted centuries. Jagged cracks appeared in the cavern walls, and loose earth fell from the ceiling in a steady rain.

MacNeil clutched the cavern wall as the ledge shifted suddenly under his feet. Thin cracks appeared in the stone, and Scarecrow Jack was thrown off balance. He fell awkwardly and threw his torch away to cling tightly to the heaving stone with both hands. The blazing brand disappeared down into the darkness and was gone. MacNeil quickly put his lantern down and moved back to help Jack. Hammer managed to keep his footing, but the liches kept pressing forward, undeterred by the destruction around them, and it was all Hammer could do to hold them off. One of the dead slipped and fell from the ledge. The falling body grew smaller and smaller, and was finally swallowed up by the darkness that hid the bottom of the cavern. The liches surged forward along the narrow ledge, which suddenly rose and fell a good foot as the cracks in the cavern wall widened still farther. Hammer lost his balance and staggered into MacNeil, who tripped over Jack's outstretched legs. He fell on top of Jack, and the two of them rolled toward the brink of the ledge. MacNeil jammed his hands into one of the cracks and pulled himself to a halt, but Jack skidded over the edge.

MacNeil lashed out desperately with his legs, and one of them kicked Jack in the chest. The outlaw grabbed the leg instinctively and stopped his fall. He hung helplessly over the long drop, clinging to MacNeil's leg with both hands. MacNeil forced his hands deeper into the crack in the stone, wedging them against the weight that was trying to pull them loose. For a long moment neither of them dared move, and then Jack started to climb up MacNeil's body. MacNeil groaned out loud at the pain that swept through his arms and hands as he fought to support the double weight. And then Jack was able to reach out and grab the ledge, and MacNeil let out his breath in a great shuddering sigh as the extra weight suddenly disappeared.

Jack clambered up onto the ledge again, and MacNeil rose painfully to his feet. He looked down at the drop and then looked away. He'd never liked heights. He handed Jack the lantern and turned quickly back to see how Hammer was faring. The ledge was still trembling under his feet, but it seemed to have steadied somewhat. All around him the cavern walls were shifting and groaning, and there was a faint continuous rumble from somewhere far away, deep down under the cavern.

The liches suddenly stopped pouring out onto the ledge from the tunnel mouth. Hammer cut down the last few corpses as they pressed forward, and their rotting bodies fell away from the ledge and out into the darkness. Hammer slowly lowered his sword and then leaned on it tiredly. MacNeil began to breathe a little more easily. The dead from the border fort had pushed their intended prey all the way back to the mouth of the original tunnel before the last of them had been destroyed. MacNeil looked at Hammer and winced. The Infernal Device was glowing brightly, almost too brightly to bear. Hammer was leaning on the sword with his eyes closed. His sides were heaving and his face was slick with sweat. For Hammer the nightmare wasn't over; it was just beginning. He groaned aloud and screwed his eyes shut rather than look at the sword he held.

MacNeil and Scarecrow Jack looked at each other. The liches might be gone, but the cavern was still breaking up. This was no place to be hanging around.

There was no sign of the Beast, and MacNeil couldn't see one good reason to stay in the cavern a single moment longer than necessary. He moved forward to stand facing Hammer. The outlaw gave no sign he even knew MacNeil was there.

"Hammer?" said MacNeil. He had to raise his voice to be heard over the constant groaning of the shifting stone all around him. "What is it, Hammer? What's wrong?"

"It's the sword," said Hammer hoarsely. His face twisted, and his knuckles were white where they gripped the long sword hilt. "It's the Damned sword. I used it for too long, tempted it too much . . . It's awake."

MacNeil glanced back at Jack, who nodded jerkily. "He's right, Sergeant. The sword is alive, and aware. I can feel it."

MacNeil turned back to Hammer. "Sheathe the sword. We don't need it anymore, Hammer. It's all right to sheathe it now."

"You damned fool!" said Hammer despairingly, "I can't sheathe it! The bloody thing's awake, and it's hungry. . . . You don't understand the power in this sword, MacNeil. There's power here beyond your worst nightmares, power to destroy all the world and leave it nothing but a rotting ball of filth. And the sword wants me to use that power."

MacNeil swallowed dryly. He didn't want to believe Hammer, but he had no choice. There was a power in the hellsword, beating in rhythm to the pulsing of the sword's brilliant light, beating so strongly that even he could sense its presence. He started to grab the sword away from Hammer while he was still distracted, but the outlaw immediately moved back out of reach and leveled the sword at MacNeil's breast.

"Stay away from me. Try that again and I'll kill you. I'll have to."

"Hammer . . ."

"I can control the Device. I can! I just need a little more time—"

A thick, vile grunt issued up from somewhere deep in the cavern. It sounded like some monstrous hog at its trough. The echoes seemed to take forever to die away. The cavern shook constantly now, and earth fell from the ceiling like a fine mist. The grunt came again, a huge, sonorous sound that shook the air like thunder. Hammer, MacNeil, and Scarecrow Jack looked down into the darkness, and a line of silver fire suddenly appeared far below on the cavern floor. Hundreds of yards wide, it stretched from one side of the cavern to the other, splitting the darkness in two. And then, slowly, the split grew wider. The shining light became brighter still as the split widened into a broad band of light. The silver glare filled the cavern, painfully bright and piercing. It wasn't until a vast golden circle moved into the light from behind the darkness that MacNeil realized he was looking at the opening of a single gigantic eye.

The huge, dark eyelids crawled open, revealing the whole floor of the cavern to be one great eye. The enormous golden pupil stared up at MacNeil with monumental disdain. He wanted to look away but couldn't. He was held by the sheer immensity of the eye below him, fixing him with the awful stare of an ancient and unforgiving god.

It's too big, thought MacNeil dazedly. *It's just too big.*

Nothing could be that size. . . . That eye must be hundreds of yards across. . . . He tried to visualize the size of the Beast and couldn't. It was just too big, too large for his human mind to cope with.

There were giants in the earth in those days.

Something beat on the air like a great commanding voice, silent but imperative. MacNeil stared down into the Beast's eye, and the unspoken voice called to him, demanding that he surrender to it. And the longer he looked, the more he wanted to. Helpless tears streamed down his cheeks, his eyes dazzled by the silver glare that illuminated the cavern, but unable to look away. MacNeil stared into the Beast's eye, and the world grew soft and dim. All the things that troubled him, all the things that scared and angered him, seemed to drift away. Nothing mattered. Nothing mattered at all, except listening to the silent voice and doing as it commanded. He was safe and warm and comfortable, and nothing would ever hurt him again. All he had to do was obey the Beast in all things, and it would set him free from the cares of the world. All he had to do was give up his duty.

Duty. The word tolled in his head like a bell. He had served as a Ranger because of his duty to the Forest Kingdom. He had fought the demons in the long night because of that duty. He had stood at his post and he hadn't run, because of his duty and his honor. In that moment MacNeil finally understood why he hadn't deserted his post all those years ago, and why he never would have, no matter what. He had been afraid then, and he was afraid now, but there was no disgrace in that. Only the foolish and the dead never feel fear. Duty and honor are important because they give us courage, the courage we need to do what must be done, to face what must be faced.

MacNeil groaned aloud and tore his gaze away from the great shining eye. He turned his back on it and pressed his face against the cold, unyielding stone of the cavern wall. His heart was racing and he was panting for breath, as though he'd just run a mile in full armor. Sweat ran down his face and stung his eyes. He'd come close to losing his mind and his soul, and he knew it. He shuddered violently, his hands clenched into fists. He made himself breathe slowly and deeply, and a little of his calm returned. He turned away from the cavern wall and put his back to it, wincing as the bright silver glare hit him again. But this time the unspoken voice was gone. He knew it for what it was, and his mind was closed to it. He looked around and saw that Hammer and Jack were still staring raptly down at the blazing eye.

Scarecrow Jack called out to the trees, but nothing answered. He'd come too far from the Forest. He was in the Beast's domain now. Its voice thundered in his mind, disrupting his thoughts and scattering his memories. He needed the strength of the trees. He reached out with his mind, fighting fiercely against the voice of the Beast, searching desperately for the communion of the trees that had always been his. The Forest was still there, far above him. The trees and the greenery still stretched for countless miles across the Forest Land, and all of its ancient strength was his to call upon. The darkness pressed in around him as the Beast grew stronger. Only newly awakened and barely come into its power, its voice was already nearly overpowering in

its intensity. Jack summoned all his defiance into one
great shout of denial, and reached out one last time.
And finally the trees heard him and lent him their
strength. The Beast's influence vanished from his mind
like the fleeting memory of a bad dream, and he was
free again. He breathed deeply, and the bitterly cold air
seared his lungs, shocking him awake. He realized how
close he was standing to the brink of the ledge and
stepped quickly backward.

MacNeil nodded briefly to him, but sensed that Jack
was still too shaken to be much help in tackling Hammer. The renegade guard's face was working horribly,
and his hands twitched around the hilt of the Infernal
Device, but he was unable to tear his gaze away from
the great blazing eye. The Beast had him now. MacNeil
swore silently and braced himself. He had to get the
Infernal Device away from Hammer before the Beast
could take control of him. Now that the Beast had
awakened, the hellsword was the only chance they had
of equaling the odds. MacNeil moved stealthily forward
and reached out to take the sword.

Hammer spun around, the great longsword sweeping
out in a viciously short arc. MacNeil dived under the
blade at the last moment, and the wind of its passing
ruffled his hair. The sword bit deeply into the cavern
wall, and as Hammer started to pull it free Jack
stepped in behind him and pinned his arms to his
sides. MacNeil lurched to his feet, but even as he
started forward again, he saw that Hammer's face was
cold and calm and empty of all emotion. Hammer had
lost his last battle, and now only the Beast looked out
through his eyes. The outlaw struggled furiously to
break Jack's hold, but the strength of the tall trees

surged through Jack's arms, and Hammer couldn't break free. MacNeil slammed a punch into Hammer's gut. The outlaw stared coldly back at him, and struggled to raise the Device and cut him down. MacNeil hit him as hard as he could on the jaw, snapping Hammer's head back. It had no effect at all. MacNeil did it again and again, and Hammer just ignored him. And slowly, despite everything Jack could do to hold him, he began to raise the Infernal Device.

"Do something!" panted Jack. "I can't hold him much longer."

MacNeil lifted his sword and cut Hammer's throat with a single stroke. Blood gushed into the air, spattering MacNeil's chest and arms, but the outlaw didn't fall. He went on struggling even as the color drained from his face and the blood pumped more and more feebly. Finally the blood stopped coming and he stopped breathing, but still he stood there, gripping the Infernal Device and fighting to break free. MacNeil stood gaping, and in that moment Hammer broke Jack's hold and sent him staggering backward. Hammer spun around to face him. Jack tripped and fell, and again the Device missed its target by only a fraction of an inch. MacNeil yelled and stamped his foot on the ledge to draw Hammer's attention away from Jack, and the outlaw turned back to face him. Hammer's chest was soaked with his own blood, but the dead eyes watched MacNeil's every movement with unblinking intensity.

He belonged to the Beast now.

MacNeil backed slowly away along the narrow ledge. He daren't meet Wolfsbane with his own blade; the Device would shear through the simple steel as though it were paper. But he couldn't just keep backing away, or Hammer would either rush him or turn on Jack. He was still groping desperately for a plan when he saw Jack move silently in behind Hammer and crouch down. MacNeil realized immediately what he had to do. He held his sword with both hands and charged straight at Hammer, roaring at the top of his voice. Hammer stepped back to brace himself to meet MacNeil's rush, and tripped over Jack, crouching down behind him. He toppled helplessly backward, and Jack gave him the last little push that sent Hammer flying away from the ledge and out into the long drop. MacNeil stepped quickly forward and brought his blade flashing down in one last, desperate stroke. The blade caught Hammer's right arm against the brink of the ledge and sheared clean through the wrist. The Infernal Device clattered safely onto the ledge, with Hammer's right hand still wrapped around the hilt. Jack and MacNeil watched Hammer's body fall until the distant speck disappeared into the brilliant light of the Beast's eye.

Finally they both turned away from the edge and leaned against the cavern wall while they got their breath back. MacNeil felt dizzy and lightheaded from the strain, and his leg muscles were trembling with fatigue, but he knew he couldn't rest yet. He looked down at the Infernal Device, glowing brightly on the ledge before him. Hammer's severed hand slowly relaxed its grip on the hilt.

"All right," said Jack hoarsely, "now what are we going to do?"

"Kill the Beast," said MacNeil.

Jack looked down at the great staring eye and then

back at Wolfsbane. A sudden chill ran down his spine as he realized what MacNeil meant to do, and he stared respectfully at the Ranger.

"You don't have to do this."

"Yes, I do. It's my job. My duty."

Jack looked at him for a moment and then nodded briefly. "You're a brave man, Sergeant. Good luck."

"Thanks. I'm going to need it. Now get the hell out of here. The tunnel that brought us down here was a part of the Beast's dreams. There's no telling what'll happen to it when the Beast dies."

"Sergeant . . . are you sure the Device can kill it?"

"Why else would the Beast be so afraid of it? Now go on. I'll join you later."

"Yeah," said Jack quietly. "Sure. Goodbye, Sergeant."

He gave MacNeil a quick salute, picked up the lantern, and then padded along the ledge and into the tunnel. MacNeil stood alone on the ledge and listened to the sound of Jack's footsteps fading away into silence. He could feel the Beast's presence beating on the air all around him. Its power was growing.

I could run and get away. I could run even now. But I won't.

He breathed deeply and was surprised at how shaky his breath was. He sheathed his own sword and looked down at Wolfsbane. His hands were sweating, and he rubbed them dry on the sides of his trousers. He didn't think he'd ever felt so scared in his life. He knelt down and took hold of Wolfsbane's hilt, being careful to avoid touching Hammer's severed hand. He straightened up slowly. The sword was uncannily light in his hand, despite the great length of the blade. It glowed brightly, but it was not a healthy light. And finally MacNeil discovered why Hammer had always been so reluctant to draw the Device.

Wolfsbane moved in his mind, a soft, seductive whisper that spoke of power and destiny, and appealed to all the dark dreams and fantasies he'd ever had. MacNeil shuddered helplessly as the alien presence seeped slowly through him like a horribly sweet poison. No wonder Hammer had fallen so quickly under the Beast's control; with two such forces warring for control within him, it was inevitable that he would fall to one of them. MacNeil shook his head to clear it, and stepped forward to the brink of the ledge. There was something he had to do, and he was going to do it, despite everything the Beast or the Device or his own fear could do to stop him.

He clutched the leather-wrapped sword hilt with both hands, and held the Infernal Device up before him, blinking at the brightly shining light that burned in the blade. He stepped carefully forward onto the very edge of the narrow stone ledge and looked down.

MacNeil remembered the demons in the long night, how he'd wanted to turn and run. He had always looked on his fear as a secret weakness, a flaw in his character he could never forget or forgive. He had always thought of himself as strong, and despised weakness in himself as he despised it in others. But now, standing alone on the ledge and looking down into the single great eye of the Beast, he finally knew the truth. There is no shame in fear, only in surrendering to it.

The Beast was awake at last, and when it came into its full power it would destroy the world and remake it in its own awful image. Once before, in the time of the Darkwood, he had vowed to die rather than to let such a thing happen. His vow still held, and scared as he was, his duty and his honor gave him the courage he needed to do what was necessary. He thought briefly, *Why me?* The answer came back: *Because there's nobody else. Because it's your job. Your responsibility.* He remembered his vow of vengeance to the dead children, and his resolve hardened a little more. He sighed once and lowered the great sword so that its point was facing down toward the huge eye.

Goodbye, Jessica, Giles. I was always proud to work with you. Goodbye, Constance. You turned out to be a damn good witch, after all. And Salamander . . . I'm sorry about that village.

The Infernal Device screamed with rage in his mind as it finally realized what he intended to do, but it was too late. MacNeil flexed his feet, feeling the ledge under his heels and the emptiness under his toes. He smiled wryly. He'd never liked heights. He took a firm hold on the sword hilt with both hands, bent forward, and jumped out from the ledge, diving headfirst toward the Beast.

The freezing air rushed past him as he fell, the Infernal Device held firmly out before him. The sword and the Beast screamed soundlessly in his mind, and he laughed at them both. The eye rushed closer, ever closer, the shimmering silver and gold rising to fill his vision, until all he could see was the eye, growing larger and larger, a sea of dazzling light. And finally the sword plunged into it, driven by the horrid weight of his long drop, and MacNeil and the sword disappeared into the body of the Beast. For a long moment there was only silence, and then the Beast screamed, on and on and on.

7

Leavetakings

The scream broke off abruptly, and the voice of the Beast fell silent forever.

In the cellar, the mists began to fade away. They sank back into the stonework and disappeared, leaving no trace of their passing. Without the gathering fog, the torch light was suddenly brighter, less diffuse, and the shadows were no longer quite so dark. The Dancer cut down the last two trolls in the doorway, and then looked around, confused, as he slowly realized there were no more. Flint sat down suddenly on the blood-spattered floor and closed her eyes. Constance let her hands drop back to her sides and bowed her head tiredly.

"It's dead," she said dully. "The Beast is dead."

"Are you sure?" said the Dancer.

"Yes. I can't feel its presence anymore."

The Dancer sighed once, shrugged, and sheathed his sword. He looked at Flint and moved quickly over to kneel beside her. He swore softly as he saw the ragged wound where her left ear used to be. He took a hand-kerchief from his pocket and pressed it gently to the side of her head. She winced and opened her eyes in protest, and then lifted a hand to hold the folded handkerchief in place. She gritted her teeth as the Dancer gently tied a length of rag around her head to hold the handkerchief securely. A sheen of sweat broke out on her forehead, and she felt sick and giddy from the pain, but she was still able to smile her thanks to the Dancer when he looked at her anxiously.

"We won, Giles. We actually won."

"Looks that way, Jessica."

"If this is what a victory feels like, I'd hate to be around at one of your defeats," said Wilde.

Flint looked around quickly, and with the Dancer's help she moved over to sit beside the fallen bowman. He lay on his back, glaring up at the ceiling with pain-filled eyes. There was a gaping hole in his gut, revealing broken and splintered ribs, and only his hands kept his intestines from falling out. Blood soaked his clothes and welled out from beneath him in a widening pool. There was more blood on his mouth and chin, and he couldn't even raise his head to look at Flint when she took one of his hands in both of hers. Flint looked at the Dancer, who shook his head slightly. Constance knelt down beside Flint.

"Can you do anything for him, Constance?" Flint asked quietly.

The witch shook her head. "I've no magic left. I used it all. It'll be some time before any of it returns."

"And I don't have that much time," said Wilde. He swallowed painfully. "Typical. My luck always was bad."

"Lie still," said Flint gently.

"What for? Can't hurt any worse. You there, Dancer?"

"Yes, Wilde. I'm here."

"This is a death wound, but it's a bloody slow one.

Going to take me some time to die, and I'd rather not be around while it's happening. End it for me now, Dancer. Let me go out with some dignity at least."

"Don't talk like that," said Flint, almost angrily. "There's still a chance."

"No, there isn't," snapped Wilde. He stopped to breathe heavily for a moment, and Flint mopped some of the sweat from his face with her sleeve. Wilde grinned harshly. "You always were the soft one, Jess. Now, how about a last kiss, eh? Just to say goodbye. And then, when we're through, the Dancer can let me go out on a high note."

Flint smiled despite herself, holding back tears. "You always were a Romantic, Edmond."

She leant forward, wiped some of the blood from his mouth with her sleeve, and kissed him tenderly. As she did, Wilde's hand came up and gave her left breast a playful squeeze. Flint straightened up, half shocked and half laughing. Wilde nodded to the Dancer, and he leaned forward and slipped his dagger expertly into Wilde's heart. The bowman stiffened and grinned up at Flint.

"Romantic, my arse."

And then his breath went out of him in a long sigh, and the light went out of his eyes. Flint reached out with a shaking hand and gently closed his eyes for him.

"Goodbye, Edmond. I wish things could have been . . . different."

"Jessica?" The Dancer met her gaze steadily. "I had to do it, Jessica."

"Of course you did, Thank you, Giles."

"What do we do now?" said Constance. "The trolls

are all dead, the Beast is dead . . . but what about Duncan and Jack and Hammer? What are we going to do?"

"We're going to rest awhile and get our strength back," said Flint. "Duncan and the others will be back soon."

"But what if they're not?" said Constance quietly. "What if they don't come back?"

"Then we go down and look for them," said the Dancer.

Scarecrow Jack staggered on through the earth tunnel, holding the lantern out before him with an aching arm. He'd lost track of how long he'd been in the tunnel, but his feet hurt and the weight of the lantern had become almost too heavy to bear. He trudged doggedly on, the faint echoes of his progress dying quickly away. He tried reaching out to the Forest as he had before, but there was nothing there. He was too tired and too faraway. His head pounded unmercifully, and he found it hard to concentrate. It was nothing serious, he knew that, just strain and tiredness. A few hours' sleep and he'd be fine. He was tempted to lie down and sleep for a while on the packed earth of the tunnel floor, but somewhere deep inside him he knew that if he lay down here, he might never find the strength to get up again. And so he plodded on, head hanging tiredly down, putting one foot in front of the other, over and over again.

Some time ago he'd heard the Beast scream, but the long, agonized howl had come and gone, and the tunnel was still here. Nothing had changed. He had wondered if the Beast's dreams would vanish with its death, and if so whether he might fade away along with the dream he walked through, but it hadn't happened. Or perhaps it had, and he just hadn't noticed. No, you couldn't feel this tired and hurt this much unless you were still alive. But if the dreams were still real, then maybe the Beast wasn't dead after all. . . .

The sudden thought shocked him out of his dazed state, and he stopped and looked back down the tunnel. The Beast was dead. It had to be. It couldn't have survived the Infernal Device. . . . But he had to be sure. He sat down cross-legged in the middle of the tunnel and cautiously opened his mind, letting it drift out, reaching for communion with the trees. He was still too faraway to be able to touch the Forest, but there was no trace remaining of the dark, oppressive presence of the Beast. It was gone, as though it had never been. Jack smiled grimly and rose painfully to his feet again. Maybe there was some justice in the world after all. Just a little. He walked on up the tunnel.

After a while the shadows up ahead seemed strangely different. Jack held the lantern higher and squinted against the gloom. His heart leapt as the patterns of light and darkness ahead of him resolved themselves into a set of rough wooden steps leading upward. He was almost there; all he had to do was climb the steps and clamber out through the trapdoor, and he would be free of the darkness and among friends again. He frowned suddenly and came to a halt at the bottom of the steps. He remembered how the steps had seemed to go on forever on the way down, and a faint twinge of fear went through him. He pushed it quickly aside. It didn't matter how many steps there were. He was almost there, and he wasn't going to be stopped by anything or anyone now. He was going home, to the trees.

He almost ran up the simple wooden slats, pushing himself on as fast as his aching legs would carry him. He held the lantern out as far ahead of him as his arm could reach, hoping for a glimpse of the trapdoor that would let him back into the fort's cellar, but for a long time there were only the stairs and the darkness. It wasn't until some of the frost in his hair began to melt and run down his face like tears that he realized the air wasn't as cold as it had been. In fact, it was almost bordering on warm. His hands and feet and face tingled with returning feeling as the numbness slowly left them. He gritted his teeth against the pins and needles that followed, and kept on climbing. He began to smile, until he was grinning so hard his cheeks hurt. The trapdoor suddenly appeared above him, and he lurched to a halt before he slammed his head into it. His smile faded away. What if the people in the cellar had bolted the trapdoor shut and had then been . . . overcome by something? He'd be trapped down here in the darkness forever. . . . Jack quickly decided he wasn't going to think about that. He reached up and pushed the trapdoor with his free hand. It rose an inch or so and then fell back. Jack cursed softly. He'd forgotten how heavy the trapdoor was. He put the lantern down on the top step and placed both his hands against the trapdoor. It shifted uneasily and then rose an inch or two. Jack took a deep breath and held it, and forced the trapdoor up another inch. MacNeil had always made it look so easy. And then suddenly the weight was gone as the trapdoor was yanked away from him. Light spilled down through the opening, and Jack blinked up into it. Strong hands reached down to help him, and finally Scarecrow Jack left the tunnels in the earth and emerged into the light of the cellar.

Flint and the Dancer let the trapdoor slam shut behind him, and Constance helped him sit down before his weary legs gave way. He grinned happily about him, and then he saw the look in their eyes, and his smile disappeared as he realized he had bad news to tell them as well as good.

"I'm the only one," he said quietly. "Hammer and Sergeant MacNeil won't be coming back."

"They're both dead?" said Constance.

"Hammer is. And I'm pretty sure the Sergeant is too. He gave up his life to destroy the Beast."

"What happened?" said the Dancer.

"Sergeant MacNeil used Wolfsbane against the Beast." Jack dropped his eyes for a moment, and then raised them to look squarely at the Dancer. "I would have used the sword, but he wouldn't let me. He said it was his duty. He was a brave man. Bravest I ever met."

"Yes," said Flint. "He was."

They stood in silence for a while, each lost in their own thoughts. Constance felt suddenly exhausted. She'd been saving what little strength she had left to welcome MacNeil back, and now it seemed she had no use for it. He was dead. She never had found the right moment to tell him how she felt about him, and now she never would.

"What happened to Hammer?" said the Dancer.

"He ran into something worse than him." Jack looked about him, taking in the dead trolls and the Rangers' wounds for the first time. "You seem to have kept busy while we were gone."

"We managed to keep from being bored," said Flint.

"We found the gold," said Jack. "It's all there. I'll draw you a map later on."

"What about the missing people?" said Constance.

"I'll tell you later," said Jack. "It's a long story, and not a pretty one." His eyes fell upon Wilde's unmoving body. Jack looked at it for a while, not sure how he felt. "Did he die well?"

"Yes," said Flint. "He gave his life to save mine."

Jack nodded slowly. "I never liked him, but he was good with a bow. At least he died in a good cause. He used to be a hero once, you know."

"Yes," said Flint, "I know." She looked hard at Jack. "Are you sure Duncan is dead?"

"He has to be," said Jack. "He knew he was going to die when he took on the Beast, and so did I."

"But did you actually see the body?"

"No. No, I didn't."

"Then there's a chance he's still alive," said the Dancer. He turned to Constance. "Can't you See where he is; what's happened to him?"

"I'm sorry," said the witch. "I've nothing left. It'll be weeks before I can See anything again."

"He's dead," said Jack. "I'm sorry, but he has to be."

Flint started to say something and then stopped, and for a long time nobody said anything.

"All right," said Flint finally. "Let's get out of here. We can clean up and sleep in the dining hall for tonight. Tomorrow we'll go down into the tunnels and see if we can recover Duncan's body."

"Right," said the Dancer. "We can't leave him here, alone."

Duncan MacNeil woke up slowly. His whole body ached, and all the length of his back was a single great stabbing pain. He groaned aloud, and tried to raise his head, but for the moment even that was beyond him. He opened his eyes, but everything stayed dark. He lay quietly where he was, gathering what was left of his strength, and tried to figure out where the hell he was. There was a hard unyielding surface beneath his aching back, but one arm and both his feet seemed to be hanging over the edges of it. An appalling smell filled the air all around him; a dank oppressive stench of rotting foulness that made him want to retch. He tried to lift his head again, and this time succeeded. He still couldn't see anything. *Of course not,* he thought sluggishly, *It's dark down here. Down here . . .*

Memories returned in a rush, and his heart missed a beat as he remembered falling toward the giant glowing eye. He thrashed about in the dark, trying to find something to grab onto, and then froze as he realized he was lying on something precariously narrow, with an unknown drop to either side. He felt about a little more cautiously, and his hands encountered something soft and unpleasantly yielding. He snatched his hands away and lay very still while his heart and breathing returned to normal. The first thing to do was to shed some light on the subject. He reached carefully into his pocket and brought out the inch of candle stub he always carried with him for emergencies. Lighting the wax stub with flint and steel from his boot whilst being very careful not to overbalance himself turned out to be a nightmare in itself, but finally he got the wick to light and held the candle up before him.

He was lying on a narrow shelf of discolored bone, surrounded by dark walls of rotting flesh. If he looked up, he could see above him the beginnings of a broad tunnel reaching up through the decaying meat. Another equally broad tunnel fell away beneath him. MacNeil sat up cautiously on the ledge of bone, cradling the candle stub carefully in his shaking hands. He finally knew where he was. He was in the body of the Beast. He'd plunged into the eye and through it, and fallen into the head of the Beast, destroying its mind. The liquid in the massive eyeball must have cushioned his fall enough so that when he finally hit the more solid flesh beyond it, the shock of the impact hadn't been enough to kill him. At some point he must have dropped the Infernal Device. It had carried on without him, rotting its way deeper into the Beast's mind, and leaving behind it the tunnel beneath his ledge. There was no knowing how deep Wolfsbane had gone, but it must have gone deep enough. The Beast was dead. MacNeil only had to look around to know that; everywhere he looked was rotten with decay. And the Infernal Device was gone, lost deep in the decomposing body of the Beast.

And there it can stay, for all of me, thought MacNeil firmly.

He clambered unsteadily to his feet and looked up at the tunnel above him. The opening was just above his head, easily within reach. It was the only way out, much as he disliked the thought. There was no telling how far he'd penetrated into the Beast's body before the bone shelf broke his fall, and in his current bat-

tered state he wasn't up to much climbing. The ledge
of bone suddenly creaked loudly and shifted under his
feet. He looked down, and saw a fine tracery of cracks
spreading across the bone. The decay was continuing.
He no longer had a choice; he had to climb out while
he still could. If he fell any farther into the body of the
Beast he might never get out, even if he survived a second fall.

MacNeil allowed a trickle of melted wax to fall onto
the absorbant cloth of the shirt over his shoulder, and
used it to stick the wax stub firmly in place. He was
drenched from head to foot with foul-smelling slime
from his passage through the eye, but the candle stub
seemed more or less secure, and he had to have both
hands free for climbing. He drew his knife from its
sheath and cut himself a series of foot and handholds
in the decaying flesh of the tunnel opening above him.
He then gripped the knife firmly between his teeth,
gagging at the awful taste, and pulled himself up into
the wide shaft. His arms groaned with the effort, but
eventually he pulled himself high enough for his feet to
find the first footholds, and then the long climb began.
In later years, he was only to remember most of it in
his worst nightmares.

The climb seemed to last forever. The flickering candlelight showed him a wall of red and purple flesh, already dark with spreading pockets of decay. Dim pulses
of light ran through the Beast's flesh occasionally, and
once MacNeil thought he saw a strange distorted face
peering up out of the meat at him. When he looked
again it was gone, and he didn't wait to look more
closely. A slow dull ache burned in his legs as he
climbed, spreading to his hips and chest and arms. His

back grew steadily worse. He couldn't even stop for a rest; his weight would have been too much for the precarious foot- and handholds he hacked out of the yielding wall before him. Occasionally slivers and promontories of splintered bones erupted out of the walls, and he quickly learned to work his way around them. They looked solid enough, but they were eaten away inside. Wolfsbane did its job thoroughly. MacNeil climbed on, slowly making his way up the decaying column of flesh.

He came at last to the enormous socket that had once held the Beast's eye. It was an open crater now, carpeted in places with a rotting, translucent jelly. MacNeil clambered out of the tunnel and into the crater, and just stood for a moment, while his various aches and pains subsided enough to be bearable. His candlelight didn't travel more than a few feet, but the glowing crystals in the cavern walls still shone with a dim, stubborn light. The curving sides of the crater stretched away in all directions, and beyond them lay the cavern wall he would have to climb to reach the stone ledge that led to the exit tunnel. Assuming of course that the damned tunnel was still there . . . MacNeil shrugged, and started off across the crater, heading for the nearest wall. There was no point in thinking about things like that. Either the tunnel was there, or it wasn't. He'd find out when he got there.

The rest of the journey passed in a kind of daze, and he remembered little of it, even in his dreams. Possibly because he was too tired to be scared anymore. He reached the edge of the crater eventually, and climbed up the sheer rock face until he got to the stone ledge. The climb wasn't too hard; the walls were cracked and broken from where the Beast had stirred briefly in its sleep, and there were plenty of ready-made hand- and footholds. He made his way along the ledge and trudged wearily back up the tunnel that led to the wooden steps and the cellar. He wasn't thinking much by this time. There was only the pain and the tiredness and his own dogged refusal to give in.

His candle stub had pretty much run out by the time he finally reached the wooden steps, and he clawed his way up the steps in pitch darkness after the light suddenly guttered and went out. The first he knew of reaching the closed trapdoor was when he banged his head against it. The shock snapped MacNeil awake again, and a horrid thought came to him. What if the others had supposed him dead, and gone away, leaving the trapdoor securely bolted? He grinned savagely. After all he'd been through to get here, a closed trapdoor sure as hell wasn't going to stop him. He braced himself on the narrow wooden slat, and his hand brushed against something on the top step. He froze, studying the feel of it in his memory. It hadn't seemed alive; it had felt cold, like metal or glass. He reached out again carefully, and his fingers found the familiar shape of his lantern. MacNeil smiled widely in the darkness. So Jack had made it back, at least. He took out his flint and steel and lit the lantern with trembling fingers. The sudden light was blinding, and tears ran down his face. He waited patiently till his eyes had adjusted to the new light, and then put his shoulder against the underside of the trapdoor. He took a quick breath, and then thrust upwards with all his strength. For one heartbreaking moment he thought the damn thing wasn't going to budge, and then it suddenly rose a good three inches, almost throwing him off balance. He quickly regained his footing and pushed again, and in a few moments the trapdoor had swung high enough for him to push it over backward. It fell to the floor with a great echoing crash, but there was no response. The cellar was dark and abandoned.

MacNeil clambered painfully out of the opening, but rested only a moment before checking through the piled up bodies for signs of his friends. But among all the trolls, there was only one human body: Wilde. MacNeil heaved a sigh of relief and started the long slow journey out of the cellar and back through the warren of passageways that would take him eventually to the outside world. Not for the first time, he wondered if the others had already gone, leaving him alone in the fort. He had no way of knowing how long he'd been unconscious in the body of the Beast. But if they hadn't left yet, they were probably still in the dining hall. He stood undecided in a dark passageway for a moment. He wanted to get out of the fort, with all its blood and death and madness, and breathe fresh, clean air again, but even more than that he needed the company of friends. So he set off in the direction of the dining hall and hoped. It took longer than he'd thought to get there, mainly because he was so much weaker than he'd realized, but finally he stood in the empty corridor before the closed hall door. He hesitated again, but couldn't hear anything. He shrugged and pushed the door open, slamming it back against the wall.

The Dancer had been sitting on guard. He was on his feet, sword in hand, before the echoes had even begun to ring, but when he saw who it was, his jaw dropped and he stood frozen in place. Jack, Flint, and

Constance sat up bleary-eyed from sleep, and stared blankly at the grisly apparition in the doorway. And then the shock of the moment passed, and all four of them hurried forward to greet him. Constance got there first and hugged MacNeil ferociously, despite the blood and slime that soaked his clothes.

"You're alive! Oh, Duncan, I knew you had to be alive! I knew it!"

Her feelings ran wild within her, making her suddenly inarticulate, but that didn't matter. There'd be time to tell him about those feelings later. There would be time for many things now.

Finally she let him go, and the others took turns hugging him and slapping him on the back and shoulders. All the exuberance was suddenly too much for MacNeil, and he had to sit down quickly before he fell down. The Dancer and Jack helped him to a chair, and MacNeil then had to spend some time assuring them all that he was fine really, and just needed a little time to get his breath back. Constance wrapped a blanket around his shoulders to keep out the cold. Flint handed him a wine flask, and he nodded his thanks.

"All right," said Constance, "tell us what happened. You've been missing for hours. Did you really kill the Beast?"

"Oh, yes," said MacNeil. "It's dead." He told them his story, and they sat around him in silent awe, like children listening to the village storyteller. When he was finished, no one said anything for a long time.

"So, Wolfsbane is lost again," said Flint finally. "I can't say I'm sorry to see the back of it. Damn thing gave me the creeps."

"Right," said MacNeil. "As far as my official report is

concerned, it's lost without trace. I think it's better for everyone if it stays that way." He yawned suddenly and allowed himself the luxury of a long, slow stretch. "And now, my friends, if you'll excuse me, I think I'm going to lose these clothes and crawl into my sleeping roll and sleep for a week. Good night . . . and pleasant dreams."

In the end, he slept about ten hours. It was late in the afternoon when he finally woke up. Every muscle he had was complaining loudly, but the long sleep had taken the edge off his pains, and he thought he could live with them now. Flint and the Dancer were sitting not too far away, talking quietly. Constance was preparing a meal of cold field rations at one of the tables. There was no sign of Scarecrow Jack. MacNeil smiled contentedly. It felt good to be alive. He lay back in his bedroll and stared up at the ceiling. In a strange way, he felt very much at peace with himself. Down in the darkness, under the gaze of the Beast, he had tested his courage and found it sound. He'd never been more scared in his life, but still, when it mattered, he had done the right thing. It meant a lot to him, knowing that.

He emerged reluctantly from his blankets and climbed into his spare set of clothes. One look at the stained and slime-drenched clothes he'd worn previously was enough to convince him they were beyond saving. He raised his hands to his face and sniffed them suspiciously. Despite a thorough washing the night before, he could still smell the foul stench of the Beast. Maybe when the reinforcements arrived they'd have someone with them who could repair the hot water boilers, and he could have a long soak in a very hot bath. MacNeil smiled, savoring the thought, and moved over to join Constance at the table. She smiled back at him and passed him some of the cold field rations. It was a continuing matter for debate among all guards as to whether field rations tasted worse cooked or cold. Most guards usually ended up deciding they tasted equally vile either way. MacNeil wasn't all that hungry anyway, but since Constance had gone to the trouble of preparing the meal, he supposed he'd better eat some of it or she'd be upset. After a few mouthfuls he discovered he was hungry after all, ate the lot, and even wished there was more. He pushed back the empty plate with a sigh, and looked up to find Constance sitting patiently beside him.

"Jack's waiting in the courtyard," she said quietly. "He doesn't like being indoors, but he didn't want to leave without saying goodbye."

"Strictly speaking, I ought to arrest him," said MacNeil. "But . . ."

"Yes," said Constance. "But."

They shared a smile, and MacNeil got up from the table and headed for the door. Flint and the Dancer broke off their conversation and got up to follow him. Constance brought up the rear, as usual.

The fort seemed somehow smaller and less impressive in the afternoon sunlight, as though the evil that had infested it had vanished with the night. In a way, MacNeil supposed it had. For all the death and spilled blood, this was just another border fort now, and that was all it would ever be. MacNeil finally led the others through the entrance hall and out into the courtyard. The storm had passed over during the early hours of the morning, and the rain was long gone. There were no clouds in the sky, and the warm sunlight had dried off most of the stonework. Scarecrow Jack was standing by the open main gates, staring out at the Forest. He looked around as the Rangers approached, and nodded politely.

"You're looking better, Sergeant MacNeil. Is there anything I can do for you before I go?"

"I don't think so," said MacNeil easily. Despite Jack's relaxed appearance, he was clearly ready to turn and run for the trees at the first sign of any attempt to arrest him. Old habits die hard. MacNeil smiled warmly at Jack to reassure him. "In fact, as far as my official report is concerned, you were never here. But do me a favor: try to stay out of trouble until we've left the area. I'd hate to be ordered to hunt you down."

Jack grinned at him. "What makes you think you could find me?"

They all laughed. Jack turned away and looked at the Forest.

"You don't have to go," said Constance suddenly. "After all your help, after all you've done, I'm sure we could get you a pardon. You could return to your home, to your family; make a new life for yourself."

"The Forest is my home and my family," said Scarecrow Jack. "I wouldn't leave it for a dozen pardons. Thanks anyway, Constance. Goodbye, my friends."

He grinned quickly at them, and then ran through the gates and out into the clearing. For a while his running figure was outlined against the bright sunshine, and then he reached the trees. His camouflage of rags blended into the Forest, and he was gone.

"I have a strong feeling we should have gone down

into the tunnels and counted those bags of gold before we let him go," said Flint.

MacNeil smiled and shook his head. "I wouldn't have begrudged him a bag or two, but I doubt he took a single gold coin with him. What use is gold in the Forest? Come on, we ought to clean up some of the mess before the reinforcements get here. And we've still got to agree on what story we're going to tell them."

"Right," said the Dancer. "They'd never believe the truth. I was here, and I don't believe half of it."

The four Rangers laughed together and went back into the fort. The sun shone down through a cloudless sky, and the fort stood clean and open beneath it.

THE WORLDS OF
Simon R. Green

The author of such fascinating bestsellers as *Blue Moon Rising, Blood and Honor*, and the upcoming *Shadows Fall* has proven himself time and again as a gifted storyteller. On the following pages is a special sixteen-page preview of *Shadows Fall*, Green's newest and most ambitious novel since *Blue Moon Rising*. In addition, just in case you've missed them, here are spellbinding glimpses of *Blue Moon Rising* and *Blood and Honor*, both set in the same captivating fantasy realm as *Down Among the Dead Men*.

SHADOWS FALL

Lester Gold and Sean Morrison walked the rest of the way in silence, each occupied with his own thoughts, and finally they came to the Unseeli Court, the Gathering of Faerie. Two vast doors swung open unassisted as they approached, revealing a great chamber packed wall to wall with the highest of the elven kind. Tall, lean and imposing, they dressed in complex robes of bright and curious colors, and every one of them wore a sword on his hip. Every face and form was perfect, without defect or blemish. They were beautiful, graceful, burning, and intense. The sheer pressure of their presence was like facing a blast of heat from an open furnace. They stood perfectly still, inhumanly still, like an insect poised to attack, or a predator watching its prey to see which way it will run. Some wore masks of thinly beaten metal that covered half their face, while others wore the furs of beasts, with the heads still attached and resting casually on the wearer's shoulder. Strange perfumes scented the air, thick and heady and overpowering, as though someone had crushed a field of flowers and captured their essence in a jar. But most of all, there was the silence, perfect and complete, unbroken by any murmur or whisper of movement. Gold and Morrison looked at the assembled elves, and the Faerie looked back, in a moment that seemed as though it would last forever.

And then the elves at the center fell back, opening up a path through the middle of the Court. Morrison stepped forward, calm and confident, and Gold went with him. The elves slowly turned their heads to watch the two humans walk among them, and Gold had to fight hard to repress a shudder. He could feel their gaze like a physical pressure, and there was nothing of friendship or welcome in it. Morrison had made it clear early on that they had no guarantee of protection. Whatever the Faerie did, no one would or could call them to answer for it. Morrison might have been here before as a bard and honored guest, but that had been at their summons. This time he'd come unannounced and without invitation, and brought a stranger with him.

Anything could happen.

Gold and Morrison finally came to a halt before a wide, raised dais, on which stood two great thrones, intricately carved out of bone. Shapes and sigils and glyphs of all kinds patterned the fashioned ivory, detail upon detail complex beyond hope. And on those thrones were two elves. The man sat on the left, fully ten feet tall and bulging thickly with muscle, wrapped in bloodred robes that showed off his milk-white skin. His hair was a colorless blond, hanging loosely about a long angular face dominated by eyes of an arctic, piercing blue. He sat perfectly still as though he had waited patiently there for an age, and would wait longer still, should it prove necessary. The woman sat on the right, dressed in black with silver tracings. She was a few inches taller than the man, lithely muscular, with skin so pale that blue veins showed at her temples. Her hair was black, cropped short and severe, and dark eyes watched thoughtfully from a heart-shaped face. She held a single red rose in her hand, ignoring the thorns that pricked her. Nobility hung about them both, like a cloak grown frayed through long use. Gold didn't need to be told who they were, who they had to be. Their names were legend. Morrison bowed low to the King and Queen of Faerie, and Gold quickly did the same.

"My Lord and Lady, most noble Oberon and gracious Titania, I greet you in the name of Shadows Fall." Morrison paused, as though expecting a response, but the silence dragged on. He smiled winningly, and continued, practically oozing charm and goodfellowship. "I apologize for this intrusion, this uninvited appearance, but matters of great urgency have arisen which lead me to impose upon your friendship and esteem. If you will permit, I would like to introduce my friend Lester Gold, a hero."

Gold didn't need to be prompted to bow again, and did so as decorously as he could. It wasn't something he was used to, and he suspected it was one of those things you needed to practice a lot before you could bring it off really successfully. He straightened up to find neither the King nor the Queen had moved or acknowledged him in the slightest. Morrison stood at his side, smiling calmly, obviously waiting for a response. But the silence still held, gathering a kind of weight and momentum that was both disturbing and dangerous. The endless stare of the packed Court seemed more and more threatening, and Gold had to fight to keep his hand from edging closer to the gun in his shoulder-holster. For the first time in his long career, he knew he was facing something that couldn't be stopped by naked courage and a well-placed bullet. Morrison smiled easily at Oberon and Titania, but Gold could sense the effort it took. The bard had been prepared for outright refusal, but the continuing silence that denied his very existence was getting to him.

"My Lord and Lady, have you nothing to say to me? I have been your bard in days past, sung your history and your praise before audiences both human and elven. In turn, you have honored me with your friendship and your ear, and I need them both now more than ever. If I presume upon your patience, it is only because necessity drives me. Something has arisen that threatens humanity and Faerie alike, and I fear the town cannot hope to stop it alone. Your highnesses, will you not speak to me?"

A short, stocky figure appeared suddenly between the two thrones, grinning unpleasantly. Gold stared. It was the only elf he'd seen who wasn't perfect. The elf was easily as tall as the two humans, but the thrones and their occupants made him seem smaller. His body was smooth and supple as a dancer, but the hump on his back pulled one shoulder down and forward, and the hand on that arm was withered into a claw. His hair was gray, his skin the faint yellow of old bone, but his green eyes were alive with mischief and insolence. At his temples there were two raised nubs that might have been horns. He wore a pelt of some animal whose fur melded uncannily with his own hairy body, and his legs ended in cloven hooves. He laughed suddenly, and Morrison flinched at the naked contempt in the soft sound.

"Back again, little bard, little man, little human? Back to trouble us with your wit and worries, your passing consequence and transitory worth? And speaking of urgency, and matters arising, as though the frantic tick-tocking of your mortal span had any interest to us. You forget your place, little human. You come when you are summoned, at our pleasure and at our convenience. You do not intrude upon our Court and our business as and when the spirit moves you."

"My Lord Puck," said Morrison easily. "A pleasure, as always. The harshness in your words pains me greatly. Am I not the bard of this Court, this Gathering? Have I not sung for you in this very hall not six days past? You honored me then with your praise, and gave me drink and bid me call you 'brother.' "

"I never liked my brother," said Puck, spinning casually on his hooves with surprising grace. "Though I like humans well enough. They make such easy prey. They run with such touching desperation, and squeal so pleasingly when they are run to ground. The smallest things please them, and they'll fawn endlessly for a smile or a pretty word from their betters. They sniff at the rump like a randy dog, and kiss our perfect arse and think that makes us friends. You come at a bad time, human. Take what is left of our good will and leave now, while you still can."

A brief movement went through the ranks of the Court, and Gold could all but feel the tension on the air. The weight of so many eyes, fixed and unblinking, was almost unbearable. Morrison didn't seem to be feeling any strain, but it was all Gold could do to stand his ground. Part of him wanted to turn and run, and keep running till he was safely back in a world he understood. The thought steadied him somewhat. He wasn't going to run. He was a hero, and heroes didn't run. Though they did sometimes withdraw, for tactical reasons. He glanced casually behind him, checking how far it was to the doors, and how many elves were in his way. He thought again about the gun under his jacket, but kept his hand well away from it. There were hundreds of elves, and he had only a handful of ammunition. Besides, he had an uncomfortable feeling these majestic beings wouldn't be much bothered by anything as simple as a gun. He decided to concentrate on standing very still, and doing his best to look calm and unconcerned.

"Something has happened," said Morrison flatly. "Something has happened here, in this Court, in this land, since I was last here. But I have not changed. I am still your friend, your bard, your voice in the world of humans. I have not forgotten the gifts you gave me, or the nature and responsibilities of my position. It is a bard's duty to say what must be said, be he welcome or no. I have come from the town to speak with you, on a matter most vital, and I will be heard. The land beneath the hill is bound to Shadows Fall by oaths as old as Time itself. Am I now to understand that the word of the Faerie has become worthless, and all agreements null and void? Have the elves forsaken honor?"

Another brief movement went through the Court, and Gold could feel the subtle change from menace to anger. Morrison ignored them all, his unwavering gaze fixed on Puck. His voice had not risen once from its calm and reasonable tone, and his arms were folded casually across his chest. The imperfect elf leaned forward, his hooves clattering quietly on the polished floor. He glared at Morrison, all trace of smile and mischief gone, but the bard didn't flinch.

"Watch your words, little human," said Puck. "Words

have power. They bind the speaker and the listener. If you would not hear words of power and portent, leave now. I will not make this offer again."

"I came to speak," said Morrison, "And I will be heard. Do as you must, Lord Puck, but I'll not move another step. There are words that must be said, and matters that must be discussed, no matter what the consequence. The next step in the dance is yours, Lord Puck. I'll not be the first to break the faith between us."

"So brave," said Puck. "So arrogant. So very, very human. Speak your piece, bard. It will make no difference. Your words have no meaning here. We do not hear them."

"I have the right to audience," said Morrison carefully. "You made me your bard, for better or worse, and whatever falls between us that cannot be undone. I respectfully demand that two ranked members of this Court hear my words, and give judgment as to whether my words have meaning, and shall be heard."

"Right? Demand?" Puck drew himself up to his full height, forcing his hump and shoulder back as far as they would go. "Does a human dare to use such words in our Court, in our land?"

"Yes. Their majesties Oberon and Titania gave me that right, in days gone past. Do you now deny their word?"

"Not I," said Puck. "Never I. Though there might come a time when you will wish I had." He giggled suddenly, a strange and unsettling sound in the quiet of the Court. He spun on his hooves again, and dropped gracefully into a crouch. "I like your gall, Sean. I always did. You remind me of someone I respect. Myself, probably. So, since you will not be told and you will not be warned, matters will proceed as they must. Lord Oisin, Lady Niamh—step forward."

Two elves made their way through the Court, and came to stand facing Gold and Morrison, with their backs to Oberon and Titania. They bowed to Morrison, who bowed deeply in return. Gold bowed too, just to show he was keeping up with things.

Puck leaned casually against Oberon's throne. "The Lord Oisin Mac Finn. Once a human, now an elf, of long-standing in this Court. The Lady Niamh of the Golden Hair, daughter to Mannannon Mac Lir. They will hear your words. Do you accept them?"

Gold studied them both while Morrison took a long time to say yes. Oisin, (once a *human*?) was six feet tall, which made him seem almost a dwarf when set against the rest of the Court. He had the same fierce eyes and pointed ears, the same lithe musculature and natural grace, but there was still something of the human in him. He was perfect, but not on the same scale. Niamh was a good eight feet tall, and looked even taller next to Oisin and the two humans. She had a sharp, handsome face and long golden hair that fell thickly to her waist, pulled back and kept out of her face with a simple headband. Gold found himself wondering, almost despite himself, how much time every day the poor girl had to spend washing and brushing and combing it.

He forced himself to concentrate on the matter in hand. Neither Oisin nor Niamh seemed particularly friendly or unfriendly. But there was something about the Court . . . the feeling he was getting from the packed hall had changed yet again. The anger and the menace were gone, replaced by something that had the flavor of resignation. As though by Morrison's insistence they had set out on a road none of them had really wanted to travel. Gold shook himself mentally. It was more than probable he was reading things into the Court's silence that weren't actually there. After all, they weren't human, and therefore weren't bound to think or feel as humans did ... He glanced at Morrison, who had finally stopped speaking. The young bard seemed calm, almost relaxed. But then, he always did. Gold had always prided himself on being calm under fire and cool in a crisis, but that was thirty-odd years ago, and he hadn't met the Faerie then. Morrison bowed to Puck, crouching half-hidden behind Oisin and Niamh.

"I have my harp with me, to hand. You taught me how to get the best out of it, Lord Puck, and I will do your teaching justice. Hear my song."

A guitar was suddenly in his hands. Gold blinked. He would have sworn it wasn't there a minute ago. It would appear there was more to being a bard than owning a pleasant voice and knowing three chords. Morrison strummed the guitar casually, the soft gentle sound filling the quiet Court. Oberon and Titania sat forward a little in their thrones. Morrison began to sing in a strong tenor voice, and the Faerie listened.

It was a simple tune with a steady rhythm that held the ear and then the mind, haunting and sublime. All who heard could no more have turned away than they could have stopped breathing. Morrison was a bard, and there was magic in his song and in his voice, the magic that comes from the heart and the soul, focussed and given shape through the man and his song. He sang and the world stood still.

He sang of Shadows Fall, and its unique nature. Of the lost and the fearful and the dying who came to the town when the world had no more use for them. He sang of the ancient and noble elves, and the long compact between Man and Faerie down all the many years. Of love and honor and duty, and how they held Man and Faerie together. And finally, he sang of the town's need in its hour of despair, of murder unfinished and unpunished. He broke off abruptly, and his music echoed on the still air for a long moment, as though it had unfinished business with those who had listened.

Tears stung Gold's eyes and there was an ache in his heart, and in that moment he could have denied Morrison nothing. He looked at the Faerie, at Oberon and Titania, Oisin and Niamh and Puck, and a cold breeze touched him. There were no tears in their fierce eyes, no sign in their faces that they had felt any of the exaltation that had moved Gold so strongly. Instead, they looked tired and sad and resigned, as though the song had merely confirmed the need for something they would rather have avoided. Oberon and Titania leaned back in their thrones, and Niamh bowed to Morrison. He bowed back, the guitar disappearing from his hands.

"Your song moves us, as always, dear bard." Niamh's gentle voice was music itself, slow and steady and remorseless, like a tide sweeping up a beach. "You have been our friend and our voice among the humans, and we would have spared you this if we could. But you have demanded the truth, as is your right, and we will give it to you, though it break your heart and ours. We know what is happening in Shadows Fall. The Wild Childe has come among you. He is the beast with every man's face, the killer who cannot be stopped or bargained with, because that is all he is. There is nothing you or we can do to stop him.

"Worse things still are coming. You are betrayed without and within. A vast army is gathering, to take the town by force. And we . . . are divided, friend Sean. For the first time in centuries, we cannot see our way. Our oracles speak of death and destruction and the ending of the Faerie. Some of us would form an army, calling up weapons and sciences long unused. Some would close the door between hill and town, and bar it shut forever. And some would destroy the town and render it to ashes, in the hope we might then escape its fate.

"And so we talk and argue and debate and nothing is decided. We cannot find our way. The only thing we are sure of is that the darkness is closing in around us, and there seems no hope for man or elf. We have no help to offer you, friend Sean; only words of doom and warnings of disaster. Divided as we are, still we would have spared you that, if we could, rather than blight your hope or damn your spirit. We tried to turn you away, and give you harsh words in place of harsher truths, but you demanded to be heard, and we could not deny you.

"I think that in the end we might yet stand beside you, against whatever form our doom finally takes. Man and Faerie are bound by compacts older than Shadows Fall itself, and we would rather die than live without our honor. And we are fond of you, in our way. You are the children we never knew. I trust we will not desert you in your hour of need, no matter what the augeries say."

"That is not yet decided," said Oisin, his voice flat and heavy. "Though many voices would rally us to humanity's need, there are as many and more who would have us stand clear of the town's fate, and turn our backs on the world of man forever. We have a duty to survive. We have done all we can for you, and if the world must move on, then let it go. Like all children, humanity must learn to stand alone, for good or ill."

"You must not go," said Morrison, and there was no anger in his voice, only urgency. "We need you. We need your glamour and your mysteries, your strangeness and majesty. The world would be a grayer place without your epic battles and intricate intrigues, your towering rages and immortal loves. You are humanity written large, and life roars within you. Don't go. We would be smaller without you to inspire us, and your going would leave a gap in us that we might never fill. You are the joy and glory of the world. You make us whole."

Niamh smiled. "Your words move us, as always, but I fear words have not the strength among us that once they had. Stay with us, Sean, and speak further. Perhaps together we can see our way clear again. You understand that I can promise nothing."

"Nothing," said Oisin, and it seemed that some of the Court whispered it with him.

Morrison bowed. "I am at your service."

"We have heard your words," said King Oberon, in a voice that filled the Court. "We shall consider them."

"In the meantime, be our guests," said Queen Titania. "Ask for anything, and nothing shall be denied you."

Niamh and Oisin turned to confer in lowered voices with the King and Queen, and the Court talked quietly amongst itself. Puck winked once at Morrison, spun sharply on his hooves and suddenly wasn't there anymore. Morrison let out his breath in a long sigh, and all but slumped against Gold, his strength gone. He looked suddenly older and smaller, as though he'd poured something of himself into his entreaties. Gold supported him surreptitiously with an arm at his elbow. He had a strong feeling it would be a bad idea to show any kind of weakness at this time. He looked around him for inspiration, and his gaze fell upon a small table conveniently to hand, bearing a bottle of wine and two golden cups. He reached out for the wine, curious to see what the label said, and then stopped abruptly as Morrison's fingers sank painfully into his arm.

"Don't touch any of it!" said Morrison in a savage whisper. "You can't eat or drink anything here; accepting it into your body ties you to the world that produced it. This is not our world, and the rules are different here. Time runs differently. As visitors, we can come and go unaffected. We'll return to Shadows Fall at the exact moment we left it, but to eat and drink here would make you subject to a different time. You could leave here after a few hours, and find that years had passed in the world you left. So please, Lester, remember what I tell you. This isn't the kind of place where you can afford to make mistakes."

"Of course, Sean, I understand. Now will you please let go of my arm before my fingers drop off?"

Morrison let go of him, and Gold nodded stiffly.

He'd never liked being lectured, but it was clear the bard knew the ground rules here and he didn't, so he kept his peace. He nodded at the surrounding Court.

"What do you suppose they're talking about now?"

"Damned if I know. They don't think as we do. There was a time I might have managed an educated guess, but things here have changed so much . . . I knew something was up when Oberon and Titania wouldn't talk to me directly, but I had no idea things would get this out of hand."

"Let me make sure I've got this right," said Gold. "Something really nasty is loose in Shadows Fall. Not only can the elves not help us, but some of them are actually seriously considering wiping out the whole town, just in case it gets them too. Have I missed anything?"

"Not really. Once, I would have said this was impossible. The very idea of an elf breaking his oath would have been unthinkable. Which only goes to show how scared they are. I've never seen them like this before."

"They said something about oracles. How accurate are these fortune-tellers?"

"Very. They tend to be a bit ambiguous, but they've got a hell of a track record. If the augurs say that the very existence of the Faerie is at risk, you can put money on it."

"But what could possibly endanger a people who can't die?"

"The Wild Childe, presumably. Whatever that is."

"That's another thing," said Gold. "I got the distinct impression they've known about this killer for some time. Why haven't they said anything before?"

"Because there was nothing they could do. They

were ashamed. That's at least partly why they didn't want to talk to me at first. Partly because they were trying to hide the worst from me, but also because they didn't want to admit that they had failed in their oath to protect the town. They really believe we're all doomed. They didn't want me to know for the same reason that you don't tell someone in hospital that they're going to die. Because it would be cruel to take away all hope."

Gold looked at him steadily. "Is it really that bad? We're all going to die, and there's nothing anyone can do?"

"I don't believe that. I won't believe it. They must have misinterpreted the oracle. Misunderstood it. I have to convince the Faerie not to give up without a fight. For their sake, as well as ours."

"For their sake? Why?"

"Because if they believe they're going to die, they will. They'll just fade away. It's happened before, when an elf loses all hope. It's one of the few things that can kill them. We've got to convince them that there's still a chance, that you can't give up fighting just because the odds are against you."

"What if it's not just odds? What if it's a certainty? James Hart has returned to Shadows Fall."

"I can't think about that now," said Morrison flatly. "If I try to think about everything, I'll go mad. We have to concentrate on what we can do."

"Pardon me for seeming dim, but what the hell can we do? What can a young bard and a hero well past his sell-by date do to save the Faerie and the town, that a race of immortal, unkillable elves can't do?"

"Beats me," said Morrison, smiling suddenly. "I guess we'll just have to improvise."

Gold looked at him speechlessly for a moment, and then both of them realized the Court had grown silent again. They looked around the Unseeli Court, and found all eyes were on them. Gold stiffened. Something had changed again. He could feel it on the charged air; a strange mixture of menace and expectancy. Gold felt like a rabbit staring into the lights of an approaching car. Something really unpleasant was headed his way, and he hadn't a clue which way to run. He looked to Morrison for guidance, but the bard looked just as thrown as he did. Niamh and Oisin bowed to them both, and after a moment Gold and Morrison bowed back.

Here it comes . . . thought Gold. *And whatever it is, I'm not going to like it one little bit.*

"This is a matter of great importance," said Niamh. Her quiet voice seemed to fill the Court. "It is not something to be decided in haste. We shall adjourn, and consider the matter at our leisure. In the meantime, their majesties Oberon and Titania will reside over the Games. You are welcome to join them, as honored guests."

"Oh shit," said Morrison, very quietly.

Gold looked at him sharply. He thought for a moment the bard was going to faint. All the color had drained out of his face, and his mouth had gone a funny shape. "Sean? Are you all right?"

"We'd be delighted to join their majesties," said Morrison. "Delighted. Wouldn't we, Lester?"

"Oh sure," said Gold, picking up his cue. "Always ready to watch some Games."

Everyone took turns to bow to each other, and then the Faerie turned to talk amongst themselves again. Gold turned to Morrison.

"Oh shit," said the bard with great feeling.

"Sean, talk to me. What have we just agreed to, and why do I think from the look on your face that I should really be sprinting for the nearest exit?"

"Don't even think about it," said Morrison sharply. "Trying to leave now would be a deadly insult. You wouldn't live long enough to reach the door."

"We're in trouble, aren't we?"

"You could put it that way. The Faerie have always been big on games. Challenges of strength and skill, wit and courage. You've already seen a duel, and their idea of betting, but they save the really heavy stuff for the Arena. They put on the kind of shows that would have shocked hardened Roman Circus-goers. They may not be able to die themselves, but they do like to watch other beings do it. Preferably in violent and inventive ways. We're talking combat to the death; man against elf, people verses all kinds of creatures, under all kinds of conditions. It's very rare for a human to be invited to attend the Games . . . except as cannon fodder."

In a moment the world changed. The ground dropped away from under Gold's feet, and slammed back again even as he put out a hand to steady himself. The massed candlelight of the Unseeli Court was gone, replaced by a brighter, harsher light. Gold looked stupidly about him, the pressure of a gusting wind on his face. The Court was gone, and he and Morrison were standing in an ornately decorated private stadium, set high above the ranked seats, looking out over a vast Arena, spread out below an open sky.

BLUE MOON RISING

Prince Rupert rode his unicorn into the Tanglewood, peering balefully through the drizzling rain as he searched half-heartedly for the flea hiding somewhere under his breastplate. Despite the chill rain, he was sweating heavily under the weight of his armor, and his spirits had sunk so low as to be almost out of sight. "Go forth and slay a dragon, my son," King John had said, and all the courtiers cheered. They could afford to. They didn't have to go out and face the dragon. Or ride through the Tanglewood in full armor in the rainy season. Rupert gave up on the flea and scrabbled awkwardly at his steel helmet, but to no avail; water continued to trickle down his neck.

Towering, closely packed trees bordered the narrow trail, blending into a verdant gloom that mirrored his mood. Thick, fleshy vines clung to every tree trunk, and fell in matted streamers from the branches. A heavy, sullen silence hung over the Tanglewood. No animals moved in the thick undergrowth, and no birds sang. The only sound was the constant rustle of the rain as it dripped from the lowering branches of the waterlogged trees, and the muffled thudding of the unicorn's hooves. Thick mud and fallen leaves made the twisting, centuries-old trail more than usually treacherous, and the unicorn moved ever more slowly, slipping and sliding as he carried Prince Rupert deeper into the Tanglewood.

Rupert glowered about him, and sighed deeply. All his life he'd thrilled to the glorious exploits of his ancestors, told in solemn voices during the long, dark winter evenings. He remembered as a child sitting wide-eyed and open-mouthed by the fire in the Great Hall, listening with delicious horror to tales of ogres and harpies, magic swords and rings of power. Steeped in the legends of his family, Rupert had vowed from an early age that one day he too would be a hero, like Great-Uncle Sebastian, who traded three years of his life for the three wishes that would free the Princess Elaine from the Tower With No Doors. Or like Grandfather Eduard, who alone had dared confront the terrible Night Witch, who maintained her remarkable beauty by bathing in the blood of young girls.

Now, finally, he had the chance to be a hero, and a right dog's breakfast he was making of it. Basically, Rupert blamed the minstrels. They were so busy singing about heroes vanquishing a dozen foes with one sweep of the sword because their hearts were pure, that they never got round to the important issues; like how to keep rain out of your armor, or avoid strange fruits that gave you the runs, or the best way to dig latrines. There was a lot to being a hero that the minstrels never mentioned. Rupert was busily working himself into a really foul temper when the unicorn lurched under him.

"Steady!" yelled the Prince.

The unicorn sniffed haughtily. "It's all right for you up there, taking it easy; I'm the one who has to do all the work. That armor you're wearing weighs a ton. My back's killing me."

"I've been in the saddle for three weeks," Rupert pointed out unsympathetically. "It's not my back that's bothering me."

The unicorn sniggered, and then came to a sudden halt, almost spilling the Prince from his saddle. Rupert grabbed at the long, curlicued horn to keep his balance.

"Why have we stopped? Trail getting too muddy, perhaps? Afraid your hooves will get dirty?"

"If you're going to be a laugh a minute you can get off and walk," snarled the unicorn. "In case you hadn't noticed, there's a massive spider's web blocking the trail."

Rupert sighed, heavily. "I suppose you want me to check it out?"

"If you would, please." The unicorn shuffled his feet, and the Prince felt briefly seasick. "You know how I feel about spiders . . ."

Rupert cursed resignedly, and swung awkwardly down from the saddle, his armor protesting loudly with every movement. He sank a good three inches into the trail's mud, and swayed unsteadily for a long moment before finding his balance. He forced open his helmet's visor and studied the huge web uneasily. Thick milky strands choked the narrow path, each sticky thread studded with the sparkling jewels of trapped raindrops. Rupert frowned; what kind of spider spins a web almost ten feet high? He trudged cautiously forward, drew his sword, and prodded one of the strands. The blade stuck tight, and he had to use both hands to pull the sword free.

"Good start," said the unicorn.

Rupert ignored the animal and stared thoughtfully at the web. The more he looked at it, the less it seemed like a spider's web. The pattern was wrong. The strands hung together in knotted clumps, falling in drifting streamers from the higher branches, and dropping from the lower in thick clusters that burrowed into the trail's mud. And then Rupert felt the hair on the back of his neck slowly rise as he realized that, although the web trembled constantly, there was no wind blowing.

"Rupert," said the unicorn softly.

"We're being watched, right?"

"Right."

Rupert scowled and hefted his sword. Something had been following them ever since they'd entered the Tanglewood at daybreak, something that hid in shadows and dared not enter the light. Rupert shifted his weight carefully, getting the feel of the trail beneath him. If it came to a fight, the thick mud was going to be a problem. He took off his helmet, and put it down at the side of the trail; the narrow eyeholes limited his field of vision too much. He glanced casually around as he straightened up, and then froze as he saw a slender, misshapen silhouette moving among the trees. Tall as a man, it didn't move like a man, and light glistened on fang and claw before the creature disappeared back into the concealing shadows. Rain beat on Rupert's head and ran unheeded down his face as a cold horror built slowly within him.

Beyond the Tanglewood lay darkness. For as long as anyone could remember, there had always been a part of the Forest where it was forever night. No sun shone, and whatever lived there never knew the light of day.

Mapmakers called it the Darkwood, and warned: *Here Be Demons.* For countless centuries, Forest land and Darkwood had been separated by the Tanglewood, a deadly confusion of swamp and briar and sudden death from which few escaped alive. Silent predators stalked the weed- and vine-choked trails, and laid in wait for the unwary. And yet, over the past few months, strange creatures had stalked the Forest Land, uneasy shapes that dared not face the light of day. Sometimes, when the sun was safely down, a lone cottager might hear scratchings at his securely bolted doors and shutters, and in the morning would find deep gouges in the wood, and mutilated animals in his barn.

The Tanglewood was no longer a barrier.

Here Be Demons.

Rupert fought down his fear, and took a firmer grip on his sword. The solid weight of the steel comforted him, and he swept the shining blade back and forth before him. He glared up at the dark clouds hiding the sun; one decent burst of sunshine would have sent the creature scuttling for its lair, but as usual Rupert was out of luck.

It's only a demon, he thought furiously. *I'm in full armor, and I know how to use a sword. The demon hasn't a chance.*

"Unicorn," he said quietly, peering into the shadows where he'd last seen the demon, "you'd better find a tree to hide behind. And stay clear of the fight; I don't want you getting hurt."

"I'm way ahead of you," said a muffled voice. Rupert glanced round to find the unicorn hiding behind a thick-boled tree some distance away.

"Thanks a lot," said Rupert. "What if I need your help?"

"Then you've got a problem," the unicorn said firmly, "because I'm not moving. I know a demon when I smell one. They eat unicorns, you know."

"Demons eat anything," said Rupert.

"Precisely," said the unicorn, and ducked back out of sight behind his tree.

Not for the first time, the Prince vowed to find the man who'd sold him the unicorn, and personally do something unpleasant to every one of the swindler's extremities.

There was a faint scuffling to his left, and Rupert had just started to turn when the demon slammed into him from behind. His heavy armor overbalanced him, and he fell forward into the clinging mud. The impact knocked the breath from him, and his sword flew from his outstretched hand. He caught a brief glimpse of something dark and misshapen towering over him, and then a heavy weight landed on his back. A clawed hand on the back of his neck forced his face down, and the mud came up to fill his eyes. Rupert flailed his arms desperately and tried to get his feet under him, but his steel-studded boots just slid helplessly in the thick mire. His lungs ached as he fought for air, and the watery mud spilled into his gaping mouth.

Panic welled up in him as he bucked and heaved to no avail. His head swam madly, and there was a great roaring in his ears as the last of his breath ran out. One of his arms became wedged beneath his chest plate, and with the suddenness of inspiration he used his arm as a lever to force himself over onto his back, trapping the squirming demon beneath the weight of his armor.

He lay there for long, precious moments, drawing in great shuddering breaths and gouging the mud from his eyes. He yelled for the unicorn to help him, but there was no reply. The demon hammered furiously at his armor with clumsy fists, and then a clawed hand snaked up to tear into Rupert's face. He groaned in agony as the claws grated on his cheekbone, and tried desperately to reach his sword. The demon took advantage of his move to squirm out from under him. Rupert rolled quickly to one side, grabbed his sword, and surged to his feet despite the clinging mud. The weight of his armor made every move an effort, and blood ran thickly down his face and neck as he stood swaying before the crouching demon.

In many ways it might have been a man, twisted and malformed, but to stare into its hungry pupilless eyes was to know the presence of evil. Demons killed to live, and lived to kill; a darkness loose upon the Land. Rupert gripped his sword firmly and forced himself to concentrate on the demon simply as an opponent. It was strong and fast and deadly, but so was he if he kept his wits about him. He had to get out of the mud and up onto firm ground; the treacherous mire gave the demon too much of an advantage. He took a cautious step forward, and the demon flexed its claws eagerly, smiling widely to reveal rows of pointed, serrated teeth. Rupert swept his sword back and forth before him, and the demon gave ground a little, wary of the cold steel. Rupert glanced past the night-dark creature in search of firmer ground, and then grinned shakily at what he saw. For the first time, he felt he might have a fighting chance.

He gripped his sword in both hands, took a deep

breath, and then charged full tilt at the crouching demon, knowing that if he fell too soon he was a dead man. The demon darted back out of range, staying just ahead of the Prince's reaching sword. Rupert struggled on, fighting to keep his feet under him. The demon grinned and jumped back again, straight into the massive web that blocked the path. Rupert stumbled to a halt, drew back his sword for the killing thrust, and then froze in horror as the web's thick milky strands slowly wrapped themselves around the demon. The demon tore furiously at the strands and then howled silently in agony as the web oozed a clear viscous acid that steamed where it fell upon the ground. Rupert watched in sick fascination as the feebly struggling demon disappeared inside a huge pulsating cocoon that covered it from head to toe. The last twitching movements died quickly away as the web digested its meal.

Rupert wearily lowered his sword and leaned on it, resting his aching back. Blood ran down into his mouth, and he spat it out. Who'd be a hero? He grinned sourly and took stock of himself. His magnificent burnished armor was caked with drying mud, and etched with deep scratch marks from the demon's claws. He hurt all over, and his head beat with pain. He brought a shaking hand up to his face, and then winced as he saw fresh blood on his mailed gauntlet. He'd never liked the sight of blood, especially his own. He sheathed his sword and sat down heavily on the edge of the trail, ignoring the squelching mud.

All in all, he didn't think he'd done too badly. There weren't many men who'd faced a demon and lived to tell of it. Rupert glanced at the now-motionless cocoon, and grimaced. Not the most heroic way to win, and certainly not the most sporting, but the demon was dead and he was alive, and that was the way he'd wanted it to be.

He peeled off his gauntlets and tenderly inspected his damaged face with his fingers. The cuts were wide and deep, and ran from the corner of his eye down to his mouth. *Better wash them clean,* he thought dazedly. *Don't want them to get infected.* He shook his head and looked about him. The rain had died away during the fight, but the sun was already sliding down the sky toward evening, and the shadows were darkening. Nights were falling earlier these days, even though it was barely summer. Rain dripped steadily from the overhanging branches, and a dank, musky smell hung heavily on the still air. Rupert glanced at the web cocoon, and shivered suddenly as he remembered how close he'd come to trying to cut his way through. Predators came in many forms, especially in the Tanglewood.

He sighed resignedly. Tired or no, it was time he was on his way.

"Unicorn! Where are you?"

"Here," said a polite voice from the deepest of the shadows.

"Are you coming out, or do I come in there after you?" growled the Prince. There was a slight pause, and then the unicorn stepped diffidently out onto the trail. Rupert glared at the animal, who wouldn't meet his gaze.

"And where were you, while I was risking my neck fighting that demon?"

"Hiding," said the unicorn. "It seemed the logical thing to do."

"Why didn't you help?"

"Well," said the unicorn reasonably, "If you couldn't handle the demon with a sword and a full set of armor, I didn't see what help I could offer."

Rupert sighed. One of these days he'd learn not to argue with the unicorn.

"How do I look?"

"Terrible."

"Thanks a lot."

"You'll probably have scars," said the unicorn helpfully.

"Great. That's all I need."

"I thought scars on the face were supposed to be heroic?"

"Whoever thought that one up should have his head examined. Bloody minstrels . . . Help me up, unicorn."

The unicorn moved quickly in beside him. Rupert reached out, took a firm hold of the stirrup, and slowly pulled himself up out of the mud. The unicorn stood patiently as Rupert leaned wearily against his side, waiting for his bone-deep aches to subside long enough for him to make a try at getting up into the saddle.

The unicorn studied him worriedly. Prince Rupert was a tall, handsome man in his mid-twenties, but blood and pain and fatigue had added twenty years to his face. His skin was gray and beaded with sweat, and his eyes were feverish. He was obviously in no condition to ride, but the unicorn knew that Rupert's pride would force him to try.

"Rupert . . ." said the unicorn.

"Yeah?"

"Why don't you just . . . walk me for a while? You know how unsteady I am in this mud."

"Yeah," said Rupert. "That's a good idea. I'll do that."

He reached out and took hold of the bridle, his head hanging wearily down. Slowly, carefully, the unicorn led him past the motionless cocoon and on down the trail, heading deeper into the Tanglewood.

BLOOD AND HONOR

The Great Jordan waited until the last of his audience had left, and then he sat down on the edge of his stage and began wiping the makeup off his face with a piece of dirty rag. Without the carefully placed shadings and highlights, his face looked younger and softer, and nowhere near as forbidding. His shoulders slumped wearily as the tiredness of the day caught up with him, and the air of mystery and command that had surrounded him on stage vanished like the illusion it was. The sword he'd used in his act poked him unmercifully in the ribs, and he pulled it out of the concealed sheath under his clothing. Seen up close, it was battered and nicked and not at all impressive. It was just a sword that had seen too much service in its time. Jordan yawned and stretched, and then shivered suddenly. Nights were falling earlier as the summer gave way to autumn, and the rising wind had a cold edge. He glanced across at the smoldering demon, but the roughly carved prop had pretty much burned itself out. He'd have to do some more work on the demon. It still looked all right from a distance, but the spring that threw it out from behind the concealing piece of scenery must be getting rusty. This was the third time in a week that its timing had been off. Any later and the damned fireworks would have gone off first. Jordan sighed. The spring wasn't the only thing who's timing was off. He was getting too old for one-night stands in backwater towns. At twenty-seven he was hardly an old man, but he just didn't have the stamina anymore to put up with an endless round of poor food, hard travel, and never enough sleep.

He got to his feet, strapped the sword to his side, and walked unhurriedly over to the offerings bowl. For a moment he allowed himself to hope, but when he looked it was even worse than he'd expected. The dozen or so small copper coins barely covered the bottom of the bowl. Jordan emptied the coins into his purse, and glumly hefted the trifling weight in his hand. Bannerwick was only a small mill town deep in the desolate North country, but he'd still looked for better takings than this. If things didn't improve soon, he'd have to go back to card sharking and picking pockets to make ends meet. He hadn't seen takings this bad since he first started out on the stage as a juvenile.

It wasn't just the Kingdom of Redhart, of course. Jordan had spent most of his professional life in Hillsdown. He'd known good times there. Not once had he ever thought he might one day be forced to leave the country of his birth by poor takings. He'd appeared three times before the duke himself, and known the company of great men and their ladies. They'd been the first to name him the Great Jordan.

Jordan frowned as he tried to work out if he had enough money to buy provisions and to get drunk, and if not, which of the two was the most important. The mental arithmetic took a depressingly short time. It would have to be provisions. Bannerwick stood alone and isolated in the middle of Redhart's moorland, and it was a good two or three days' traveling to the next town.

Still, there was no denying he'd been in excellent form tonight. The times might be hard, but he was still the Great Jordan, and the High Warlock was one of his best roles. He shook his head. It was getting too cold to sit around brooding. He threw a blanket over the smoldering demon prop to douse the last of the flames, and then set about transferring his props and scenery into the back of his small caravan. He gathered up his stage lights and counted them carefully twice, just to make sure none of them had disappeared with some unprincipled member of his audience. He stacked the lanterns and lamps in their proper places, and then went back for his stage. It was supposed to break easily into sections, but Jordan had to struggle with each square until he was red in the face and short of breath. He scowled as he slid the last section onto the floor of his caravan. He was going to have to do more work on the stage before it would come apart properly, and he hated working with wood. No matter how careful he was, he always ended up with splinters in his fingers. His scowl deepened as he laced up the caravan's back flaps. He shouldn't have to do scut work like this. He was an actor, not a carpenter.

Jordan smiled sourly. That was his past talking. Stars might not have to do scut work, but actors did. If they wanted to eat regularly. And if nothing else, exercise did help to build a healthy appetite. He set off down the main street, looking for a tavern. Late as it was by country standards, the town inn would still be open. Such inns always were. *I don't care if the speciality of the house is broiled demon in a toadstool sauce, I'm still going to eat it and ask for seconds,* he thought determinedly. Halfway down the narrow street, his nose detected the smell of hot cooking, and he followed it eagerly.

As he passed an opening between two houses, Jordan thought he heard someone moving surreptitiously, deep in the gloom of the alley. He slowed to a halt just past the opening, and scratched thoughtfully at his ribs, letting his hand drift casually down to the sword at his side. Surely it was obvious to anyone with half the brains they were born with that this particular actor had nothing worth the effort of taking it, but it was best to be wary. A starving man would murder for a crust of bread. Jordan's hand idly caressed the pommel of his sword, and he eased his weight onto his left foot so he could get at the throwing knife hidden in that boot if he had to. And if all else failed, there were always the flare pellets he kept concealed in his sleeves. They might not be quite as effective as they appeared onstage, but they were dramatic enough to give most footpads pause. He swallowed dryly, and wished his hands would stop shaking. He was never any good in a crisis, particularly if there was a chance of violence. He let his gaze sweep casually over the dark alleyway, and then stiffened as his hearing brought him the rasp of boots on packed earth, and something that might have been the quiet grating of steel sliding from a scabbard. Jordan whipped his sword from its sheath, and backed away. Something stirred in the darkness.

"Easy, my dear sir," said a calm, cultured voice. "We mean you no harm. We only want to talk to you."

Jordan thought seriously about making a run for it. Whenever anyone started talking that politely, either they were intent on telling him something he didn't really want to know, or they wanted to sell him something. On the other hand, from the sound of it there had to be more than just the one man hidden in the alley darkness, and he wasn't that fast a runner at the best of times. Maybe he could bluff them . . . He held his head erect, took on the warrior's stance he used when playing the ancient hero Sir Bors of Lyonsmarch, and glared into the gloom of the alley.

"Honest men do their talking in the light," he said harshly. "Not skulking in back alleys. Besides, I'm rather particular about who I talk to."

"I think you'll talk with us, Jordan," said the polite voice. "We're here to offer you an acting role—a role beyond your wildest dreams and ambitions."

Jordan was still trying to come up with an answer to that when the three men stepped out of the alley mouth and into the fading light. Jordan backed away a step, but calmed down a little when they made no move to pursue him. He quickly resumed his warrior's stance, hoping they hadn't noticed the lapse, and looked the three men over carefully from behind the hautiest expression he could manage. The man in the middle was clearly a noble of some kind, for all his rough peasant's cloak and hood. His skin was pale and unweathered, and his hands were slender and delicate. Presumably this was the owner of the cultured voice. Jordan nodded to him warily, and the man bowed formally in return. He raised one hand and pushed back the hood of his cloak, revealing a hawk-like, unyielding face dominated by steady dark eyes and a grim, humorless smile. His black hair was brushed flat and heavily pomaded, giving his pale skin a dull, unhealthy look. He was tall, at least six foot two, probably in his early forties, and looked to be fashionably slim under his cloak. He wore a sword at his side, and Jordan had no doubt at all that this man would know how to use it. Even standing still and at rest, there was an air of barely contained menace about him that was unmistakable.

"Well?" growled Jordan roughly, trying to gain the advantage before his knees started knocking. "Are we going to stand here staring at each other all night, or are you going to introduce yourself?"

"I beg your pardon, Jordan," said the noble smoothly. "I am Count Roderik Crichton, adviser to King Malcolm of Redhart. These are my associates: the trader Robert Argent, and Sir Gawaine of Tower Rouge."

Jordan nodded to them all impartially, and then sheathed his sword as an act of bravado. It seemed increasingly important to him that they shouldn't think they had him at a disadvantage.

"You mentioned an acting role," said Jordan to Count Roderik.

"The greatest role you'll ever play," said Roderik.

"What's the money like?" asked Jordan.

"Ten thousand ducats," said Robert Argent. His voice was flat and unemotional, and his cold gaze fixed unwaveringly on the actor.

Jordan kept his face calm with an effort. Ten thousand ducats was more than he'd ever earned in a year, even at the peak of his career. And that was a long way behind him. Ten thousand ducats . . . there had to be a catch.

"Assuming, for the sake of argument, that I'm interested in this job," he said carefully, "what kind of role would I be playing?"

"Nothing too difficult," said Roderik. "A prince—the middle of three sons. There's a great deal of background information you'll have to learn by heart, but an actor of your reputation shouldn't have any trouble with that. After all, you are the Great Jordan." He paused, and frowned slightly. "Is Jordan your real name, or would you prefer I used another, offstage?"

The actor shrugged. "Call me Jordan. It's a good name, and I earned it."

"I was most impressed with your performance this evening," said Roderik. "Did you write the material yourself?"

"Of course," said Jordan. "A strolling player has to be able to adapt his story to suit the level of his audience. Sometimes they want wit and eloquence, sometimes they want conjuring and fireworks. It varies. Did you like my High Warlock? I created the character after extensive research, and I flatter myself I caught the essence of the man."

"Nothing like him," said Sir Gawaine. His voice was harsh, with bitter undertones.

"Is that so, Sir Gawaine? Perhaps you'd care to tell me what he was really like?"

"He chased women and drank too much," said Gawaine.

"He was a great sorcerer!" said Jordan hotly. "Everybody said so! He saved the Forest Kingdom from the demon prince! All right, there were a few rumors about him, but there are always rumors. And besides . . . it makes for a better show my way."

Sir Gawaine shrugged, and looked away.

"If we could return to the subject at hand," said Roderik icily, glancing angrily at the knight. "You haven't yet said if you'll accept the role, sir actor."

"I'll take it," said Jordan. "I've nothing better to do, for the moment." For ten thousand ducats he'd have played the back end of a mummer's horse, complete with sound effects, but he wasn't going to tell them that. Maybe he could hit them for an advance . . . He looked at Count Roderik. "Well, my lord, shall we get down to business? What exactly is this role, and when do I start?"

"You start now," said Argent. "We want you to return with us to Castle Midnight, and impersonate Prince Viktor of Redhart."